OMEGA MISSILE

BOB MAYER

COOL GUS

1

THERE WASN'T A cloud in the sky and the air temperature in the eastern end of the Mediterranean was eighty degrees. The temperature of the water was a comfortable seventy-two. The surface of the sea was so smooth and flat that any disturbance of the water could be spotted easily. The moon was almost full and it reflected off the mirror surface, giving sixty-five percent illumination, aiding any prying eyes.

The American submarine lay eight kilometers off shore, due west of southern Lebanon. It was dead in the water a hundred feet down. On the back deck, just behind the conning tower, a hatch opened in the hull, leading to a pressurized compartment, the dry deck shelter —DDS—which was bolted onto the deck.

The two men climbing through the hatch into the DDS wore wet suits and carried their gear in waterproof rucksacks. As soon as they were inside, the hatch was closed behind them and sealed.

The two men ran through the pre-operations checks on the vehicle tied down inside the DDS: the Mark IX SDV (Swimmer Delivery Vehicle). The Mark IX was a long, flattened rectangle with propellers and dive fins at the rear and a Plexiglas bubble at the front for the crew to see through. A little over nineteen feet long, it was only slightly more than six feet wide and drew less than three feet from top to bottom.

After five minutes both men were satisfied with the craft. The batteries were at full charge and all equipment was functioning properly.

The divers slid inside the SDV, closing the hatches behind them. They hooked the hose from their mouthpieces directly to the interior air valves to breathe from the vehicle's tanks.

The man on the right spoke into the radiophone which was connected by umbilical to the sub. "Amber, this is Topaz. We are ready to proceed. Over."

"Roger, Topaz. We read all green here. Over."

"Request flood and release. Over."

"Flood and release will be initiated in twenty seconds. We'll leave the porch light on. Umbilicals cut in five. Good luck. Five. Four. Three. Two. One."

The radiophone went dead. With a heavy gurgle, water began pouring into the dry dock shelter. The pilot worked at keeping the SDV at neutral buoyancy as the chamber filled. Water also flooded into the crew chamber inside the SDV where the two divers lay on their stomachs peering out the front canopy. The Mark IX was a "wet" submersible meaning that the only waterproofed sections were the engine, battery, and navigational computer compartments. The two crewmen could feel the warm water seep into their wet suits and they forced out small pockets of air, trying to get as comfortable as possible in their confined space.

Once the chamber was full, the large hatch on the end of the DDS slowly swung open. The pilot activated the twin, three-bladed propellers and the SDV cleared the DDS. The long length of the submarine lay beneath them for another two hundred feet. Once in open ocean, the pilot directed the Mark IX up and down and from side to side using stabilizers, both horizontal and vertical, that were aligned to the rear of the propellers. A throttle controlled the speed of the blades, and thus the speed of the sub.

The second diver was the navigator and he was currently punching in numbers on the waterproofed panel in front of him.

"Fixing Doppler," he announced over the internal communication link between him and his partner. The computerized Doppler radar navigation system was now updated with their current location, received from the submarine prior to departure, and would guide them on their underwater journey, greatly simplifying a task that previously was a nightmare in pitch-black seas. The SDV also boasted an obstacle-avoidance sonar subsystem, which provided automatic warning to the pilot of any obstacles in the sub's path—an essential given that at their current depth they could see little more than a foot in front of them and would be "flying" blind, trusting the Doppler and their charts for navigation. The SDV had a pair of high-power halogen lights facing forward, but they were not an option on this mission.

"Course set. All clear," the navigator announced.

The pilot increased power to the propellers and they moved away from the sub, heading due east.

"What do you think, Chief?" the pilot finally asked, now that they were alone and out of the presence of higher-ranking officers. They both wore dive masks and mouthpieces, with transmitters wrapped around their necks. When they spoke, their voices sounded strangely garbled because the mouthpiece was held with the teeth while the speaker articulated with his throat.

The navigator, satisfied that everything was running smoothly, finally looked up from his panel at his cohort. "The politicians and bureaucrats ought to get their heads out of their asses and go public with this crap. That's what I think, Captain," Chief Petty Officer McKenzie replied.

"Always the big view," Captain Thorpe said with a low laugh that sounded like gargling to McKenzie. "I meant what do you think about our chances of spotting the transfer, if there is one?"

"They'd be a lot better if we went in with a big hammer right from the start and knocked these shit-birds on the head," McKenzie said. "I hate this sneaking andpeeking crap. What I really want to know is why I'm the navy guy and you're the army guy, but you're the one driving this sled?"

"Brains," Thorpe said. "Brains over muscle. You SEALs can do push-ups until the sun goes down but I'm a Green Beret. We got the brains and the looks."

"Yeah, right," McKenzie growled. "If you're so smart, how come you're in here with me?"

That was a good question, Thorpe silently acknowledged. Although they were from different branches of service, as McKenzie had pointed out, they, along with several dozen other members of the military's elite special operations forces, had been co-opted to form covert Department of Energy SO/NESTs teams—Special Operations Nuclear Emergency Search Teams.

At least that was the official jargon on their orders and the explanation given to the congressional oversight committee. In reality, he and McKenzie represented the spear point of much more than simply a search team.

They were actually part of the unit the Department of Defense used to patrol the world to keep the cauldron of nuclear weapons and materials from boiling over. Regular DOE SO/NEST teams were designed to clean up the mess after a nuclear problem occurred. They were reactive. DOD SO/NEST teams were proactive. People like McKenzie and Thorpe searched out potential nuclear problems before they escalated and a mess had to be cleaned up. So far they had been successful, but all it took was one failure and no one on the teams dwelled on that. The pressure was intense and men serving on SO/NEST rarely lasted more than a couple of years before they burned out.

Thorpe had been with SO/NEST for six months. McKenzie was the senior man in the group, with over four years of experience. The stress had aged him.

"You ever think about the insanity of what we do?" McKenzie suddenly said.

Thorpe was startled. That wasn't exactly the sort of question one asked on the inbound leg of a dangerous operation. "It's our job," he replied.

"Job?" McKenzie said. "Cutting grass, now that's a job. Being a doctor, that's a job. A doctor does an operation that saves somebody's life everybody thinks he's a god. He gets paid like one, too."

"We save millions of lives and what do we get? Shit, that's what we get. Hell, we don't even get hazardous duty pay."

"We don't get hazardous duty pay," Thorpe said, "because then the Department of Defense would have to tell Congress what we do in order to authorize it. And what we're doing is not exactly legal in the eyes of U.S. or international law. Not only are we not supposed to be operating overseas like this, it would scare the piss out of the civilians if they knew how close things get sometimes."

"Maybe the civilians need a scare," McKenzie argued. "Everyone thinks the world is safer now that the Cold War is over, but they're fooling themselves. Everything's gotten a lot more dangerous. Too many bombs, too much nuclear material floating around. Too many people playing shady games."

"You know I got passed over on my last promotion, don't you? The promotion board OK'd me, but then some fucking civilian oversight board noticed that I'd been at Tailhook. Fuck, I wasn't even in the goddamn hotel when those aviators were doing their stuff. I was representing SEAL Team Two at the convention."

"Sorry about that," Thorpe murmured, keeping his eyes on the control panel. He'd known McKenzie for the past six months, but had never worked this closely with him. Listening to him, Thorpe was beginning to wish he wasn't on this mission with the man.

"Fucking civilians," McKenzie said harshly, drawing a concerned look from Thorpe across the flooded chamber. "They're talking about chaptering me out, taking away my pension. We're the ones getting screwed while they sit at home and bitch about taxes and cut our fucking benefits. Fuck them all."

"Nav update?" Thorpe asked, trying to draw the older man's attention back to the task at hand.

After McKenzie gave him their present location, they both lapsed into silence. While his hands were steady on the controls, Thorpe felt the tension in the rest of his body and had to force himself to relax.

Thorpe's six-foot-two frame was cramped in the limited space allowed him. Under his wet suit, his body was well muscled, the result of a fierce daily workout routine.

His face, hidden by the mask he wore, was the deep brown of a man heavily exposed to the harshest of the sun's rays. He already carried the deep lines and crevasses that signaled late middle age. Only his blue eyes hinted that he was just thirty-four. If he had allowed his hair to grow beyond the thick, short stubble he favored it would have been dark and liberally sprinkled with gray.

Next to Thorpe, McKenzie had a better lengthwise fit at slightly less than five-foot-six, but his barrel chest and massively muscled arms made it difficult for him to move around. Before joining SO/NEST, McKenzie had carried the label of strongest man in the SEAL teams, quite a feat among a group of men who prided themselves on their physical conditioning. During physical training Thorpe had seen the older man bench press over three hundred pounds. McKenzie had as much pride in his body as a two-thousand-dollar-an-hour-model.

Both men stayed as still as they could during the run in, trying to keep the trim of the SDV steady.

"Running clear," McKenzie eventually said in a level voice. "I put us at three klicks off coast. Change heading to one-one-zero degrees."

"One-one-zero degrees," Thorpe confirmed, as he manipulated the controls. He glanced at his partner. The earlier outburst seemed forgotten, as McKenzie's demeanor eased.

"Two minutes."

"Roger."

The SDV slid through the water, the propellers leaving no trace fifty feet below the surface. As they drew closer McKenzie directed Thorpe nearer the surface as the ocean floor rose beneath them.

"We have one hundred feet under us," McKenzie announced. "Thirty above."

"Eighty down, twenty up."

"Sixty down, ten up. Hold vertical."

Thorpe slowed their forward speed and held their depth steady.

McKenzie was watching his screen intently. "Forty down. Route still clear."

Thorpe slowed until they were at a crawl.

"I've got solid contact," McKenzie said. "Shoreline," he confirmed. "New heading, eight-zero degrees."

"Eight-zero degrees." The SDV turned slightly left.

"Easy, easy," McKenzie muttered as he watched numbers tick off on his screen. "On my mark. Ten down, ten up. Hold."

Thorpe brought the SDV to a halt, then slowly let the craft sink until it rested on the bottom, in twenty feet of water, two hundred yards from shore.

Thorpe reached out and flipped a switch on the control panel. "Beacon on." He checked what looked like a large wristwatch strapped to his left forearm. A small red dot glowed. "I read the SDV beacon six by six."

McKenzie did the same. "Six by six."

Thorpe was doing everything by the book, following a checklist taped to the left side of his compartment. "Begin shutdown."

Each man turned off their parts of the SDV until all that was functioning was the beacon and the air supply.

"Switch to personal air," Thorpe ordered before he turned off the SDV's air supply. He glanced over. McKenzie pulled out his air hose, which also disconnected him from the internal communication system. McKenzie gave him a thumbs-up. Thorpe switched on his own rebreather then flipped a switch cutting off the internal air.

They pushed open their hatches and slid out, pulling their water-proofed rucksacks with them. Leaving the Mark IX resting on the bottom, they swam toward the shore, the rucksacks towed on six-foot lines attached to safety lines at their waists.

The two men ascended until they were just below the moonlit surface. Their fins flickered back and forth, propelling them smoothly toward shore. Thorpe held a nav board right in front of his face, following the azimuth determined from their mission briefing.

After a few minutes both men could feel the sea change. They knew they were close to shore from the increasing swell. Thorpe tapped McKenzie on the shoulder. McKenzie held position while Thorpe surfaced. Thorpe rode a wave up and looked shoreward. He could make out lights to the left but the shore ahead was dark. Thorpe hoped their underwater navigation had been accurate. He returned to McKenzie.

Together, they moved forward until they could feel the tips of their fins hit the bottom. Thorpe edged ahead, the surf lifting him and then slamming him down into the sand. Before the water pulled him back, Thorpe dug his hands into the sand and held his place, then scuttled forward a few more feet. He could feel McKenzie behind him, pulling off his fins. McKenzie then crawled to his side and Thorpe returned the favor. Each retrieved his rucksack and unfastened the submachine gun tied to it, pulling back the slide and making sure there was a round in the chamber, ready to fire, then pulling the muzzle plug out. They slipped an arm through the shoulder strap of their ruck and lay at the edge of the surf, listening carefully.

Thorpe stood and sprinted across the sand, McKenzie right on his heels. They reached the concealment of the dunes. The dry desert air felt good against their faces, the only part of their skin exposed.

Thorpe carefully unsealed his ruck, making sure it made no noise. He pulled out a small handheld device and turned it on. The GPR—Global Positioning Receiver—quickly accessed the nearest three DOD satellites overhead and pinpointed their position to within five meters.

"We're four hundred yards south," Thorpe whispered. He didn't think that was too bad for an eight-kilometer underwater infiltration. Both he and McKenzie donned their night-vision goggles. Thorpe waited a moment for his eyes to adjust to the slightly green and depth-distorted display.

Thorpe shouldered his ruck. He stood and led the way, carefully moving through the dunes to the north, McKenzie behind him and to the right.

They now heard another noise over the pounding surf: heavy diesel engines. Thorpe slowed, searching for the guards that would be near. A high dune lay across their path and they crawled until they could just see over it.

"Shit," McKenzie muttered. Four large military-style trucks were parked with their open tailgates pointed toward the beach. But the trucks were not the focus of McKenzie's comment. Rather he was referring to the two tanks, one with its main gun aimed out to sea, the other guarding the sandy road that led inland.

"They're Merkavas," McKenzie said, confirming what Thorpe had already determined from their distinctive shape. "What the hell are the Israelis doing here?"

Thorpe didn't have an answer. His and McKenzie's need-to-know had only extended to a rumor that there would be transfer of a large amount of weapons-grade plutonium. The plutonium, supposedly smuggled out of Russia, was to be delivered to the buyer tonight on this beach. They had not been informed who was doing the smuggling or who was doing the buying, but the assumption that an Arab group was involved on the receiving end had seemed likely since they were lying on Lebanese sand.

Thorpe and McKenzie had no idea how even this limited information was obtained. They had received only the filtered-down classified version from Department of Defense intelligence channels.

Both men flinched as the seaward tank turned on its high-powered searchlight. The beam spread across the water and Thorpe was glad they had come in four hundred meters to the south. He could see armed men walking around the perimeter, the nearest only twenty meters away on the far slope of the dune.

"What now, Mr. Brains?" McKenzie whispered.

"We get our air and ground support on station and we film," Thorpe said.

"Those are Israelis," McKenzie hissed. "Not some ragheads. Something heavy is going down here."

Thorpe retrieved the handset for the small backpack satellite radio from his ruck. The radio was hooked to a specially designed frequency-jumping scrambler that made it impossible for the transmission to be intercepted. "Heaven, this is Topaz. We are on target. Over."

Heaven was the code name for their commander on board an aircraft carrier two hundred miles to the west.

"This is Heaven. Read you five by. Give us a description of what you have. Over."

"Four trucks waiting on the beach. Also we've got two Merkava tanks standing guard, so your people better have something to take care of that. Approximately two dozen men on foot armed with automatic weapons. Over."

"Did you say Merkavas? Over."

Thorpe glanced at McKenzie who only grunted as he opened his ruck. "Roger. Over."

While Thorpe was talking, McKenzie pulled out a palm-sized digital video camera with a specially designed night lens. Instead of recording the image on film or tape, the camera computerized and digitized directly onto a small CD-ROM disk. McKenzie began filming.

After a few seconds of silence, Thorpe keyed the mike. "Request support stand by, over."

"This is Heaven. Your support is standing by and coming on this channel. Call sign Angel. Will be monitoring. Update us any changes. I still reserve final go. Out."

Thorpe keyed the mike. "Angel, this is Topaz. Over."

The voice that came over the air had a distinct dull roar in the background that indicated the speaker was sitting in a cockpit moving at several hundred miles an hour. "This is Angel. Standing by. We're four minutes out from your location and waiting. Over."

"Roger," Thorpe said, "stand by. Over."

According to their briefing, Angel consisted of several Harrier jets and four helicopters full of heavily armed Marines flying in from the carrier. Thorpe knew the Harriers could make short work of the tanks and the Marines could finish the job.

Something slid into the light sent out by the searchlight. There was the sound of a strong wind, then a hovercraft came into view, rapidly approaching the shore, coming up onto the beach and blowing sand about. There were no markings on the vehicle.

Thorpe pulled the mike close to his lips. "This is Topaz. We've a got a hovercraft coming in. The deal is going down. Request Angel come on in. Over."

The hovercraft pulled up directly behind the four trucks and slowly settled down. Men ran up to the rear deck and began rolling barrels down a plank onto the sand and then four men lifted each one into the rear of a truck. The barrels were painted bright red.

"Pay dirt," McKenzie muttered. "I'll bet you every cent of my measly salary that those barrels contain cased plutonium."

"I wouldn't take the bet," Thorpe whispered. "The question is, who's the supplier?" Thorpe keyed the mike, wondering why he had not received a reply to his previous message. "Angel, this is Topaz. We have positive confirmation of hot materials. Request Angel come in. Over."

"Topaz, this is Heaven. Negative. I am switching you over to call sign Loki. Take all orders from Loki. Out."

Thorpe looked at McKenzie in confusion. There was a brief break of static, then a new voice came on. "Topaz, this is Loki, over."

"This is Topaz," Thorpe replied.

"Abort mission. Return to home base. Over."

Thorpe glanced at McKenzie. "This is Topaz. I say again. Confirm hot materials here. Request Angel. Over."

"Angel is heading home, suggest you do the same. Out." The radio went dead.

"Fuck!" McKenzie hissed. "They've left us!"

At that moment, they both heard a slight noise to their rear. Thorpe was still putting the mike down and turning when he heard the low popping of McKenzie's submachine gun spewing rounds.

Thorpe caught a glimpse of a figure tumbling back down the dune. Someone else was there and a muzzle flashed. Thorpe didn't hear anything, but he reacted instinctively, firing at the flash.

Leaving their rucks behind, Thorpe and McKenzie slid down the slope to where the bodies lay, scanning the area for more guards. Both men were dead. They were dressed in khaki and armed with automatic rifles with bulky silencers on top.

McKenzie swore as he peered down at the face of the man at his feet. "They're Agency!"

"What?" Thorpe said.

"I know this guy," McKenzie said. "He's fucking CIA." McKenzie stood. "It's a set-up! That's it. I've had it with this bullshit! No wonder they aborted us." McKenzie popped the CD out of the camera and slid it into a pocket on the inside of his wet suit.

Thorpe grabbed the chin of the man he shot and turned the face up. He spotted the small boom mike attached to the headset the man wore and immediately knew what that meant.

He turned to McKenzie. "We've been made!"

"What?" McKenzie said, then both spun around as the whine of a turbine engine revving up came over the top of the dune, followed by the tip of a 105-mm muzzle.

The Merkava tank was moving at thirty miles an hour as it crested the dune and it flew almost ten feet before the heavy treads crashed down onto the sand.

Thorpe and McKenzie barely had time to roll out of the way as the steel behemoth tore by, showering them with sand and pieces of the dead bodies it had crushed.

The driver of the tank pivot steered, reversing one tread while keeping the other going forward and the tank abruptly turned. Thorpe fired on automatic, more a gesture of defiance than with any hope of causing damage. The bullets ricocheted off the metal in a spray of sparks.

"Run!" McKenzie screamed. "The water!"

Together they scrambled toward the surf two hundred yards away. The tank ate up the distance at four times their speed.

"Split!" McKenzie yelled when the tank was less than twenty feet behind them. Thorpe jigged left while McKenzie went right. With an instant decision to make, the driver turned left. Thorpe looked over his shoulder and saw the blunt edge of the tank's front slope five feet behind him. He dove into the sand, rolling onto his back and watching as the treads came toward him. He rolled once more and the right tread clanked by less than a foot away.

Thorpe was in total blackness and smothered with diesel fumes. Worse though, was the overwhelming sense of weight on top of him, the metal bottom of the tank eight inches above his body, the treads blocking movement to either side.

The tank kept going and Thorpe reached up, grabbing a loop of the tow cable overhanging off the back deck and was dragged through the sand as the tank turned around to the right. The driver briefly searched for Thorpe's body. When he couldn't find it, he decided to go after the other man.

McKenzie was running like a halfback through the defensive backfield, cutting back and forth, hoping to be able to turn quicker than the tank. But the driver was very good, matching McKenzie's moves and closing the distance. At the last second, McKenzie did what Thorpe had done, throwing himself down in a shallow ditch between the treads.

The tank rolled over the trench and McKenzie was safe, directly between the treads, but this time the driver was prepared. He slammed on the brakes, then pivot-steered back and forth, digging the treads down into the sand and moving the tank left and right in two-foot arcs.

McKenzie realized that if he didn't move soon the treads would settle down in the sand and the bottom of the tank would crush him. He scrambled through the sand trying to get from under the tank to the rear. At that moment, the driver unexpectedly made a ninety-degree turn to the left.

McKenzie couldn't move fast enough. The tread racing by caught his left forearm and sucked it into the gnashing metal. If there had been a hard surface underneath, there would have been nothing left of the limb, but the sand gave slightly.

From his position still hanging on to the rear of the tank, Thorpe heard McKenzie's scream over the roar of the engine. Thorpe let go and rolled away, then got to his feet. The tank was still churning sand, back and forth. Thorpe ran forward timing his jump to coincide with the tank's movements. He slammed onto the rear deck and grasped for a handhold.

His left hand closed around a ridge of metal and Thorpe hauled himself up. He quickly climbed onto the turret. The tank commander's hatch was slightly open, enough for the commander to look forward. Thorpe pulled his 9-mm pistol out of its holster and stuck it in the hatch and fired, hitting the commander in the side of the head, blowing brains and blood all over the inside of the turret.

Thorpe ripped open the hatch and dove in headfirst, sliding past the dead body. He was firing as he fell and he kept firing as he hit the metal grating on the floor of the turret. When the magazine was finally empty, the entire three-man crew was dead, riddled with bullets. Thorpe got to his feet as he slammed another magazine into the pistol.

The driver's dead foot slipped off the pedal and the tank came to a halt, engine still rumbling. Thorpe was just climbing out the top hatch when he spotted the second tank, a quarter mile away and closing fast.

Thorpe dropped back down into the turret. He grabbed the tank commander's override control lever and turned the turret, looking out the top of the hatch until he had the barrel lined up. The tank was heading directly for him.

Now he could only hope there was a round in the breach. Thorpe pulled back the trigger on the front of the override. There was a blossom of flame from the end of the muzzle and the blast blew back over Thorpe, a sudden surge of warm wind.

The kinetic sabot round crossed the distance between the two tanks in less than one-tenth of a second. It hit at the turret-body junction of the second tank, punching through the front and out the other side, leaving only two small, four-inch-circumference holes in its wake.

But the metal that had been in those holes killed the crew as the shrapnel ricocheted around the inside of the tank, the armor protection turning deadly as it kept the metal shards trapped inside like a swarm of angry bees. The crew was torn to shreds.

One piece of shrapnel hit the stowed rounds at the rear of the turret and ignited one of them. The round blew, taking with it those packed next to it, and the turret popped off in the tremendous secondary explosion.

Thorpe climbed out and jumped over the side to the sand. He momentarily froze as he spotted McKenzie, crawling with one arm toward the water, leaving a trail of blood in his wake. Thorpe ran over and knelt next to him.

"Oh, shit," Thorpe exclaimed when he saw the man's crushed limb in the glow of the burning tank. McKenzie's left forearm was a mess of mangled flesh and bone, hanging from his elbow by half-ripped tendons.

"Go!" McKenzie hissed. "Get out of here."

Thorpe pulled a length of parachute cord and a small Maglite out of his combat vest. He wrapped the cord around McKenzie's upper left arm. Thorpe tied a square knot in the thin rope as tight as he could, leaving the Maglite inside the knot. Thorpe then twisted the Maglite around several times, cinching down the cord and cutting most of the blood flow with the makeshift tourniquet.

Thorpe was reaching for his first-aid packet attached to his vest to get a painkiller when a string of tracers split the night, flying over their heads. He could hear voices in the distance, shouting, getting closer, firing wildly into the night.

"Go!" McKenzie insisted.

Thorpe grabbed McKenzie and, with a surge of adrenaline, threw the bulky man over his shoulders.

McKenzie was protesting, demanding that Thorpe leave him behind, but Thorpe staggered to his feet and headed for the surf.

"I'm dead," McKenzie yelled in Thorpe's ear. "Leave me."

Thorpe didn't have the breath to answer, his feet sliding in the sand as he ran for the water. Another burst of tracers went by, this time a bit closer.

Thorpe hit the water running. As the water splashed up around his legs, he reached up and grabbed McKenzie's safety line and hooked it into his own belt. He lowered McKenzie into the water, then dove forward. The line momentarily brought him to an abrupt halt, then Thorpe began the difficult business of swimming, pulling McKenzie behind him.

Thorpe swam as hard as he could, trying to put distance between them and the shore. Those on the shore were still firing wildly, tracers whipsawing in all directions.

After a couple of minutes, Thorpe pulled on the line and brought McKenzie in close to check on him.

"Leave me," McKenzie said, his face white from loss of blood. He'd popped his inflatable vest because he was too weak even to float.

"Shut up," Thorpe said as he continued to kick with his legs. "We'll make it."

"My blood will draw sharks," McKenzie warned. "Go while you can."

Thorpe hit the homer on his wrist and checked the direction. The SDV was to the southwest. Thorpe grabbed McKenzie and pulled him along as he swam in that direction.

"How far to the SDV?" McKenzie asked in a dazed voice.

Thorpe looked at his monitor. "About a hundred yards."

"I can't dive," McKenzie muttered, then he passed out, his head lolling back on the preserver.

Thorpe swam farther, towing McKenzie, and checking the homer again. They were over the SDV. In the dark, Thorpe turned to look at McKenzie. The older man's face was white, the muscles slack. As best he could in the dark and swelling waters, Thorpe made sure there was no blood passing through the tourniquet, and that McKenzie's face was out of the water. After letting the wounded man go, Thorpe inserted the mouthpiece for his rebreather and dove. His own lacerations pulsed with pain in the salt water, but Thorpe ignored them.

He was at the SDV in half a minute. Forgetting the checklist, Thorpe powered up. He retraced his route and surfaced. Kneeling in the hatch, Thorpe looked about. McKenzie was nowhere to be seen.

Reaching down, Thorpe gave power to the screws and anxiously began driving the SDV in slowly increasing circles. The six-foot swells knocked him against the side of the hatch and made it difficult for him to see. The SDV wasn't designed to operate on the surface and was tossed about like an empty canoe.

Thorpe spotted something to his left and turned the SDV in that direction. Relief flooded through him as he saw that it was McKenzie. Thorpe brought the submersible next to the unconscious figure. He tied off his safety line to a hitch on the top, then slid into the water. He paddled over to McKenzie and grabbed hold of the other man's safety line. McKenzie was still alive, but barely.

Then Thorpe felt something slide underneath him. He looked down. In the moonlight he could see a large gray form lazily swim by. Glancing up, Thorpe saw the dorsal fin of an eight-foot shark less than two feet in front of him, slicing through the calm water. Thorpe kept his legs moving as he watched the fin turn and head back. Thorpe pulled McKenzie to his chest.

Putting his body between McKenzie and the shark, Thorpe pulled on his safety line, drawing them toward the SDV, expecting at any moment to feel the rip of razor-sharp teeth in his back.

Thorpe reached the edge of the SDV and with a surge of adrenaline, shoved the older man up over the side, rolling him into his cocoon. Thorpe swiftly scrambled up the same side. Clinging to the top, he sealed McKenzie's hatch, then climbed over into his own, sealing it behind him.

Grabbing the controls, he adjusted the radar to home in on the submarine's beacon and opened the throttle all the way.

2

T HE COMBAT TALON came in low through the desert mountain pass, wingtips less than forty feet from the rock walls on either side. Inside the cockpit of the modified C-130 cargo plane, the pilots were flying by computer and long experience: watching their low-light television displays and terrain-avoidance radar while listening to the instructions from the navigators sitting in front of their computer consoles in the forward half of the cargo bay.

The flight south from the air base in Turkey had been easy, as had been the approach over Lebanon, but as the Israeli border drew closer, the Talon went lower and lower, until it was now skimming along, less than forty feet above ground level, well below even the best Israeli radar.

The Talon was just west of the Golan Heights in the jumbled terrain of northern Israel. It was uninhabited terrain and satellite imagery had confirmed this low-level course through the canyon was free of military forces.

There was near-total darkness outside, the moon having completed its cycle, and only the stars giving the faintest hint of light. Inside the cargo bay, behind the black curtain that sealed off the Talon crew from the people and equipment in the rear half, four black-clad figures waited, gathered around a canister that was rigged with a cargo parachute. The four also wore chutes, along with rucksacks rigged in front under their reserves and weapons strapped across their chests.

"Six minutes!" the loadmaster screamed, straining to be heard above the four super-charged turboprop engines that powered the plane.

One of the four kneeled down and unhooked the snap link from the cargo chute on top of the bundle and hooked it to the steel cable running over their heads along the right side of the plane. Then the four hooked up their own static line snap hooks right behind the bundles.

"Three minutes!"

The four were struggling to stay on their feet as the plane jigged its way through the canyon, the pilots staying below the rim of the walls. A particularly hard cut to the right threw all four against the other side of the plane, but their eyes were on the canister which teetered for a second, before settling back down in its specially designed holder.

The noise level increased even more as a horizontal crack appeared in the back, open to the chill night air. The crack widened as the back ramp lowered on hydraulic arms until it was level and the top disappeared into the cargo bay roof under the large tail.

They now had the pilot's view in reverse and watched as rocky walls flew by and disappeared as the plane shifted and turned. The deck slanted up as the plane gained jump altitude.

"One minute!" The crew chief knelt with a razor-sharp knife in his hand, the blade against the nylon strap holding the canister. With his free hand he cracked a chem light tied off on the apex of the cargo chute.

All eyes were riveted to the glowing red light above the opening. The seconds stretched out as adrenaline altered their sense of time, slowing it down, forcing the team into an agonized tension.

The light turned green. The knife sliced through the nylon and the canister slid out the back, its chute instantly billowing open. The four raced out, stepping off the ramp into darkness, their specially designed chutes opening within a second of exiting the ramp.

And they needed that quick opening as they were only two hundred and fifty feet above the canyon floor. Triple canopies exploded above each jumper, jarring their forward speed from the aircraft's hundred-and-twenty-five knots to zero in less than two seconds. Each jumper quickly pulled eighteen-inch attaching straps and their rucksacks fell to the end of fifteen-foot lowering lines to dangle below their feet. Just as quickly, each jumper reached up, found their toggles, and steered their chutes toward the green glow of the chem light on top of the bundle's chute. They barely had time to turn in the correct direction before the ground came rushing up and they rotated their elbows in tight against their faces, put their feet together and flexed their knees, waiting for impact.

The bundle hit sand and the four jumpers followed. Each rucksack touched down, followed by the hard slam of rapidly descending bodies all within forty feet of the bundle.

Three of the four were on their feet immediately, unhooking their parachutes while shaking off the shock of landing. Throwing rucksacks over their shoulders, weapons at the ready, they ran over to the canister, pulling their chutes with them.

"Where's Scanlon?" Brinn, the leader, asked, checking the other two faces.

They turned and looked at the fourth chute lying on the sand about thirty feet away, and the motionless dark form at the end of the suspension lines.

"Shit," Brinn muttered as they ran over. Brinn was tall and built like a linebacker. His face was weathered with age and stress and his crew cut hair was mostly gray. Like the others, he was dressed in black fatigues with a combat vest covering the top half of his body. Adorning the vest were the assorted tools of Brinn's chosen trade. A pair of night-vision goggles were looped around his neck and he pulled them up.

Reaching the body, Brinn unsnapped the man's helmet, grimacing as he was greeted by the sight of dark red blood mixed with gray brain matter. Looking aside he spotted the sharp boulder that had caused the injury. Scanlon's luck had run out. It could have been any of them, Brinn knew, but of the four, Scanlon was the one they could least afford to lose.

But there was a plan for that, an extra body for that contingency. He turned and stared at the person directly across from him who was looking down, ashen-faced, at the dead man. He had doubts about Scanlon's backup, never a good thing on a mission.

"You're primary weapons now, Parker," Brinn said. "Sanchez is your backup."

Parker looked up from the body without comprehension.

"You are primary weapons," Brinn repeated. "You got that?"

Parker slowly nodded, fighting the shock of Scanlon's violent death.

"Don't fuck up," Brinn added as he took off his helmet and placed it next to the body.

Parker followed suit. "I'll do my duty." Long brown hair, tied in a ponytail fell down her back as she shook it free of the confines of the Kevlar helmet. Parker was in her mid-thirties, five-and-a-half feet tall and slender. Her face had high cheekbones and was creased with worry lines around the edge of her mouth and eyes. At the present moment, those lines were furrowed as she turned from the body and looked at the canister.

"Let's move," Brinn ordered.

"Wait. What about Scanlon?" the third member of the party, Sanchez, asked. He was a wiry Hispanic, with dark skin and close-cropped black hair. He was kneeling over the body, his voice betraying his emotion.

"Rig a thermal grenade on the body to go off in four hours," Brinn ordered. "There'll be nothing left but bone and teeth. His gear is sterile anyway, so he's deniable. We sure as shit can't carry him with us." He tapped Parker on the arm. "Let's get the package and get ready to move."

Parker caught the gaze that Sanchez had focused on her. It was difficult to see his features but for a moment his black eyes held her with an intensity that caused her to turn back to the canister. She saw that her hands were shaking and she drew a deep breath.

An hour later, the three lay sweating in the chilly early morning air just below the east canyon rim. The five-hundred-foot climb carrying the slung canister had been harder than they'd anticipated and time was growing short.

Brinn pulled a small GPR—Global Positioning Receiver—out of his combat vest. He checked the data on the small screen. Sanchez was pulling a radio and small satellite dish out of his rucksack, opening the dish and setting it at the proper azimuth and elevation to their designated satellite. Parker was unsnapping the clasps on the side of the canister.

"We're in the right spot," Brinn said. He looked up at the crest ten feet above and gestured for the other two to stop what they were doing and follow him. The three slithered up on their bellies until they could see over.

A quarter mile away, set against the side of a steep mountain, a road led up to a massive steel and concrete portal, which was surrounded by rows of barbed wire and armored vehicles. The door set in the opening was big enough to accommodate six vehicles side by side and was over thirty feet high. The door was protected from overhead observation by huge camouflage nets draped on steel poles. In the bright green glow of their night-vision goggles, they could see not only the door, but the guards surrounding it, and the bright glow of infrared searchlights that illuminated the entire area for the guards' own night-vision goggles.

"That's the tip of the iceberg," Brinn said, indicating the door. "The Israelis have hollowed out most of that mountain." He tapped his hand on a flat rocky space to his right. "Put the special here," he instructed Parker. "Get me up on MILSTAR," he ordered Sanchez.

The other two scurried back to their equipment. Straining, Parker dragged the sixty-pound canister to the indicated spot. She finished removing the snaps and flipped open a panel, revealing a computer keyboard and LED display set into the side of the canister.

She pushed an inset button and the screen came alive, scrolling through its own internal systems check.

"I have access to MILSTAR," Sanchez whispered from the radio.

Parker opened a small door to the left of the keyboard and pulled a thin cable out. She handed the free end to Sanchez who screwed it into a corresponding portal on the top of the SATCOM radio.

She typed a command into the keyboard and watched the screen. "We have secure connection from the REACT computer to MILSTAR," she announced in a low voice.

"I've sent our infiltration report burst to Cheyenne Mountain," Sanchez said. "They know we're in location and ready."

Brinn nodded. He took one last look at the tunnel entrance, then slid down next to Parker. "You sure on your procedure?" he asked.

"I'm sure," she replied.

He looked at her long and hard, clearly unhappy about the turn of events. His stare was broken by words forming on the screen.

"I have an incoming Emergency Action Message," Parker said. The screen cleared and new words formed, followed by a six digit code. "Emergency Action Message received," Parker said. She reached inside her black fatigues and pulled out the thin steel chain she wore around her neck. Attached to it was a laminated card wrapped in black plastic. She peeled the plastic back and checked the numbers on it against those on the screen.

"EAM code is current and valid," Parker called out.

"Code current and valid," Sanchez repeated, checking his own card.

"Code verified," Brinn said. "Prepare weapon," he ordered.

Parker typed in the sequence of commands that she had long ago memorized and practiced day after day. After precisely forty-seven seconds she stopped. "Weapon prepared."

"Check the EAM," Brinn ordered. "What's the delay set for?"

For a moment the trained routine broke as all three sets of eyes met over the canister. Parker looked back down. "As briefed, I read a delay of two hours from activation to blast if the bomb is initiated."

"Yeah, right," Sanchez muttered, earning himself a glare from Brinn.

"Hopefully we won't have to find out if the computer's telling the truth," Parker said.

Sanchez laughed bitterly. "Yeah, hopefully."

Brinn's voice had a hard edge to it. "Captain Sanchez, I don't like that tone."

Sanchez kept quiet, merely lifting his eyes to Parker as if they had some silent pact. Parker ignored him, wishing she could leave the bleak desert landscape and this blighted mission. She tried not to dwell on the next few hours, but instead thought of exfiltration and home.

Parker looked at the sky. There was no sign of dawn yet. They had another two hours of darkness. Brinn pointed across the canyon and down to the left where a knoll was silhouetted against the night sky about three miles away. "That's our overwatch and exfiltration point. I hope we can make it in two hours if we have to."

Brinn leaned back against his rucksack. "Might as well make yourself—" he paused as there was a low beep from the computer in the side of the canister.

"Oh, fuck," Sanchez muttered.

Parker read the new message with a trembling voice. "We are ordered to free firing locks so the bomb can be remotely controlled by the REACT computer through MILSTAR."

"Great, just fucking great," Sanchez said. Freeing the firing locks took activation control away from the team.

"Free firing locks," Brinn ordered, ignoring Sanchez.

"Something's not right about this," Sanchez said flatly and with certainty.

Brinn shook his head. "Listen, we got sent in here with this thing. We have an EAM. Let's do our job, people."

"Jesus, what if this is some mistake? We're going to set this thing off—" Sanchez said, but Brinn cut him off.

"We're not setting it off. We're just removing the safety firing locks. Someone from the National Command Authority will give the order to fire this bomb and that order will be relayed from Cheyenne Mountain through MILSTAR to the REACT computer and that will set this thing off."

"But we're not at war with Israel," Sanchez argued. "I mean, what's the purpose here?"

Brinn's voice sharpened. "Do you want to sit here and discuss this until we get scarfed up by the Israelis or are you going to do your job, Captain?" He turned to Parker. "Remove the safety firing locks."

Parker took a deep breath and flexed her fingers before she began typing into the keyboard, entering the code words she had memorized during the mission briefing. She entered the two words, then put her finger over the enter key.

"Do it!" Brinn hissed.

Parker pressed the enter key and the screen cleared. A highlighted box blinked, waiting for Sanchez's code word.

Sanchez didn't move. Brinn's hand slid down toward the pistol grip of the submachine gun slung over his shoulder.

Sanchez saw the move. "Hey, Major," he pleaded, "we could be starting World War III here. I just feel like something's wrong. There's no reason to arm this thing. I tell you there's something fucked up going on and we're about to add to it."

"You don't need a reason, Captain," Brinn said stoically. "Your job is to type in your code."

"Don't you think I know that, sir?" Sanchez replied. "This isn't my first mission. But we never went as far as removing the firing locks before."

Parker silently watched the two men arguing, alarm and fear swimming across her fine features. She was having a difficult time accepting that this, her first Red Flyer mission, would probably be her last. Nuclear weapons were her specialty and beyond Sanchez's concerns about the mission, she had her own fears about removing the locks. They'd been assured that there would be a two-hour delay if the locks were removed and the weapon activated by the REACT computer from afar. A certain twisted logic in the back of her brain told her that there might not be a delay. The bomb could go off the second the locks were removed and a firing code transmitted. Why would the powers-that-be leave the bomb sitting here for two hours unattended? To allow the four—check that, three—of them to get away? A lousy three people weighed against a tactical nuclear strike on Israel's secret nuclear weapons storage bunker made for a very uneven equation in her mind.

Despite that concern though, she had entered her code. What other option was there? They were here and they'd received their orders. Parker felt strangely detached from reality; even her fear felt like someone else's pressed upon her. Sixteen years of military training from her first day at the Air Force Academy was allowing her to function and follow orders.

"We do our duty," Brinn said. "Enter your code."

Sanchez didn't move.

The muzzle of Brinn's sub was now centered on Sanchez's forehead. "Enter your fucking code to remove the locks, Captain, or I guarantee you'll never leave this place alive. Your only chance is to do your duty."

"Scanlon was primary weapons," Sanchez said. "Maybe he knew something we don't. We don't know exactly what's going on. We—" Sanchez was again cut off by Brinn.

"We're not supposed to know exactly what's happening. We're supposed to do what we're trained to do when we're given the correct orders!" His finger tightened on the trigger. "You have five seconds, Captain, or I blow your head off. And you know I'll do it." The muzzle moved ever so slightly. "You have three seconds," Brinn warned.

Sanchez looked at Parker but what could she say? She'd already entered her code. She looked down into the canyon, unconsciously holding her breath, fearing either outcome of Sanchez's decision.

With shaking hands, Sanchez took Parker's place and typed in his code word. "May God forgive us," he whispered.

All three tensed as the screen cleared. They each, to varying extent, expected the bomb to go off in their faces. As the seconds passed and nothing happened, they slowly relaxed.

A new message came up. "Locks are removed," Parker read. "Weapon is armed and ready for incoming commands."

Another message flashed and numbers began counting down on the screen.

"Bomb is armed and firing sequence initiated," Parker whispered in disbelief. "Two hours until firing." Without consciously thinking of it, her fingers set the timer on her wristwatch for two hours and she pressed the start button.

Sanchez stared at the bomb. "I am the destroyer of worlds," he whispered.

Brinn, his professional demeanor cracked by the last couple of minutes, jabbed a finger in Sanchez's chest. "You're a crazy fuck. If it's the last thing I do, you're out of Red Flyer. You can kiss your career good-bye."

Sanchez looked at the star-filled sky. "You are both just another button on that panel."

"Another word and I'm placing you under arrest," Brinn snarled. "Now, let's get out of here."

The other two didn't need any further urging as they gathered up their rucksacks and slithered down the canyon wall.

I t took them one hour and forty-eight minutes of hard climbing to make it to the overwatch position. Breathing heavily, they threw their rucks to the ground as they reached the top of the knoll. Brinn quickly undid the flap on his rucksack and pulled out three long plastic tubes. He unscrewed the ends and slid out the stock, receiver, and barrel for a fifty-caliber sniper rifle. With practiced hands, he quickly bolted the three parts together and slid the eight-power scope on top. The first hint of dawn was showing in the eastern sky, lighting up the Jordanian border.

He pulled back the bolt and chambered one of the five-inch-long rounds. He sighted in on the bomb. It sat where they had left it, undisturbed. His finger trembled lightly on the trigger as he watched, protecting the bomb in its final moments.

"Prepare to record for the damage report," he told Sanchez, the first words spoken since they'd left the bomb.

Sanchez pulled a digital video camera out of his rucksack and trained it in the general direction of the bomb.

Parker leaned back against her rucksack, feeling the sweat beginning to dry on her back. She checked her watch. Six minutes before detonation.

The three were silent as the minutes passed. Parker looked at her watch once more. A minute. She pulled her goggles down and turned them back on. She felt pain in her shoulders and realized she was hunched over behind her ruck, putting it between her and the bomb. She forced herself to straighten up. She knew the effects the bomb would have, knew that they were safe at this distance. But although her mind knew the facts, her body still felt and feared the worst.

Brinn put a special cover over the end of his scope, a device that would protect his eye from the effect of the flash. "Give me a time hack," he ordered.

"Fourteen seconds," Parker said. "Ten." She watched the numbers. "Five. Four. Three. Two. One."

She flinched as there was a sharp flash of light in the direction of the bomb, but just as quickly, the light was gone and nothing happened. No shock wave ... no mushroom cloud ... nothing.

"Malfunction?" Sanchez was looking through binoculars.

"Something blew," Brinn muttered. He jabbed a finger at Sanchez. "Come up on FM radio and see if our exfil chopper is inbound. If you get contact, tell them we have a malfunction."

"They don't malfunction," Parker said in a low voice, but Brinn ignored her.

Sanchez turned on the small FM radio secreted in his vest and put the small headset on. "Condor this is Eagle, over."

He pressed a finger to his ear as he got a reply. He relayed the information to the other two. "Condor is five minutes out."

"Tell them about the malfunction," Brinn insisted. "Tell them the mission is a no-go."

Sanchez repeated the information. He listened to the reply, then slowly looked at the other two. "They know. It was a test," he said.

"What?" Brinn was confused.

"A test. They had a small conventional explosive rigged in the canister, not a nuke," Sanchez said.

"Why the fuck would they have us come out here for a goddamn test?!" Brinn exploded.

"To see if we'd do it," Parker said in a quiet voice.

MAJOR BRINN, Major Parker, and Captain Sanchez were directed into a dimly lit conference room by the taciturn lieutenant who'd been their escort since their arrival at Cheyenne Mountain two hours earlier.

The trip to Colorado had required a series of rides with plenty of time to reflect, from the moment the HH-53 Pavelow helicopter had swooped in to pick them up in Israel and fly them to Turkey, where a U.S. Air Force jet had been waiting to take them to Germany, then on to the United States. They'd been debriefed by several men, some wearing civilian clothes, on the flight back to the States. Parker, Brinn, and Sanchez had spent the flight anxiously awaiting this after-action review of the exercise. Not once had they been told why they'd been sent on a test mission into Israel with what they thought was a nuclear bomb. Nor were any regrets or concerns over Scanlon's death expressed.

The conference room was located inside Cheyenne Mountain, on the southwest side of Colorado Springs. Cheyenne Mountain was a massive granite mountain along the front range of the Rocky Mountains. Pikes Peak was a few miles to the northwest, Colorado Springs to the northeast. The complex inside the mountain had been built in the early 1960s by the Department of Defense to house NORAD, the North American Aerospace Defense Command.

Parker looked around the room. There were several colonels and majors seated around the conference table with junior ranking officers in plastic seats along the walls. Two men, seated all the way at the rear of the room, were shrouded in shadow, only their silhouettes and the dim glow of a pipe. Parker was surprised the man was smoking in here, given that smoking in federal facilities had long ago been banned. The scent of the pipe smoke lay heavy in the room.

Parker and the others snapped to attention as General Willoughby walked into the conference room. The two men in the back remained seated.

"Take your seats," Willoughby ordered as he sat at the head of the table. The general looked about the room, his gaze lingering on Brinn, then Sanchez, and then shifting past Parker to the rear of the room.

"Mr. Lugar," he was looking at the man to the left who didn't acknowledge the introduction. "Mr. Lugar," Willoughby continued, "represents the National Command Authority." Willoughby's head turned to the man smoking the pipe next to Lugar. "Professor Kilten," he said with a nod of his head.

"General," Kilten returned the greeting.

Parker started at the name. She, and every other officer in nuclear weapons command, knew who Kilten was: the designer of the REACT computer system and practically every other piece of computer hardware and software used in the nuclear weapons business. He was the man who had designed and pulled together the entire nuclear command and control structure, from the design of the bombs themselves to the strategic planning for their use.

While military men switched jobs every few years in keeping with their career paths, Kilten was one of the many civilians at the Pentagon who provided long-term expertise in certain fields. Because of that, he knew more about the field than the military men he worked for.

"Let's get this over with," Willoughby said.

The colonel to Willoughby's right got up and stood at the lectern. He opened his portable computer. It had the record from the mission debriefing loaded into its hard drive, from jump-in to the chopper ride out. The colonel went into the after action review, speaking rapidly and succinctly, using the computer display when necessary. It was all recorded and it was pointless to argue the facts.

The colonel flipped down the cover on the laptop after the brief outline of events. "In summary, sir, the exercise was successful although there was a problem when it came to releasing the arming locks on the weapon."

Willoughby nodded. "Thank you, Major." The general turned to the people seated around the table. "I cannot overstate the importance of exercises such as the one we have just debriefed." Willoughby glared at Sanchez. "The security of this country rests on our potential adversaries' certainty that we will not hesitate in the slightest to use our nuclear arsenal. It is our duty. It is the very purpose of our entire command and control system.

"An EAM is a lawful order coming from the National Command Authority," Willoughby continued. "You do not have the option to question that order or any that follow it. If you cannot do your duty, what the hell are you doing in the Air Force, Captain Sanchez? What are you doing in my command?"

"I am doing my duty, sir," Sanchez said, meeting the general's angry gaze straight on.

"Your duty was to disarm the locks, Captain!" Willoughby slapped his palm on the tabletop.

Parker twisted in her seat, wishing she could disappear. She was looking down at her hands, rotating the Air Force Academy ring on her finger.

"Sir, with all due respect, I tried to do the correct thing," Sanchez said, his voice tightly controlled.

Willoughby stared at him, momentarily speechless.

At the rear of the room, Kilten leaned forward into the light. "Why do you say that, Captain Sanchez?"

Sanchez turned in his seat. "The EAM we received was not, as the general said, a legitimate National Command Authority order, but rather a test, as was the entire mission given that the bomb was not nuclear. Therefore General Willoughby's argument is false," Sanchez said. "Because the mission was only a test, my hesitation to disarm the lock was not a factor. I just felt something was wrong."

Willoughby looked stunned by the bizarre logic. "You didn't know it was a test," Willoughby found his voice. "You thought the bomb was real."

Sanchez's words were clipped but still carried a deferential tone. "I felt there was something wrong. I didn't know it was a test, but I didn't feel that it was the real thing either."

"You operate on orders, Captain, not feelings," Willoughby snapped. "The EAM we sent was legitimate as far as you were concerned. You get that order, you do what you are trained to do!"

Sanchez, sensing the inevitable, was emboldened. "Like we're just part of the machine?"

"You are part of the machine. You're the last switch," Willoughby said.

"Gentlemen," Kilten said, his voice quiet in contrast to the other two. "Let us calm down."

Sanchez spoke up. "I may not have done what I was trained to, but I did what a person with some feelings would do."

"Feelings?" Kilten repeated, one eyebrow raised.

General Willoughby had reached the boiling point. "Captain, you are relieved as of this minute!"

Kilten turned his head toward the irate general. "If I may, General, I would like to hear about Captain Sanchez's feelings. Maybe he can articulate why we had the problem removing the locks. And isn't that the point? To perfect the system?"

Sanchez dropped all pretense of military hierarchy and interrupted the older civilian. "Perfect the system? That's what I mean. How do you perfect something that has a basic flaw? The whole thing's nuts!"

Kilten seemed to take Sanchez's words as a personal affront. "Captain, you have no business playing a role in a system you apparently don't understand or believe in."

"I did believe in it once," Sanchez countered. "Nuclear deterrence sounds pretty good until you have your finger on the button and there's no good reason why. Until you're sitting right on top of the bomb and you just left one of your buddies dead with his brains smashed out. You don't want me to think, you just want me to push that button like a rat at a food bar. Well, I'm a man. I have a gut and it tells me things."

General Willoughby snorted. "We're not running the defense of this country on your gut, Captain."

Sanchez was beginning to look tired and defeated and Parker felt a blanket of sadness settle over her. She had never imagined that Sanchez would so completely destroy his own career. She wondered what he could possibly do now. She and Brinn were invisible, barely moving lest some of the attention find them.

Sanchez's voice broke the momentary quiet and he spoke with firm conviction. "You believe that the weakest link in the nuclear system is the human factor. I suppose I'm proof of that, at least from a certain perspective. I believed that bomb was real. I believed we were destroying a big chunk of a nation we've always considered an ally. I felt that was a mistake, so I didn't do my duty. What if it hadn't been a test? What if it was a mistake?"

"You think you're making the system foolproof. You're just taking the checks out. Someday the big mistake will come and you'll just have a bunch of robots listening to the computers. The whole thing will be a machine."

"But a human being will make the decision," Kilten said. "The machine won't act on its own."

"I'm a human being and I made a decision," Sanchez argued, "and you're frying my ass and getting rid of me."

"You're not the National Command Authority," Lugar spoke for the first time. "I represent the NCA and that's who makes the decision to use nuclear weapons."

"Who made the decision to run this training mission in Israel right next to their nuclear weapons storage facility?" Sanchez asked. "If we had been captured by the Israelis, the political repercussions would have been staggering. Scanlon's body being left there, despite the thermite grenade I had to put on him, could still cause trouble if it's found. The casing for that bomb, even after the conventional explosion, will be found."

"We did it there to push you to the limit," Lugar said. "And I'm damn glad we did."

Kilten leaned forward toward Sanchez. "If what you're saying is—"

But Lugar cut in. "Captain, I've heard enough from you. We're not here to debate the system, we came here to talk about what happened on this mission."

"You have to look at the system," Sanchez argued. "If you don't examine the—"

"The system is fine," Willoughby growled. "It's people like you who screw it up."

"Then get people out of the system," Sanchez yelled, finally losing his patience, "and just leave the machines there. If I have no discretion and am not supposed to use my intuition, my human mind, to decide whether or not to unlock the arming control on that bomb, then get us the hell away from the bombs. Have the machines take total control."

"You are being taken out of the system, Captain!" Willoughby snapped. "You'll never work near a damn nuclear weapon again!"

"Fine, sir!" Sanchez ripped the weapons badge off the breast pocket of his coat and tossed it on the table. He stood. "Then I guess I'm done here."

"You're done in the Air Force, young man," Willoughby said to the captain's back as he walked away.

Sanchez paused, his hand on the doorknob and faced the room. "What about Captain Scanlon? Is he just a statistic in all this? What did you tell his widow? Killed in a plane crash during training? Body lost at sea?"

"That's none of your business," Lugar said.

"Scanlon died in your test," Sanchez said, glaring at Kilten.

"I'm sorry about—" Kilten began, but Sanchez opened the door.

"You people are fucked," Sanchez said. He walked out, slamming the door behind him.

Willoughby looked to the rear of the room in the awkward silence that followed. He regained his composure. "Mr. Lugar, Professor Kilten, I'd like to thank you for your assistance in setting up this exercise. Your system worked; it was my people who failed to use it efficiently." Willoughby got to his feet. "You are all dismissed."

They stood. The general walked out the door, the other officers right behind him. As Parker approached the door a low voice called out to her. "I'd like to speak with you for a moment, Major."

Parker turned toward Kilten. The man stood and walked forward into the light. Now that she could see him, Parker saw that Kilten was an old man, nattily dressed in a brown wool suit with a bright bow tie. He was frail and slender, his face hatchet-thin. He wore thick glasses with gold rims. Behind the lenses his eyes were a bright green and sparkled with intelligence.

"Major Parker, if you don't mind, I'm interested in your opinion of what just happened in this room." Kilten's voice was soothing, the antithesis of the general's.

"I don't know if I have an opinion," Parker said. "I do believe Major Scanlon's death played a greater role than any of us are admitting."

"Why do you think that is?"

"I believe Scanlon and Sanchez were friends, sir."

"Friends, oh, yes." Kilten repeated the word with relief, as if it explained everything that had just happened. "It was a pleasure to meet you, Captain," Kilten said. The discussion was apparently over. He turned for the door.

Parker found herself momentarily confused by his reaction.

"Sir—" Parker began and Kilten paused. "Sir," she continued, "why did we go into Israel? I don't understand why we ran such a high-risk operation on foreign soil."

Kilten turned in surprise. "You don't believe Mr. Lugar's explanation that it made for a more realistic test situation?"

"No, sir, I don't."

"Why did you release the arming locks, then?"

"Because I had a lawful EAM to do so, as we discussed. And at the time I had to believe my orders. But now, after what happened, I have to wonder about those orders. Nothing that I heard in this room really justifies what we did in Israel."

Kilten tapped his pipe against his palm, his eyes regarding Parker thoughtfully. "You want to know the truth?"

Parker nodded.

"I don't know either, but I should, shouldn't I?"

Lugar stuck his head in the door. "Are you ready, Professor?"

Kilten nodded and walked out.

Parker was left alone. Slowly she sat down and stared at the ring on her finger.

3

WASHINGTON, D.C. IS the nation's capital. It also leads the country in murder per capita. Just blocks from the hallowed halls of Congress, the quality of life and housing diminishes quickly.

Nestled among the rotting and decaying buildings stood a two-story house painted a fading, dingy red. The house to its right had been abandoned and was now home to transients whose primary interest was stealing enough money to maintain a twenty-four-hour-a-day connection to their crack pipes. The building to the left of the red house was the headquarters for the local crack-and cocaine-dealing gang. Traffic to its back door was steady, day and night.

No one in the neighborhood had ever seen anyone go into the red house, but they knew it was occupied. All the locals knew that. And it was accepted, even by the gang members, that no one was to mess with the red house. There were vague stories of would-be burglars disappearing. The word was that they had been killed.

The man who occupied the red house had indeed killed—and more than once. Not just the few unfortunates who tried breaking in, but on the battlefield in a very different part of the world. It had not been necessary in the strictest sense to kill anyone breaking in upstairs since the four-inch-thick steel door blocking the way to the basement would have denied the criminals access to his lair, but he felt it was wise to keep any potential threats at arm's reach. There was also the possibility that some intruder might stumble across the coaxial cable that led to the satellite dish hidden in an old pigeon coop on the roof. The cable and satellite dish must never be interfered with. The man inspected both each morning and evening. Every day. He had performed the ritual for the past twenty-one months and sixteen days without missing a single one.

His tour of duty would be up in less than three months, but he had not allowed himself the luxury of anticipation. He would not think of home until he was there. To think of anything other than this job would take his mind off the task and that was when things went wrong. Combat had taught him that.

Not that anything was happening in the basement. His job was to make sure the satellite link worked and the object in the basement was secure. He slept in the basement, a cord from the satellite link tied around his wrist. If the link came alive while he slept, an electric shock would be sent through the cord.

When he'd assumed his tour of duty, the men who had brought him here had unloaded enough food for two years from the U-Haul truck they had driven. The electricity, water, and sewage bills were taken care of by others. The man had one job. There was an official title to his job, but he was known by the select few aware of his existence by an informal, but apt, title. He was the man who waited.

TWO BLOCKS AWAY, out of direct view of the red house was an old fire station. Inside the blacked-out windows, a dozen hard men with cold eyes also waited. Their weapons were in racks along the walls, next to an M-2 Abrams Fighting Vehicle whose turret housed a 40-mm automatic cannon and TOW missile launchers. A belt of rounds was loaded into the cannon and the two TOW launchers held live missiles. The Abrams had been brought into the firehouse several years ago on a lowboy carrier hidden under a tarp, the operation conducted under cover of darkness.

In the troop bay of the Abrams, several specially designed charges were carefully secured, blasting caps inserted, primers ready. The charges were checked four times a day.

These men had their own satellite receiver on the roof of the firehouse. They waited on the man who waited.

4

THE PATIENTS REFERRED to the room as the torture chamber. Its location belowground next to the VA hospital's parking garage added to that image. There were no windows and the echo of car doors being slammed and engines running echoed dully through the cinder block wall separating it from the garage. Inside, the rows of machines with their Velcro belts and gleaming metal would have done the Spanish Inquisition proud. Patients sweat and cried while they were strapped to those machines as they worked to rehabilitate damaged parts of their bodies or to compensate for missing ones. On one end of the room, rows of prostheses, crutches, canes, and wheelchairs added a macabre tilt.

McKenzie liked the physical-therapy room because it reminded him of the weight rooms where he used to spend all his off-duty time. It was the only part of the hospital where he felt comfortable. His ward upstairs was full of whining old military retirees too afraid to die. The little park in the back of the hospital where he was supposed to go every day for some sun depressed him with its view of jets landing and taking off at nearby Miramar Naval Air Station. McKenzie had staged out of Miramar several times when he was on SEAL Team Two back in the late eighties and those memories only brought bitter bile to the back of his throat. In the other direction lay the Pacific Ocean off of San Diego and it was in those waters that McKenzie had received his SEAL training when he was a much younger man. It also wasn't a direction he favored.

"Are we ready?" Nurse Stedman was a petite, wizened brunette in her early fifties who had seen a generation of men, old and young, through physical therapy here. When she'd first started they'd handled loads of Marines, their bodies torn and maimed in the jungles of Vietnam. She'd thought she'd seen and heard it all but this SEAL, McKenzie, was someone very unique, in even her experience.

"Ready," McKenzie growled, hopping onto the rubdown table. He pulled off his shirt without being asked and extended the stub of his left arm.

The arm had been gone when he'd arrived here two months ago, but he'd needed an operation to smooth off the stump and then he'd been confined to his bed as he fought off several infections from what had been a very dirty wound. He had told her he lost the arm to a tank. He'd also said that he and his partner had knocked out that tank as well as another. Stedman had instinctively thought he was lying at first. Marines and SEALs would come up with anything to try to impress a nurse. But she'd checked his medical records and discovered to her surprise that he was telling the truth. There was no hint in the records telling where this had happened but despite her world-weariness, and maybe because of it, Stedman had an itching desire to know McKenzie's story.

The doctors had been forced to take the arm four inches above the elbow. The mangled joint had still been attached when he'd arrived, the original amputation being below the elbow, but there was too much damage to the joint. Besides, the original surgical amputation had been crudely done. Stedman had checked the records and discovered that that initial procedure had been done by a ship's doctor on board a submarine. She shuddered to think of the scene inside the cramped, insufficiently equipped infirmary onboard that vessel. It must have been a desperate situation for the sub's doctor, a general practitioner, to do the surgery. And the submarine must have been someplace where an aerial evacuation had not been possible, which further fueled Stedman's interest given that there wasn't an ocean in the world where the U.S. Navy couldn't get a medevac helicopter in a few hours' time.

Stedman picked up the artificial arm which had undergone several adjustments based on their last attempt at fitting. She'd had to stand over the bored specialist to get the job done right, but she felt McKenzie was worth the time and effort.

"Let's see how it works now." She attached the arm, using a Velcro and leather harness that slipped over both of McKenzie's shoulders and hooks that went into loops left at the end of the stub. The massive muscles in his upper arm had been salvaged and the hope was that the operation of the prosthesis could be linked to those muscles. It took them twenty minutes to get it on.

"How does it feel?"

McKenzie looked at her. "Feel? It's metal. I don't feel a damn thing. I feel like my arm is still there, but every time I try to use it I'm reminded it isn't."

"Your nerves will keep firing as if the arm were there for a long time," Stedman said. "What I meant was how does the prosthesis feel?"

McKenzie hopped off the table and walked. "Strange. I don't know. Maybe it's normal. It was strange not to have the rest of my arm there. I'll have to get used to the weight. The balance." The arm twitched as he attempted to move it.

"Sit down, please," Stedman said. She took the metal hand at the end of the arm and carefully lifted the arm up until it was standing straight out. "How does that feel?"

"Fucked," McKenzie muttered. "It's fucked. It's never going to be the same."

Stedman was used to that. The feeling of irrevocable loss hit every amputee sooner or later. She sensed a deeper level to what McKenzie was saying though. As she began working him out, teaching him how to use the arm, she questioned him about what had happened.

"I looked at your file. You weren't B.S.'ing me when you said a tank caused your injury."

McKenzie stared at her. "Injury? Is that what they call it? An injury? Like I was lifting weights and hurt myself? Tripped over a rock?" He tapped the artificial limb with his good arm and his voice dripped bitterness. "This was a wound sustained in the service of my country."

"Your VA status and the—" Stedman began, but McKenzie cut her off.

"I lost my arm in Lebanon," McKenzie said.

As she worked, he talked, telling the story of what had happened for the first time since he'd been debriefed during the medevac flight from Italy back to the states. He'd been ordered under an oath of secrecy never to discuss what had happened, but such oaths meant nothing to him now.

"Captain Thorpe got me on board the SDV," McKenzie said as he neared the end of the story. "Then he headed for the sub. Only it wasn't there. Seems like when Loki pulled the plug on us, he pulled everything."

"The only thing that saved us," he said, "was that the captain of the sub picked up our transponder as he was beating feet out of the area. He didn't check in with anyone higher or else we'd still be out there. He came back and picked us up. I heard he was relieved afterward for disobeying orders."

Stedman had heard many horror stories in this room but she had to shake her head. "I can't believe they would abandon you."

McKenzie snorted. "They didn't just abandon us. Someone gave us up to the Israelis and the CIA. If that sub captain hadn't disobeyed orders, Loki would have gotten his wish and Thorpe and I would be dead."

"Why would we be supplying plutonium to the Israelis?" Stedman asked. A part of her wanted McKenzie to be lying, but her instincts told her he wasn't because there was no bravado in what he said. If his story was true, it was a story she wasn't supposed to know.

"Politics," McKenzie said. "Why was Oliver North sending arms to the Contras? Why'd we fight the Gulf War? Who the fuck knows why?" he said.

"I do," a low voice said behind them.

McKenzie turned. An old man, dressed in a brown wool suit with a wildly colored bow tie, stood behind them. He looked ill, his gray hair missing in spots, his body rail thin, his skin splotchy with red, raw areas.

"Who are you?" McKenzie demanded.

"My name is Kilten." The man waved an ID card at Nurse Stedman. "Might I have a few moments alone with Chief McKenzie?" he asked.

Stedman nodded and walked over to the other side of the room to help a patient working on a Cybex machine.

"I'm a friend," Kilten said.

"Friend?" McKenzie said. "I don't have any friends."

"What about Captain Thorpe? He saved your life."

McKenzie frowned. "What do you know about me and Thorpe?"

"I read a classified file, code name Delilah, that contained the CIA's debriefing on your SO/NEST mission into Lebanon."

"Who are you?" McKenzie asked. "I saw your ID card. You work for the government."

"I work for the same government you work for."

"Worked," McKenzie spat. "Get the tense right. I don't work for them anymore. I gave them my arm and damn near gave them my life and it was all just an administrative screw up. That's what they told me during the debriefing. Can you believe that bullshit? They were dealing nuclear materials to the Israelis for God knows what reason and if they happened to kill me in the process of doing that, well, that's just too bad, right?"

Kilten nodded. "The CIA was keeping it a secret and the Department of Defense accidentally learned of the deal, not knowing exactly who was involved. So there you were, secretly watching our own government at work."

McKenzie frowned. "How do you know that?"

Kilten plowed on, ignoring the question. "Then when your

commander became aware that the Israelis were involved, he bounced the whole thing up the chain of command until someone who knew what was going on pulled the plug on you."

"Loki," McKenzie hissed. "Who is he?"

"He's just a lackey who works for someone else," McKenzie said. "We'll get to that. I've run into him also. We have much in common, McKenzie. It seems we have both become cynics. The source of your dissatisfaction is rather obvious. I suppose mine is more complex. Suffice it to say my eyes have been opened. Better yet, I have a gut feeling that something bad is about to happen."

"Fuck bad. Look at my arm," McKenzie angrily said.

Kilten gave a sad laugh. "Your arm?" He rubbed a thin hand, blue veins sticking out, along his chin. "You see my hair? My skin? Radiation poisoning. Someone put a lethal dose of isotopes in my food sometime in the past month."

"Loki?"

Kilten nodded. "I would suspect so."

"Why?"

"Because I was asking questions that people don't want asked."

"Why didn't they just kill you outright?" McKenzie asked, drawing on his own violent background.

"I suppose they thought this would look like an accident. I work around nuclear materials all the time in the lab and field. Unfortunately for them I'm not that stupid, although they have succeeded in killing me."

Kilten stared at the angry man wearing the prosthesis. "I believe that you and I together can accomplish much. How would you like to profit from your misfortune as well as ensure the survival of the planet?"

"Fuck the planet," McKenzie growled. "I want what's due me."

"I think this is the start of a beautiful but short relationship," Kilten murmured, satisfied that he had found his man.

5

M AJOR PARKER AND her partner, Captain Lewis, walked to the surface entrance of the Launch Control Center, gravel crunching beneath their boots. Parker ran a hand across her forehead, feeling the perspiration despite the early morning position of the sun on the eastern horizon. The humidity was overwhelming. Coming from the low humidity of Colorado to the oppressive heat of Louisiana had sent her internal temperature control into a tailspin. It had only been two weeks, but she hoped she would acclimatize soon.

The surface entrance to the LCC was set in the middle of an open grassy space, about the size of a football field, surrounded on all sides by thick forest. Thirty feet from the edge of the forest on all sides surrounding the surface building was a twelve-foot-high fence topped with razor wire. One gravel road led to the building. No TRES-PASSING signs were hung every ten feet on the fence. The signs also informed the curious that the use of deadly force was authorized against intruders. Video cameras, remote controlled machine guns, a satellite dish, and a small radar dish were on the roof of the building, the latter two pointing at the cloudless sky.

Parker and Lewis had arrived moments ago in a blue Air Force pickup from Barksdale Air Force Base—the 341st Missile Wing Head-quarters and their home base. The pickup was parked right behind them, waiting to take the off-shift crew back to base.

Parker punched a code into the outer door and it opened. They stepped into an anteroom and approached a massive vault door guarding the elevator. A crest with a mailed fist holding lightning bolts and the stenciled words OMEGA MISSILE was bolted to the elevator door.

Both Lewis and Parker were dressed in black one-piece flight suits. On their right shoulders they wore a copy of the crest on the door. A Velcro tag on their chest gave their name, rank, and unit.

Lewis was a skinny, redheaded man, an inch shorter than Parker. He sported Air Force issue black-framed, thick-lensed glasses. Perched on his small nose, the bulky glasses always seemed ready to fall off.

Parker put her eyes up to the retinal scanner on the left side of the door. A mechanical voice echoed into the room.

"Retina verified. Major Parker. Launch status valid."

Lewis followed suit, lifting up his glasses so his eyes could push up against the rubber.

"Retina verified. Captain Lewis. Launch status valid."

There was a brief pause, then the computer spoke again.

"Launch officers on valid status verified. Please enter duty entry code."

On a numeric keypad next to the vault door, Parker entered the daily code they'd been assigned when departing Barksdale.

"Code valid. Look into the camera for duty crew identification."

Parker and Lewis stepped back and looked up into a video camera hanging from the ceiling.

"On-duty crew identifies," the computer intoned. "Opening door."

Parker made a mock bow in the direction of the speaker. "Thank you, REACT."

Lewis shifted the small daypack on his back. "You act like that computer is alive."

"That computer controls the lives of more people than God. Believe me, it is alive."

The vault door slowly swung open. They walked into the elevator and the door shut. The elevator hurtled down a hundred feet and abruptly halted, causing them both to flex their knees.

The elevator opened on the rear of the Launch Control Center and it was the only connection to the surface. To the right of the elevator, a door went to a separate, small room that held four bunks, a bathroom and a kitchen area. A door to the left went to a small area that contained enough stores for a crew of four for three months.

They walked into the Omega Missile Launch Control Center. There were rows of machinery in the forty-by-forty room. There was a gray tile floor and the walls were painted dull gray up to three feet, and then Air Force blue to the ceiling. Twelve years ago, when Parker started in missiles, the LCCs had been painted colors that psychologists had determined would be conducive to the crew's mental health during their extended tours of duty. That policy had been rescinded because of budget cutbacks and a change in command that had brought in a no-frills policy.

The entire facility was actually a capsule suspended from four huge shock absorbers, theoretically allowing it to survive the concussion of a direct nuclear strike overhead. The theory had yet to be put to the test and there was much speculation among missile crews as to whether that bit of 1960s engineering was outmoded. In the old days of the Cold War a facility such as this LCC would have had several warheads targeted at it anyway.

The main feature of the control room were the two REACT consoles at the front of the room. Above those consoles, various screens showed scenes from the surface directly above, as well as the silos that this center controlled. Many of the screens had the brightly colored display that indicated thermal imagery.

A major, happy to be done with his twenty-four-hour shift, stood up and halfheartedly saluted Parker. "Omega Missile LCC is all yours. Nothing of note in the duty log. Status green."

He reached inside his flight suit and removed a set of two keys—

one red, one blue—on a steel chain from around his neck and handed it to Parker. His partner did the same with Lewis.

Parker looked over at the large red digital clock overlooking both consoles. "You stand relieved as of zero-seven-zero-four."

She reached into a pocket of her flight suit and handed him a key attached to six-inch piece of wood.

The officer being relieved took the pickup truck key with a laugh. "I get a ten-thousand-dollar pickup truck; you get a half billion dollars' worth of computers and missiles and nuclear weapons. I'm not sure I got a good deal in the trade."

"You get to go home and take a shower," Parker said. "That's a good deal." She looked over at the main console. "How's REACT?"

On top of the main computer console there was a sign spelling out the acronym: RAPID EXECUTION AND COMBAT TARGETING. The system was relatively new, having been brought on line in the past two years as part of an overall upgrade of the entire nuclear missile arsenal. The computer consolidated what six separate systems inside the LCC had previously controlled. Besides being linked back to 341st's Emergency Operations Center (EOC), at Barksdale, REACT was also tied in to the MILSTAR secure satellite communication system and all the other REACT computers at every nuclear weapon control location.

The officer being relieved pocketed the truck key. "She's running smooth. No glitches. Have a good shift."

He and the other officer walked to the elevator and got on board. The doors shut and they were gone. Parker and Lewis took the seats at their respective terminals. Parker watched the video screens, seeing the two crewmen get off the elevator in the upper facility. One screen showed the pure video feed, the other the thermal. On the thermal screen the two men were glowing red figures against a blue background. When they got in the truck the thermal sight picked up a perfect outline of their sitting forms. Then the engine started, showing up as a bright red glow in the front of the truck.

"Surface door secure," Lewis reported. "Hatch secure."

On the screen, the pickup truck pulled away. The gate in the fence closed behind it automatically.

"Fence secure," Lewis said. "LCC secure."

"Turn the sensors and automatic guns on," Parker ordered.

Lewis threw a switch activating the machine guns on the roof of the surface LCC building. They were connected to motion sensors and would fire at anything moving inside the perimeter.

There was a moment of quiet and in the background Parker could hear the rhythmic thump of the powerful pumps that drained the water flowing from the high water table in this part of Louisiana into the space outside of the LCC. They were only thirty miles from the coastal swamp that extended for sixty miles before hitting the Gulf of Mexico. Not the smartest place to build underground control centers and silos but pork-barrel politics had determined the location, not military practicalities.

Parker leaned back in her seat and tried to adjust to working silo duty again. Two years ago she had left this type of work when she was selected to be part of the elite Red Flyer nuclear weapons team. Not long after the exercise in Israel she had been transferred off the team and spent a couple of months doing nothing at Cheyenne Mountain until she had been reassigned to this posting. Although Omega Missile was the apex of missile duty, she felt a sense of failure.

She had filled the previous two weeks with training and study and now that her background knowledge of the Omega Missile system was up to speed, she would have to deal with the inevitable boredom of twenty-four-hour shifts.

Omega Missile was considered a good career move in the regular Air Force. There were eight officers assigned to man the Air Force's lone Omega Missile LCC and, given its mission, they were the elite of the Missile Corps. Parker had started in missiles upon graduation from the Air Force Academy. Personally, though, the thought of resuming a career in the field was numbing to her.

When she'd graduated, her eyesight had not been good enough for her to get flight training. Therefore, her options had been limited: she could get a job in support or missiles. At the time, the latter had offered excitement and career potential. After a few years of sitting in silos for twenty-four-hour shifts, though, the thrill had worn off. She'd searched for something more exciting and when the classified request for volunteers for the nuclear weapons Red Flyer team had come down, she'd volunteered. She'd been the only woman to make it through training—check that, she suddenly thought, as she realized she hadn't made it through training since they'd transferred her out. At least she hadn't ended up like Scanlon, she thought with a shudder.

Parker noted Lewis was taking a stack of books out of his backpack. "What have you got there?"

Lewis held up a book. "Stuff for my master's degree. Can't beat a Sunday morning in here for studying."

Parker pulled out a binder. "Let's run through our checklist on REACT and make sure we're running smoothly first. Then you can study."

She flipped open to the first page. "Cable link?"

Lewis looked at his console. "Cable link check."

"Satellite dish?"

"Satellite dish check."

6

"I NEED YOU and Tommy," Thorpe said.

"I know you need us," Lisa said. "But I want you to want us."

Thorpe pulled a green drive-on rag out of the cargo pocket of his camouflage fatigues and wiped it across his face. They were standing on the edge of the flight line at Barksdale Air Force Base, eight miles from Parker's LCC. Thorpe wore a combat vest over his camouflage fatigues. He had a pistol strapped high on his right thigh in a special operations rig.

Thorpe reached out, taking Lisa's left hand in his. He nodded down at the matching rings. "Please come back."

Lisa was about to answer when a twelve-year-old boy came running around the corner of a hangar. Upon seeing Thorpe he broke into an all-out sprint. He wore a pair of jeans and a camouflage shirt with a bright set of captain's bars pinned on the collar. He had short blond hair and his wide smile at seeing his father exposed a set of teeth covered with braces.

The boy stopped just short of Thorpe and threw him a salute.

"Hey, Tommy," Thorpe returned, his hand automatically starting to go up in a salute, then pausing as he caught the look Lisa gave him.

Tommy squinted, looking up at his father. "You look tired, Dad."

Thorpe tried to smile, but couldn't quite succeed. "I am tired, Tommy." He was twenty pounds lighter than he'd been on the beach in Lebanon. His face was gaunt, circles under his eyes.

"I told you to stay by the car," Lisa said to Tommy. "It's dangerous here by the flight line."

Tommy scuffed the toe of his sneaker into the tar. "I'm sorry, Mom, but Uncle John taught me about the flight line and all the aircraft. We're safe here."

"How long are you going to be in the area?" Lisa switched her attention to her husband.

Thorpe glanced over his shoulder at a Blackhawk helicopter sitting empty about fifty yards away near another hangar. "Just today, then we move on."

There was a long, awkward silence.

"Uncle John is a lot of fun," Tommy finally said. "He took me to work. I got to sit in the cockpit of a C-141." He pointed at his feet. "I got new sneakers."

Thorpe winced and turned his face away for a second, then turned back with a forced smile. "I'm glad you're having a good time, son. I like your sneakers."

Another silence ensued, then finally Thorpe spoke. "I'm looking forward to you coming home. We can go hiking in the mountains. Maybe do some climbing."

Tommy stepped closer to his father and spoke in a low voice. "I miss you, Dad. I want to come home."

Lisa gave Thorpe a warning glance.

"Your mother and I have to talk about some things first," Thorpe said.

"I just want to go home," Tommy repeated.

"I know that, dear," Lisa said, a hand on his shoulder gently separating the two. "Your dad and I need to talk. Can you go wait by the car like I asked you?"

"I have to go to the bathroom," Tommy said.

Thorpe pointed at the hangar. "There's one in there."

"Hope we can go hiking soon," Tommy said, giving him another salute.

"I hope so, too, Tommy."

Tommy disappeared into the hangar.

"I was surprised to get your call saying you were here," Lisa said.

Thorpe was looking at the hangar. "I'm just passing through. I'm not even supposed to be here. The rest of my team is at Fort Polk but the chopper had to fly here to refuel and pick up a part. I have to get back to the chopper soon."

"That's not what I meant when I said I was surprised to hear from you."

Thorpe looked at her, his face resigned because he knew what she meant. "I'm still deployed most of the time," he said. "We were surprised ourselves to get orders to come here this weekend. We have to check out some nuclear materials storage facilities for security."

"I know very well that you are deployed most of the time," Lisa said. "I lived with it for thirteen years."

Thorpe didn't say anything.

"I'm not going to let you do to Tommy what you did to me," Lisa said. "He deserves better."

"What did I do that was so bad?" Thorpe asked resignedly.

"You put me second. I could live with that until I realized you were putting Tommy second. You can't do that to your child."

"I do all I can," Thorpe said. "I've taken care of you and Tommy as best I can."

"You don't understand, do you? There's more than rules and form. There's substance. There's priorities. There's being a human being, a father. A husband. Being those things before being a soldier. If you'd understood those things, we wouldn't be in this situation right now."

"Please, Lisa," Thorpe begged. "Come home. We can work it out."

Lisa shook her head. "You wouldn't even be there if I went home tomorrow, would you?"

"I'll be back at the end of next week," Thorpe said. He wiped his face again.

"See?" She leaned close. "You're sweating out last night's drunk, aren't you? I can smell it."

Thorpe looked down at the tar.

"You've been like this since you came back from the Middle East. Something happened to you and since you can't talk about it, we can't help you. I'm angry, and maybe a little jealous."

Thorpe shook his head. "I've never given you a reason to be jealous, Lisa. Not in—"

Lisa dismissed his plea with a wave of her hand.

"I don't mean that. Don't you see, you're falling apart. You're destroying yourself and us because of some crap in your beloved job. There's nothing in your life with Tommy and me that could have brought you to this. The army has all of you, even your pain. I can't even hurt you like it does."

"That's bullshit, Lisa. Why, if something happened to you or Tommy, I'd die."

"Something has happened to me and Tommy— we've left," Lisa said. "But I don't think you know what to feel. You're drinking too much to feel anything. You're too caught up in the army to stop for a moment and try to feel." She moved closer. "What is so bad? What's gone wrong?"

Thorpe closed his eyes. "I don't know. I don't know what I believe anymore. All I know is I want you back."

"We can't come back like this. Not to the same thing," Lisa said. "Tommy looks up to you too much to see you like this."

Thorpe looked over his shoulder. Two pilots in flight suits, one man and one woman, were walking toward the Blackhawk. "I have to go." He turned back to Lisa. "Please come back."

"Not now. Not with you like you are. When you want us, then maybe we can talk."

Thorpe lifted his hands helplessly. "Lisa, I don't—"

"Go," Lisa said. "Before Tommy comes back. It only makes it worse for him to see you like this."

~

A MILE from Thorpe and Lisa's location, a half dozen dump trucks and two Humvees were parked off the edge of a dirt road that ran alongside a chain link fence with RESTRICTED U.S. GOVERNMENT PROPERTY signs hung on it. On the other side of the fence, through a hundred yards of trees that blocked the view, was the Barksdale flight line with helicopters and aircraft tied down in neat rows.

Inside the lead Humvee, two men sat, both dressed in black combat fatigues. The man in the passenger seat pulled a cellular phone out of his vest and punched a number in.

"Sim Nuke is in position," he said as soon as the other end was answered.

FOUR MILES from that location and on the other side of the Anaconda River, two more Humvees and a backhoe were parked along a gravel road. The hydraulic shovel on the backhoe was carefully excavating earth from a six-foot-deep hole on the side of the road, right next to a sign that spelled out BURIED CABLE in large letters. Smaller letters informed anyone wanting to dig in that area to contact the BARKSDALE AIR FORCE BASE FACILITIES ENGINEERS.

Inside the lead Humvee McKenzie listened to the report from the man outside the flight line. "All right, Drake. Just wait for further orders."

He put the phone down and looked at the man in the backseat. "Sim Nuke is in position."

"Sir!" the driver, Aldrich, called out, bringing McKenzie's attention to the front. A Security Police car was coming around the curve in the road, slowing as it neared their location.

"We've got company," McKenzie said.

A low voice spoke from the shadows of the backseat. "That's what you're here for," Professor Kilten said. "Remember, no one is to get hurt," he added.

McKenzie spit out the window. "What do you think will happen when you set off your simulated nuclear device outside the air base?"

The military police car had stopped and the two cops were talking to the man operating the bucket loader. The operator was shrugging and pretending he didn't know what they were asking.

"You know the plan. No one will be injured," Kilten said. "The flight line will be clear of personnel."

"Accidents happen," McKenzie said with a twisted smile. "After all, that's why we're here, isn't it?"

Kilten didn't answer.

McKenzie pushed open the door of the Humvee. He was dressed in black fatigues. His artificial left hand was covered with a black glove, his right hand was empty. Aldrich also got out and joined him. Aldrich had on a red beret with a distinctive badge above the left eye.

The two air force policemen turned, not quite sure what to make of the men in black with combat harnesses but no weapons in their hands. Both cops drew their side arms.

"Hold it right there," one of the policemen yelled.

"What's wrong?" McKenzie held up his right hand, palm empty.

"I said hold it!"

"Hold what?" McKenzie asked. He reached with his right hand and lifted his left arm. It stayed in place, straight out from his side. McKenzie tapped on the sleeve and produced a dull metal sound.

"You going to shoot me?" McKenzie asked. "A wounded veteran?"

McKenzie was walking closer as he spoke, now only ten feet away. Both cops stepped back, the muzzles of their weapons not quite steady.

"Ever shoot anyone?" McKenzie asked. "You going to shoot me for digging on the side of the road?"

McKenzie and Aldrich finally halted about six feet from the two policemen.

"This is a restricted area," one of the men said. "You can't dig here. You're on a military reservation."

McKenzie turned as if to talk to Aldrich and a steel dart flew out from under his left sleeve. It hit one of the cops in his chest. McKenzie turned slightly and another dart hit the second one. Both men dropped.

McKenzie and Aldrich picked up the bodies and loaded them into their patrol car. McKenzie waved reassuringly at Kilten as his partner drove the patrol car down a dirt path into the woods. Soon the lush Louisiana foliage surrounded them.

Once out of sight of Kilten and the road they stopped. McKenzie and Aldrich rolled the two bodies out of the backseat onto the ground. The two cops were just beginning to recover from the effects of the nerve agent.

McKenzie drew a silenced pistol from his shoulder holster. Without hesitation he shot one of the miltary policemen right between the eyes, spraying the white side of the car with gore.

The second policeman's eyes were wide over the top of McKenzie's gun. He made a noise as if to beg, but he couldn't articulate. McKenzie fired again.

"No one's supposed to get hurt," he muttered to himself. "Fuck Kilten and his idealistic bullshit. If you don't hurt people they don't listen. And the whole idea is to get people to listen. This is just the beginning of a world of hurt." He looked at Aldrich and smiled, his eyes dancing strangely. "And you can take that to the grave, my friend. To the grave."

THORPE STOOD on the flight line with a small handheld fire extinguisher as the left engine on the Blackhawk helicopter began making a high-pitched whining noise. He could see Lisa still waiting at the edge of the flight line.

After half a minute, the voice of the pilot sounded tinnily in his ears. "Starting right engine."

Thorpe dutifully walked around the front of the helicopter and stood fire watch over that engine. Since they had brought no crew chief with them on this parts run, he had to fulfill those duties.

"If that engine catches on fire," he said into the headset, "you think this thing will put it out?" He could see the copilot who'd identified himself as Chief Warrant Officer Maysun look out the cockpit at him.

"Hell, no, sir. We just want you to start spraying so we know something's wrong and we can get the hell out of here."

Both engines were now running and very slowly the four large blades began turning.

"Come on board," Maysun ordered and Thorpe coiled up the headphone cord as he walked around to the left cargo door and climbed on board. The rear of the chopper was crammed full with empty fuel bladders and equipment boxes. Thorpe squeezed himself into the front of the cargo bay and pulled the door shut. He sat down right behind the pilots and waited as the engines slowly built up RPMs and the pilots completed their pre-flight checks.

He looked out at the flight line for Barksdale Air Force Base. He could see Lisa. She wasn't looking in his direction.

7

As the president's national security adviser, Michael Hill had his choice of tee times at the Andrews Air Force Base golf course. But this Sunday morning he was able to mix business with pleasure. An hour and a half ago he'd waved good-bye to the president as the chief executive departed for a G-7 meeting in Paris. Then Hill had his driver take him over to the golf course which was practically deserted at this early hour except for Hill and his aide, Keith Lugar.

With the president gone, Hill was looking forward to a busy week, beginning this afternoon. He always managed to get more work done with the president out of town. No briefings to give, no silly questions to answer, no ego to stroke.

Hill was a tall man, topping out at six-foot-four, and he carried himself so rigidly that he seemed even taller to those who stood near him. He was slender and blessed with distinguished white hair. Hill had been in Washington for over thirty years and knew not only where all the skeletons were hidden, but he'd put many of them in other people's closets. Hill considered himself to be part of the "real" power in Washington. He wasn't a politician who came and went at the whim of an ignorant voting public, but someone who stayed in the halls of power year after year in various appointed positions, gaining experience and helping the latest incumbent avoid the mistakes of ignorance and naivete.

He worked with a network of other longtime bureaucrats throughout the highest levels of government and while the politicians hemmed and hawed, Hill and his cohorts got results and kept the country running. From the National Security Council to the State Department, from the Department of Defense to the CIA, a handful of men wielded a tremendous amount of power.

Hill pulled the golf cart to a halt at the third green. As he was selecting his club, the cellular phone buzzed three quick times, indicating an incoming fax. Lugar opened the briefcase in the back of the cart and plugged the phone to the portable printer/fax inside.

Hill set his ball down. He was eying the green when Lugar called out, "Sir!"

"What is it?" Hill demanded irritably.

Lugar held up a piece of paper. "You need to read this."

The fax was still humming, working on a second page when Hill snatched the paper out of Lugar's hand. Hill quickly started reading, his eyes slowing down as the import of the words struck him.

TO: NATIONAL SECURITY ADVISER HILL
    FROM: PROFESSOR KILTEN
    RE: OPERATION DELILAH, OPERATION
    RED FLYER
    I KNOW WHAT YOU'RE DOING!
    SOON EVERYONE WILL!

"WHAT THE HELL?" Hill said to himself. He would think it a joke except for the reference to Operation Delilah and that it came from Kilten. There were only three people in Washington who were supposed to know that code name and Kilten wasn't one of them.

Lugar was holding up the second page. It was a fax of a digital photo showing men loading a barrel into an army truck on a beach. In the background a tank had its searchlight on. "Son-of-a-bitch," Hill muttered. He glared at Lugar. "How did Kilten get ahold of this?"

"I don't know, sir."

"I thought this entire incident was sterilized," Hill was shaking the photo.

"I thought it was, too, sir."

"Then where did this photo come from?" Hill didn't give him a chance to answer. "I thought you took care of Kilten and he was no longer a problem."

"I did, sir," Lugar said.

Hill shook the paper. "This is a problem. Obviously, Kilten is still alive."

"Yes, sir, but your specific instructions called for an accident. He is dying as we speak of acute radiation poisoning. We've used it before with no trouble. I thought in this case the irony would—"

Hill swung his golf club close enough to Lugar's head that the man stepped back, ashen-faced.

"Who the fuck told you you could think, moron? An accident is a piano crate landing on his head, not a lingering disease. Don't you think a nuclear expert would know he's been deliberately exposed? He's an old man. Anything would have looked like an accident for Christ's sake. You've done nothing but create a time bomb with our names on it."

Lugar picked up the crumpled fax sheet from the green where Hill had tossed it in his fury. Hill calmed down and was lightly tapping the head of the club on the carpet of grass. "I want the Agency to find Kilten. ASAP. And terminate him immediately before he does something stupid. Is that clear?"

"Yes, sir."

"Good." Hill turned and walked back to tee off. Lugar flipped open his secure portable phone and began punching in numbers.

8

M CKENZIE LOOKED INTO the pit the backhoe had dug. Aldrich was next to him. Kilten was in the pit, kneeling in the dirt next to a cluster of exposed cables. He'd spent twenty minutes using a specially designed saw to slice through the six inches of lead shielding encircling the cables. The scientist was now using a sophisticated-looking tool to cut through the black rubber shielding wrapped around a red cable.

"I'm already through the anti-tampering shielding," Kilten said. "This last part is the EMP guard."

"EMP guard?" Aldrich asked. There was an accent to his voice. Aldrich was French-Canadian, as were over half of the men McKenzie had recruited.

Kilten continued working as he spoke. "Electromagnetic pulse. When a nuclear weapon goes off, it fries everything electronic that isn't shielded. We've spent billions putting special protection on our cables and equipment to guard against it."

Aldrich shook his head. "You fucking Yanks. We didn't worry about shit like that in the Canadian army. Figured if the big boys started throwing the heavy stuff, our ass was grass."

Through the shielding, Kilten attached leads from a laptop

computer to the cable itself. "We have access into the LCC REACT. It will take five minutes for everything to shift over to my laptop, then we'll be ready." He looked up at McKenzie. "Tell the Sim Nuke team to be ready to initiate in about ten minutes."

McKenzie flipped open his cellular phone and called Drake, giving the appropriate orders. Then he punched in a new number.

FOUR MILES AWAY, on the banks of the Anaconda River, the call was answered by a man sitting in the cab of a Humvee. A large dump truck was parked directly behind it, off the side of a two-lane tar road. The road crossed the Anaconda on a sturdy steel and concrete bridge, the muddy waters gently flowing beneath the bridge's supports.

"Bognar," the man answered the phone.

"This is McKenzie. Put it on the bridge and arm the charges."

"Roger," Bognar said. "Be with you in a few minutes."

Bognar leaned out the window of the Humvee and waved. The driver of the dump truck threw it into gear and slowly drove onto the center of the bridge. He parked in the center, leaving one lane open. Opening the hood, he used a knife to cut through wires, making sure the engine wouldn't work. They had yet to see any traffic on the bridge except the pickup truck with the outgoing LCC crew earlier in the morning. That was to be expected since they were in the middle of a massive military reservation, off-limits to civilian traffic.

The Anaconda flowed southeast until the banks of the river fell away and the waters merged into the bayous on the west of the Mississippi. The river separated Barksdale Air Force Base from some of the missile silos that were assigned to the base: the missiles controlled by the Omega Missile Launch Control Center. The next bridge over the Anaconda was fifty miles to the north.

The driver from the dump truck came running back and climbed into the backseat of the Humvee. Bognar flipped open the cover on a small metal box. A light next to a single switch glowed green. "We're hot," he announced. He turned to a group of six heavily armed men, all wearing black fatigues and red berets gathered around the Humvee. "Take your positions."

The men moved to a small rise overlooking the bridge and sighted their weapons. They had two M-60 machine guns, two Mark-19 40-mm automatic grenade launchers and two RPG-80 rocket launchers. Bognar picked up the phone and reported, "Bridge hot and covered."

ON THE EAST side of the river, in the lead Humvee, Drake acknowledged a call from McKenzie. The six dump trucks were spaced out ten feet apart along the fence facing the flight line, the drivers crammed into the trail of two Humvees. "We're moving to secondary position," he told McKenzie. He opened his own small metal box and the light glowed green.

"Sim Nuke is hot," he added.

Inside each of the dump trucks, a receiver rested on top of a double row of stacked fifty-five-gallon drums. Wires ran from it to each drum. A light glowed bright green underneath the tarps that stretched over the top of the bed.

Drake slid the cellular phone inside one of the many pockets on his combat vest and thrust his arm out the window. "Let's move," he ordered the driver. "There's enough explosives in those things to make a damn big hole in the ground. So let's go a little faster, please."

THE BLACKHAWK ROLLED down the runway, until the wheels slowly lifted from the ground. The pilots continued above the concrete runway, staying within the flight path as dictated by the Barksdale control tower until they reached the outer markers for the field, then they banked west.

In the rear, Thorpe settled back in the crew chief's seat. As they cleared the edge of the airfield, Thorpe noted dump trucks lined up along the outside perimeter road. Tarps covered the back part of each truck. Thorpe leaned out and peered, trying to make out details but the chopper banked and the trucks were out of sight.

"SHOWTIME," McKenzie said, checking his watch.

Kilten tapped the enter key on his portable computer and the screen rewarded him with:

message sent

9

"VERIFY EMERGENCY ACTION Message," Major Parker tersely ordered as she reached over her shoulders and pulled the straps for her seat down and buckled them in, pulling the slack out. A red light was flashing and a nerve-jarring tone was sounding throughout the LCC. She locked down the rollers on the bottom of the seat. Then she hit the keys on her computer.

"I have verification of an incoming Emergency Action Message," she announced.

Lewis was reading his terminal. "I have verification of an Emergency Action Message."

The screen cleared and new words formed. "Emergency action message received," Parker said. She pulled a sealed red envelope out of the safe underneath her console and ripped it open. She checked it against what was on the screen. "EAM code is current and valid."

"Code current and valid," Lewis repeated, checking his own envelope.

Parker's fingers flew over the keys. The blinking message on her screen cleared and new words flashed:

EAM: Launch Omega Missile

"EAM execution is to launch Omega Missile," Parker announced.

"What about our warhead missiles?" Lewis asked.

"REACT says we have orders for just Omega Missile. Give me the launch status of Omega Missile."

"Omega Missile silo on line. Missile systems show green."

New words formed on the computer screen. "I have confirmation from Barksdale emergency operations center that this is not a drill," Parker announced.

Lewis frowned. "Shit, they could be pushing us. Seeing if we'll fail to launch."

That had been Parker's first thought. "Everything says it's real. If it's a drill, we'll find out before we launch. Let's do our end. Open silo."

FOUR HUNDRED METERS from the surface entrance to the Omega Missile LCC was another fenced compound. Inside the razor-wire topped fence, two massive concrete doors slowly rose until they reached the vertical position. Inside, a specially modified LGM-118A Peacekeeper ICBM missile rested, gas venting.

"I'VE GOT green on Omega Missile silo doors," Captain Lewis announced, verifying what one of the video screens showed.

"Green on silo," Parker confirmed.

KILTEN SAW the confirmation of silo doors open on his laptop. He looked up at McKenzie. "Fortunately for us this cable goes both ways —to the Omega Missile LCC and also to the Emergency Operations Center for the 341st Missile Wing in the tower at Barksdale Air Force Base."

McKenzie didn't say anything. His right arm was across his chest, his hand wrapped around the joint where flesh met metal on his left arm. His fingers were slowly rapping out a cadence, the first two giving a shallow thud on metal, then quieter as the last two hit flesh.

Kilten typed a new command into the computer, then pressed the enter key. "Step two."

THE TOWER at Barksdale Air Force Base served two functions. In the top, air traffic controllers ran the day-to-day operation of the airfield itself. On the floor below the top, the duty staff for the 341st Missile Wing ran the day-to-day operation of the LCCs and missiles under their control. The duty staff also controlled the security reaction force responsible for safeguarding those LCCs and missiles.

At the precise moment Kilten hit the enter key, alarms began going off and red lights flashed. The duty officer immediately gave the orders he had been trained to.

"We have an incoming nuclear strike warning! Sound strike alarm. All personnel to the EOC bunker!"

Everyone in the room immediately sprinted for the stairs except the duty officer and one enlisted man. The duty officer sat down at a computer terminal and quickly accessed his command link. Outside, Klaxons were going off and the few personnel on duty along the flight line this Sunday morning ran for bunker entrances.

"We have no orders to launch," the duty officer announced. "Switching REACT computer to automatic." He turned a key and looked at the enlisted man. "Let's get out of here." The two fled the room and the tower was empty.

THORPE FELT A POUNDING in his left temple. He reached into his pocket and pulled out several aspirin. His hand was shaking and one of the three pills fell onto the cargo bay floor and rolled back under a large cardboard box.

"Damn," Thorpe muttered. He reached down and froze as he saw the tip of a new sneaker sticking out from under the cardboard. Thorpe pulled up the box and Tommy was sitting cross-legged on the floor, looking up at him with wide eyes.

"You're not mad at me, are you, Dad?"

AT BARKSDALE, Lisa ignored the Klaxons as she ran out of the empty hangar, screaming for Tommy. A Security Policeman spotted her and paused in his own flight.

"Ma'am, we have to get to a shelter," he yelled at her.

"My son is in here somewhere!" Lisa yelled.

"Ma'am, that's a strike warning. We have to take cover."

"Not without my son."

ON BOARD THE BLACKHAWK, Thorpe had Tommy in the seat next to him and was talking through his headset to the pilots. "We have to go back to Barksdale," he said.

"That's your son?" Kelly asked, twisting about in her seat. "He sure didn't inherit your ugly mug, Captain." She turned to the front and had the chopper banking and heading back the way they had come before Thorpe could think of a reply.

"You're not mad at me, are you, Dad?" Tommy repeated.

Thorpe put an arm around his shoulders. "No, son, I'm not mad."

INSIDE THE LCC there was controlled tension as the pair of officers ran down their checklists.

"What's the targeting matrix for Omega Missile?" Lewis asked.

Parker had already checked that information. Since the end of the Cold War, the United States and Russia had reached an agreement where all ICBMs would no longer rest in their silos targeted at each other's countries. Instead, the standing targeting information programmed in each warhead was for a site in the middle of an ocean, called a Broad Ocean Area. This was to prevent disaster in case of an accidental launch. In case disaster actually was desired and the missiles really had to be used in a conflict, a target matrix would be fed through REACT into each missile and they would be quickly reprogrammed with the new destinations for the warheads.

"We don't have a target matrix," Parker said. "We're to launch Omega Missile with control accessed to MILSTAR through REACT. Whoever's left alive can program the targeting matrix once the missile is up."

Parker knew that was one of Omega Missile's assets to the nuclear launch infrastructure. Omega Missile, once launched, could be used not only to launch but also to input target matrices to every ICBM and every other nuclear platform, including bombers, submarines, and even Red Flyer teams.

"Let's stop yakking and get our missile up," she ordered. But even as she was saying the words, she looked up at the TV at the end of the row of security scenes. This last one showed CNN still coming in over the cable and there was no sign of any special report or trouble. As she was watching it, the screen went blank and then static refilled the tube. "We've lost cable," she announced. Parker picked up the phone. "Phone's down," she told Lewis. "I can't get landline verification."

She put the phone down and looked at her computer screen. "We still have access to Barksdale on REACT. Still shows EAM verified and Omega Missile launch verified."

Parker sat still for a few seconds. Lewis waited on her for the next command. When she spoke, it was hesitant, the flow of action finally slowing down. "That's enough to launch, but I'm going to check with the 20th Air Force in Cheyenne Mountain through MILSTAR to confirm launch."

"We're supposed to launch with what we have," Lewis said.

"I'm in command here," Parker said.

"You're wasting time," Lewis replied, glancing at the clock.

KILTEN LOOKED UP AT MCKENZIE. "NOW!"

McKenzie was waiting, cellular phone in hand. He spoke into it. "Initiate Sim Nuke!"

DRAKE and his Humvee had crossed the bridge just two minutes earlier. He was parked a safe distance away from the bridge.

Drake heard McKenzie's order and pushed the button. The green light went out and the red one lit.

Six miles away, the line of dump trucks spaced out along the flight line fence disappeared in a massive explosion. The fence was blown away like a thin piece of paper in a strong wind. The blast wave flattened trees and roared across the flight line, destroying everything in its path.

Over two million pounds of a special diesel fuel/ammonium nitrate composition went up in that split second. It had taken McKenzie and his men over a month to carefully buy that much ammonium nitrate in much smaller segments in nine different states throughout the south. Then Kilten had directed the loading and mixing of the composition in the trucks.

Not only was there enough ammonium nitrate in the trucks to cause a massive explosion, Kilten had layered the tops of each pile with special chemicals to simulate the flash effect of a nuclear explosion. The entire thing was also configured to produce the trademark mushroom cloud of a nuclear bomb.

Kilten had done this before—for the government at White Sands Missile Range. After the ban of nuclear testing, the United States had still needed a way to test equipment in a simulated nuclear blast. Sim

Nuke had been the result and Kilten had appropriated it for his own purposes here.

Bognar slapped a soldier wearing a red beret on the shoulder. "All yours, Mitchell."

Mitchell nodded and walked back to the other five men overlooking the bridge as Drake and Bognar drove away to link up with McKenzie.

SEVEN MILES from the epicenter of the Barksdale explosion, Thorpe spun about as he heard a yell. A bright flash had blinded both pilots and Thorpe turned in time to see the blast wave rumbling toward the helicopter, a surge of pure energy, pushing debris along its forward edge. A mushroom cloud was rising behind the blast wave.

"I can't see!" Maysun cried out.

"Keep it steady," Thorpe said as the shock wave hit the helicopter. He wrapped both arms around Tommy and pulled him to his chest. The explosion hit the chopper head on.

"We're going down!" Kelly yelled. "I've got the controls! Brace for impact!"

The helicopter nosed over, hitting trees. The blades splintered branches and cut through the trunks of two large trees. One of the blades broke off and slashed through the pilot's side of the chopper.

Thorpe had only one agenda: holding Tommy with all his might as the sound of metal ripping and tearing reverberated through the cargo bay. He was thrown from side to side but his seat belt held and his arms clung tight to his son.

The chopper finally came to a halt, tangled in the wreckage of the trees it had crashed through.

INSIDE THE OMEGA MISSILE LCC, Parker and Lewis stared in stunned silence at the video image from the security camera on top of the silo closest to Barksdale Air Force Base. A mushroom cloud was rising over the horizon in the direction of the base.

Parker slowly put down the satellite phone. They could feel the ground rumble from the force of the explosion.

"Barksdale's been nuked!" Lewis exclaimed.

Parker tore her gaze from the video. "We launch now!"

IN THE HOLE, Kilten disconnected the computer. He took a pair of bolt cutters and severed the remaining cables. Then he climbed out and joined the others. McKenzie and his men were staring at the mushroom cloud.

"It looks just like the real thing," McKenzie said, impressed for the first time today.

"It should look like the real thing," Kilten replied. "It took us four years to develop after the testing ban went into effect."

"In-fucking-sane," McKenzie muttered. Then he shifted his gaze back to the immediate area. "Let's get moving. They'll launch for sure now and we need to be ready."

"TO LAUNCH CONTROL," Parker ordered. Unlocking their seats, they both rolled along their respective tracks to the middle of the launch control room. The launch consoles faced each other but were separated by ten feet and a Plexiglas, bulletproof wall bisecting the room. A speaker in the wall allowed Parker and Lewis to communicate. They both locked their seats down in front of their respective consoles.

Parker put her eyes against the retinal scanner and the REACT computer's voice echoed out of a speaker on the console.

"Launch officer verified. You may insert key."

Parker pulled her red key from under her shirt and inserted it into the appropriate slot.

The REACT computer verified Lewis's retina and instructed him to insert his key, which he did.

THORPE UNBUCKLED WITH ONE HAND, the other still holding Tommy.

"Daddy!" he yelled, trying to control his fear.

"It's all right, son, it's all right." As soon as he was free, Thorpe picked Tommy up and climbed out of the buckled door. He carried his son thirty feet away and set him down at the base of a large oak tree. "Wait here, Tommy. I'll be right back."

Tommy was wide-eyed, staring at the remains of the chopper.

"Wait here, you understand?" Thorpe repeated, putting his hands on either side of Tommy's head and staring into his eyes.

Tommy slowly nodded.

Thorpe ran back to the chopper and slithered between the seats. He grimaced as he noticed that one of the blades had splintered through the cockpit and hit Kelly in the chest. He reached out and felt for the artery in her throat. Nothing. He felt Kelly's blood soaking into his fatigue pants as he pushed himself farther into the cockpit and turned his attention to the copilot, who was thrashing about. He unbuckled Maysun's belt, then pulled the copilot out the door and dragged him to Tommy's location.

Maysun was blinking, trying to clear his eyes of the bright image that had blinded him. "Where's Kelly? Do you have her?"

Thorpe looked back at the chopper. "I'll get her in a second. Take it easy."

A small fire had broken out in the engine compartment. Thorpe ran back to the cargo bay and pulled out the fire extinguisher he had held at the airfield. He quickly doused the flame.

"ON MY THREE," Parker said, staring through the glass at Lewis. "One. Two. Three."

They both turned their keys at the same time.

Inside the Omega Missile silo, the solid first stage of the LGM-118A ignited. Umbilicals fell away and the rocket slowly began lifting on a tail of flame, clearing the silo.

THORPE WAS KNEELING OVER MAYSUN, doing a primary survey of his injuries when he heard a loud, roaring noise to his right rear. Just over the far tree line, a large rocket appeared, accelerating straight up. Thorpe watched, mesmerized.

"What's that noise?" Maysun demanded.

"Dad, look!" Tommy cried out, pointing. "What is it?"

Thorpe continued to watch the rocket as it raced up toward the white clouds. "That's an ICBM from one of Barksdale's silos," he said quietly.

"Oh, man," Maysun muttered. "It was a nuke that took us down." He grabbed Thorpe's arm. "Do you have Kelly? Is she all right?"

Thorpe lowered his voice so Tommy couldn't hear. "She's dead."

Thorpe felt pain as Maysun's hand squeezed tight. "Oh fuck! No! Check her, man. Maybe she's just hurt. She can't be dead!"

"She's dead. There's no doubt."

MCKENZIE WAS LEANING out the side of the Humvee watching the long red tail of the ICBM. "It worked."

"Of course it worked," Kilten wasn't even bothering to watch. The convoy of Humvees was racing along a gravel road. "Have your people at the LCC reported anything?"

"All secure there."

Kilten nodded. "The crew will need a couple of minutes. We'll be there before they take any further action."

THE FIRST STAGE of the Peacekeeper had finished its sixty-second burn and separated, the second stage immediately taking over. The missile had been going straight up, simply absorbing the upward thrust of the first stage, but the second stage had some thrust-vector and the rocket turned slightly to the north and west, heading up at over a thousand miles an hour and still accelerating.

10

"OMEGA MISSILE IS away clean," Parker said, checking the telemetry readouts. "First-stage separation clean and tracking proper vector for command orbit." She leaned back in her seat and wiped the sheen of sweat off her forehead.

~

"WHAT HAPPENED TO HER? I mean, did she suffer?" Maysun was blinking his eyes, trying to clear the glowing spots that prevented him from seeing.

"No," Thorpe said. "She didn't suffer." He looked over at Tommy who was sitting with his back against the trunk. He had his knees pulled up to his chest. "You all right, Tommy?"

"I want to go home," he said.

"We will," Thorpe assured him. "I have to take care of this man first."

Maysun was rocking back and forth. "Kelly saved us. I was blinded and she took the controls and kept us from inverting. We'd be dead if we'd inverted."

Thorpe pulled the radio out of Maysun's vest. "I'm going to try your survival radio. Call for help."

Maysun's voice was high. "Help? From who, man? Barksdale just got nuked and the survivors are launching missiles in retaliation. Besides, the EMP would have fried the radio."

Thorpe was adjusting the frequency. "My operations sergeant is at Fort Polk, Master Sergeant Dublowski. He's monitoring on a set frequency. Maybe I can get him."

Maysun shook his head, tears coursing down his cheeks. "That radio doesn't have the range to make it to Polk."

"I know that," Thorpe said, "but I'm going to try anyway. Maybe somebody around here is listening."

Thorpe tried the emergency frequency and, as he expected, received no answer. "What's the frequency for the tower at Barksdale?" he asked Maysun. Thorpe set it on that frequency.

Thorpe keyed the radio. "Any station this net, this is Army Helicopter Seven-Eight-Six. Any station this net, this is Army Helicopter Seven-Eight-Six."

There was no response, just a steady dribble of static when Thorpe released the send key. "The radio seems to be working," Thorpe noted. He tried one more time, then put the radio back into Maysun's vest. He looked about, getting his bearings. The forest was thick, just short of being a swamp. Undergrowth cut visibility down to less than forty feet in any direction.

"You need medical attention."

"I'm not worried about my leg," Maysun said. "Kelly's dead. And we probably caught enough rads from that explosion to kill us in twenty-four hours."

Thorpe leaned down. "Take it easy, all right. Don't scare my son any more than he already is."

Maysun shook his head. "There'll be more missiles coming down any minute. You can be sure the Russians have targeted Barksdale for more than one strike."

"How do you know it's the Russians?"

"Well, somebody dropped a nuke on Barksdale. I'll pick the Russians, you pick someone else if you like. Does it really matter?"

Thorpe looked at the wreckage of the helicopter and the mushroom cloud still clearing on the horizon, then over at Tommy. He leaned close to Maysun again and spoke in a low voice into his ear. "Listen, I know your friend is dead. I know you're hurt. But my son is here and he's scared. You've got to get your act together or you're going to scare him even more."

Maysun turned his head toward Thorpe and blinked, trying to see. The pilot took a few deep breaths and then nodded. "All right, Captain. I'll be cool. I'm sorry."

IN THE WOOD line surrounding the surface entrance to the Omega Missile LCC, Kilten, McKenzie, and the other men were waiting in the trees, looking at the small building. McKenzie held a large 50-caliber sniper rifle in his hands, the end of the barrel resting on a bipod he had set up. He looked through the high-power scope and slowly squeezed the trigger. The half-inch-diameter bullet smashed into a small satellite dish on top of the building, destroying it.

THORPE COCKED his head as the sound of a shot echoed through the woods.

"What was that?" Maysun asked.

"Someone's firing," Thorpe said. His hand had unconsciously slid down and cradled the handle of his pistol.

"IT WOULD BE EASIER if you let me shoot out the video cameras, too," McKenzie said. "The thermal might pick us up even here."

"We've got our own satellite dish," Kilten patiently replied, "but we'll need the cameras once we get in. Plus the crew needs to feel the surface is secure. The cameras only pan the open area, not into the tree line."

Two of McKenzie's men were slowly making their way across the field, crawling in the knee-high grass. They wore ghillie suits, strips of muslin woven into a camouflage netting, that for all practical purposes made them invisible if one didn't know exactly where to look. To counteract the thermal capabilities of the cameras, the suits were laced with special cooling lines that made the surface thermal image of the men the same as the surrounding grass. It was top of the line and expensive gear but McKenzie had the money to get the best.

"You sure the crew will come up?" Bognar asked. "If they don't open that vault door, there's no way we're ever going to get in there."

McKenzie looked at the younger man. Bognar and all the others besides Kilten and Drake were former Canadian paratroopers. After allegations of severe misconduct by the paratrooper unit, including the killing of civilians under interrogation on peacekeeping missions, the Canadian government had finally reacted the previous year and disbanded the Canadian Airborne Regiment. While the act had removed a severe blight on the international reputation of Canada's armed forces, it had left several hundred extremely dissatisfied, unemployed soldiers wandering the northern country. Out of several hundred, it wasn't hard to find two dozen who were willing to break the law for a high payoff.

McKenzie had worked with the Canadian Parachute Regiment on some joint operations when he was in SEAL Team Two. He'd brought in the selected men three weeks ago and they'd been prepping for this mission ever since, hiding from both their own government and the authorities in the U.S. at a remote site in the New Mexico desert. For security reasons, none of the Canadians had been told the purpose of their training or the target until this morning.

This morning was the culmination of weeks of planning. After their meeting at the VA hospital, McKenzie and Kilten had combined their knowledge. Kilten had watched the digital disk of the beach transfer in Lebanon and given McKenzie the identity of Loki and the man he worked for: National Security Adviser Hill.

"I wrote their rules," Kilten said in answer to Bognar's question. "They'll come up. They've lost all communication with their chain of command. They've launched their primary mission, Omega Missile, according to the orders I sent them. They weren't ordered to launch the ICBMs this facility controls but they won't think that's strange since Omega Missile can still launch those in addition to every other nuclear weapon in the U.S. arsenal.

"More importantly, I've taken their main computer off line. That's because I have REACT right here with me now." Kilten tapped his laptop computer.

"REACT?" Bognar asked. Bognar was not very bright but followed orders well, which was all McKenzie expected.

Kilten was still explaining things to Bognar, which McKenzie thought was a complete waste of oxygen. "REACT is the acronym for the name I gave the control computer. I invented and programmed it."

"Why can't you get REACT to open the vault door?" Bognar asked.

McKenzie wanted to smash his artificial arm over the man's head. Didn't the idiot realize they would have thought of that in their planning and done it if it were possible?

"The vault door is on a separate, manual system," Kilten patiently explained. "The security people who designed the facility are experts. You never put everything into one system. The vault door works on a code and a retinal scan. It will also open if you have a special override code. It can't be opened through REACT."

Kilten looked at the surface building. "They'll be up soon. Their priority now is to reestablish contact with their chain of command. If they can't do it from the control facility, and I have made that impossible, they have to do it physically."

"And they'll turn off the motion-controlled guns?" McKenzie added.

"Yes, they'll turn them off," Kilten confirmed.

THE SECOND STAGE burned out and explosive bolts fired, causing the large metal casing to fall away. The Peacekeeper was now almost out of the atmosphere as the third stage fired cleanly.

LEWIS HAD BEEN TRYING the computer while Parker held the satellite phone in her hand. "Satellite is out," she told Lewis. She looked at her telemetry board and blinked in surprise. "I'm not reading anything! Do you have third-stage ignition?"

"I've got nothing," Lewis said. "Our link to Omega Missile is down."

"How about REACT?"

"REACT is off-line."

"Shit!" Parker exclaimed. "We're down and no one knows. We have to get in touch with higher headquarters and let them know we're off-line on Omega Missile!"

Lewis looked up at the security cameras. "Hell, what makes you think there's a higher headquarters left?"

Parker was looking at the same screens. "Everything looks all right up top. Sensors aren't picking up any radiation." She paused. "That's strange."

Parker walked to the back room and opened a wall locker. She pulled a holster and pistol out and strapped them on. Then she put on an Air Force survival vest. Lewis did the same.

"We have to go up," Parker said. "We're cut off in here. We can try our emergency FM radios on the surface. Maybe get Barksdale Emergency Operations Center."

Lewis paused in fastening his vest. "My family lived on post!"

"It'll be all right," Parker said. "If we got a launch alert, they must have gotten some warning and they probably made it to the shelters."

"Shelters? You think those shelters on post can protect someone from a nuke?"

Parker tapped him on the arm. "Come on. Let's go and find out."

Lewis turned and flipped a switch. "I'm turning off the surface guns," he said. "We don't want to get shot by our own weapons," he added.

"I WANT MOM," Tommy cried out.

"We'll get her," Thorpe said. "But it will take a little while."

Thorpe had bandaged Maysun as best he could, using the first-aid kit from the chopper. He had been thinking about the mushroom cloud. If Barksdale was gone and there had been no warning, then that meant that Lisa had been searching for Tommy at the airfield when the nuke went off. He felt a crack widening in his chest and tried hard to focus on the task at hand. That there had been no answer to his radio call to the tower didn't bode well. Barksdale was easily within range of the survival radio.

"I'm going to check out whoever fired that shot," Thorpe said. "I'll get some help."

Maysun was lying on his back, staring straight up. "I don't think it's going to matter much."

Thorpe knelt at his side. "Hey, you're alive. Hang on to that. I don't know what's going on, but I'm going to find out. You keep trying your survival radio."

Maysun blinked. "I think I can see a little bit."

"That's good," Thorpe said. "I need you to look after my son while I get help."

Maysun turned his head toward the chopper and blinked hard several times. "Oh God." He broke down crying, tears flowing down his cheeks.

Thorpe stood, anxious to get going, but not liking the thought of leaving Maysun in this condition with Tommy. He glanced over at the body then back at Maysun. "Were you two ...?"

Maysun cut him off. "It doesn't have anything to do with her being a woman. She was the best damn pilot I've ever flown with. She was my friend!"

"I'm sorry."

Maysun shook his head. "Maybe I'll see if I can get the chopper's radio working once I can see better."

"Good idea. I'll be back in a little bit. Monitor your radio on that frequency." He knelt down next to Tommy. "I've got to go look for help. I'll be back as soon as I can. I need you to stay with this man and help him. Can you do that for me?"

Tommy blinked hard.

Thorpe reached into his pocket and pulled out the green beret he had stuffed in there. He pulled the Special Forces crest off the beret and pinned it just above the pocket on his son's shirt. "I need you to be brave, Tommy. I need you to take care of things here."

Tommy reached up and fingered the crest and nodded. "I'll take care of things, Dad."

"I know you will." Thorpe began walking in the direction of the shot.

THE THIRD STAGE stopped firing but did not separate. There was still fuel left, enough for the payload to be further maneuvered, if needed. The Peacekeeper was now in space, at a point above the middle of Kansas. Small thruster rockets fired as the on-board computer checked its position with various satellites to settle the rocket into a geosynchronous orbit.

After a few moments of firing they too fell silent and the Peace-keeper was in place.

MASS CONFUSION RAGED inside the operations center in the Barksdale Tower as the duty crew regained their stations. Shattered glass covered everything and anything not fastened down had been blown about.

The duty officer and his crew were all dressed in yellow radiation suits and wearing full head masks. He looked out at the flight line and swore. Every aircraft he could see was damaged. Helicopters had been blown up against battered hangers; planes had been flipped like toys.

Emergency crews were racing around the flight line in their own protective suits, putting out fires. Fortunately, the damage seemed confined to the flight line. Looking around, the duty officer could see that some of the hangars were damaged, but the administrative buildings further away, along with the housing areas, seemed structurally undamaged. He had no doubt that windows had been blown out, but thanked God that the blast seemed limited. He could hear the whine of ambulances.

"Give me a reading." The duty officer's voice sounded distant coming out of his mask.

An enlisted woman held a suitcase-size device in her hand. "It's clean," she said.

"What do you mean clean?" the duty officer demanded.

The woman's shoulders rose in a shrug under the heavy material. "Normal reading, sir. No sign of any radiation."

"Try another counter," the duty officer ordered.

"I've tried primary and backup, sir. The air's clean."

The duty officer stared at her for a few moments, then slowly pulled his hood and mask off. "If there's no radiation, what the hell did that to the flight line? And where did the strike warning come from?"

An enlisted man called out from his console. "Sir, I've got Cheyenne Mountain on the horn. They want to know what's going on! They say the warning center has picked up a launch from one of our silos."

The duty officer ran over and looked at his status board. "Our link with the Omega Missile LCC is down. Everything else shows secure."

He turned to the communications specialist. "Get me Omega Missile Launch on MILSTAR."

"I'm not getting an answer, sir."

"Status on Omega Missile LCC silos?"

"Omega Missile silo is empty, sir! ICBM missile silos are still secure and in place."

The duty officer grabbed the mike. "This is Barksdale EOC. Did you transmit a missile strike warning to us?"

The voice on the other end from Cheyenne Mountain was succinct. "Negative."

"Did you track any missile incoming to our location?"

"Negative.

"Did AFTAC pick up any nuclear detonations at our location?" the duty officer demanded. AFTAC stood for Air Force Technical Applications Center. It operated more than fifty sites around the world in thirty-five countries. Its job was to tie seismic disturbances with information from the Nuclear Detonation Detection System, an imaging system aboard NAVSTAR satellites, to detect a nuclear explosion anywhere on the surface of the planet.

Cheyenne Mountain was on top of it. "AFTAC reports an explosion at your location but not, repeat, not nuclear."

The duty officer grabbed an orange phone. "Get me the War Room in the Pentagon!"

DOWN ON THE FLIGHT LINE, firefighters heard the sound of a woman calling for help. They followed the voice to the shattered wall of a hangar. The voice was coming from underneath the wreckage.

"We'll get you out," one of the men called from under his mask.

Beneath the wreckage, Lisa Thorpe could only grit her teeth as the pain from her broken legs kept her from passing out. Despite that, she called to the firemen to search for her son.

"I NEVER THOUGHT it would be like this. They're all dead. All of them." Lewis's voice echoed inside the close confines of the elevator.

"We don't know what happened," Parker said, wishing the ride to the surface would go quicker. "Just hang in there."

"My wife never liked me doing this. She used to have nightmares about it. That's why I was going to graduate school, so I could get transferred out. But the money ..." Lewis's voice trailed off.

"Just hold it together," Parker said. "We'll be able to check things out in a little bit."

The elevator came to a halt at the top and the vault door ponderously opened. Parker stepped out. Lewis paused. "I think one of us should stay in the LCC," he said.

"That's not SOP," Parker argued.

"I know. But if we shut the door we can't get back in without the override. And if Barksdale was nuked then ..." His voice trailed off.

Parker shook her head. "We have to secure the vault door and make sure it can't be opened except by override code."

"I'll stay," Lewis said.

Parker frowned. "What about—" she began, then froze as Lewis drew his pistol and pointed it at her face.

"I'm staying, Major."

"What are you—" Parker began but Lewis shoved her off the elevator and the vault door began closing.

Parker threw herself at the opening. Lewis fired and Parker could feel the bullet whiz by. She ducked and the door finished closing. She pounded a fist on the metal. "You son-of-a-bitch!"

THORPE MOVED through the woods carefully, pistol at the ready. He crossed a gravel road and then paralleled it as he ran in the direction of the shot. Soon he came to the edge of a clearing. Thorpe paused and looked out. He could see the fenced compound and knew what it was, but couldn't see who had fired a gun. He was about to move forward when he noticed the grass slightly swaying on the far side of the compound. It was difficult because the camouflage was good, but he finally spotted two men in ghillie suits low-crawling toward the compound.

One of the men popped up and attached what looked like a length of hose to the fence, then just as quickly disappeared back into the grass. Then nothing moved for a few seconds until the door to the building inside the compound swung open and a woman in a black Air Force flight suit stepped out.

"Oh, fuck," Thorpe muttered. He raised his pistol and sprinted out of the woods. The concrete next to the woman's head exploded. The cracking sound of the shot being fired followed less than a second later. The woman dove for cover behind a low concrete barrier several feet in front of the door, which had swung shut.

The hose that the two men had placed on the fence flashed and a man-sized hole appeared in the fence. The two men in ghillie suits rushed through, weapons at the ready. Thorpe had covered half the distance to the compound by now. He could clearly hear one of the men calling out to the woman: "Stand. With your hands up!"

Thorpe began firing, his first rounds hitting the lead ghillie-suited figure. As he did so, the woman popped up, firing her own pistol. Between the two of them, they put five rounds into the second ghillie suit and he fell less than ten feet from her location.

The boom of a large sniper rifle sounded and a bullet smashed into the concrete near the woman, spraying her with chips. She flinched as a second round smashed into metal and ricocheted off.

Thorpe halted at the fence. He could see at least a dozen figures breaking out of the far wood line, weapons at the ready. "Come on!" Thorpe called to the woman, as he fired at the new targets.

Thorpe slapped his spare magazine into the pistol and rapidly fired at point blank range at the links in the fence, blowing fourteen of them apart. He grabbed the jagged edges and pulled them wide.

The woman dashed past the two bodies and toward the hole he was making. She slithered through, tearing her suit in the process.

Thorpe could see one of the intruders raising a large sniper rifle. Thorpe froze as he recognized the man. The 50-caliber rifle roared and a round whistled past the woman, spurring her to even greater speed. She tumbled onto the ground and regained her feet. Together they sprinted for the safety of the woods.

THE CAPSULE on the end of the Peacekeeper rocket split in two, both shells falling away. Bolted inside, the Omega Missile payload activated itself. Solar panels slowly unfolded, gathering the sun's energy to complete the boot-up of the computer and communications system.

A satellite dish twisted and turned, seeking out the closest MILSTAR satellite. It found one that was in its own geosynchronous orbit two hundred miles away. An inquiry burst was transmitted from Omega Missile to the MILSTAR satellite. A positive link burst was sent back by the MILSTAR computer, indicating that Omega Missile was now online with MILSTAR.

Inside, the REACT master computer checked itself and found all systems to be functioning. Omega Missile was ready.

11

Mckenzie stood next to the door of the Omega Missile LCC and barked out orders. "Bognar, you and Reynolds go after those two." He pointed toward the tree line and the route Thorpe and Parker had taken.

The Humvees were coming out of the tree line with the rest of the men. Machine guns were now mounted in the top center hatches and the vehicles took up defensive positions around the compound.

McKenzie jabbed a finger at Drake. "Set up the satellite dish, then join me below." He turned to the outer door and slapped a charge against it. "Fire in the hole!" he called out as everyone took cover.

There was a brief blast and the door was gone. McKenzie stepped through the debris into the foyer. He halted in surprise at the sight of the closed vault door.

"I thought you said they would leave it open," he demanded.

Kilten ignored McKenzie. He waved at the video camera just above the door and with a hiss, the door swung open.

McKenzie turned to Kilten. "Where's the other crewman?"

"In the LCC," Kilten said.

"He opened the door for you?"

"Yes."

McKenzie looked at Kilten in a new light. "Got any other surprises that you didn't tell me about?"

Kilten walked to the elevator. "Let's go down. We don't have much time."

As the vault door slowly shut on them, Kilten had a question of his own. "Why did you shoot at the other launch officer?" Kilten asked. "That wasn't the plan."

"Not your plan," McKenzie agreed. "But it seems things are changing a bit now."

Kilten looked at the soldier. "I knew you would do this."

"Do what?" McKenzie asked.

"Change things."

"Well, that's real good," McKenzie said. "Cause then you shouldn't be surprised by anything that happens, right?"

"Not likely," Kilten said with a sad expression on his ravaged face. "That's part of my job, remember? Predicting and planning. I expected you to deviate from the plan we agreed on."

McKenzie wasn't really paying attention to what Kilten was saying. "Your job invented this and now we're taking it down. And taking things down is my job. Do you have a problem with that?" The powerfully built man spoke with the firm conviction of someone taking control.

Kilten held his hands up. "I said it would be a short relationship, didn't I?"

THORPE GLANCED to his left at the female officer running next to him. "I'm out of ammunition. Do you have any?"

Parker pulled the clip out of her weapon and looked. "One round."

"Shit," Thorpe said. He halted. "Hold on for a second." He looked at her uniform. Her name tag indicated she was Major Teresa Parker, U.S. Air Force. "Do you know what is going on, Major?"

Parker was taking deep breaths. "No." She looked at his uniform. "Who are you?"

Thorpe stuck out his hand. "Captain Thorpe, Army Special Forces."

Parker took his hand, her grip firm. "Major Parker, U.S. Air Force. This was all a setup. Lewis was in on it. I should have stayed there and stopped them!"

Thorpe didn't understand what she was talking about. "If you'd have hung around there another couple of seconds that guy shooting the big bullets would have nailed you." Thorpe cocked his head, listening. Then he led her into a small gully and pointed down it. "You keep going."

Parker hesitated. "What are you going to do?"

"We've got people right behind us. I'm going to take care of them."

"How are you going to do that with no bullets?"

Thorpe could hear someone running through the underbrush, not too far away. "Damn it, just do as I say. Keep going."

Parker seemed about to say something, but then she too heard their pursuers. She took off down the gully. Thorpe stepped off to the side and hid behind the thick trunk of a fallen tree. Five seconds later, two men came rushing by, their pace increasing as they spotted Parker fifty feet ahead in the shallow trench.

Thorpe watched them race by his position. One of the men stopped and lifted his submachine gun to fire at Parker. Thorpe stepped out and threw his knife, catching the man in the neck. Blood spurted from the severed jugular. Thorpe followed through on the throw, taking two quick steps and striking out at the other man with his right leg, the toe of his boot connecting with the weapon in Bognar's hand. The submachine gun went flying. Bognar whirled, blocked Thorpe's next kick, and the two men backed off, circling.

Parker came running back, pistol at the ready. Thorpe saw her out of the corner of his eye. "Don't shoot!" he called to her.

Bognar took advantage of the distraction to reach down and draw a knife. Thorpe glanced over at his own knife, still embedded in the other man's throat. "All right," he yelled to Parker, "shoot."

Parker lifted her pistol but didn't fire; the men were too close to each other.

Bognar stepped forward and jabbed. Thorpe leaped to the side, captured the other man's knife arm under his own and levered at Bognar's elbow. But Bognar was ready, sliding out of the trap and slashing. His knife tore a gash down the side of Thorpe's sleeve.

Bognar moved forward, knife flashing, and Thorpe stepped back unsteadily, his foot slipping. He fell onto his back. The knife rose high and was coming down toward Thorpe's chest when a shot rang out and the bullet spun Bognar sideways, wounding him.

Thorpe immediately rolled onto the other man and slammed the palm of his free hand into Bognar's nose, smashing the bone into his brain, killing him instantly.

Thorpe slumped onto his back, lying next to the dead man, breathing hard.

"Are you all right?" Parker asked.

Thorpe could only nod.

"You look sick," Parker added.

"I'm all right," Thorpe said angrily. "He was lucky, that's all."

Parker stared at him without saying a word.

Thorpe got to his knees, then stood up. He swayed for a second, shaking his head. Thorpe knelt and quickly stripped Bognar of his ammunition and cell phone. He walked over and retrieved the submachine gun.

Parker grabbed Thorpe's arm. "We have to get back to the LCC entrance!"

"The LCC?"

"Launch Control Center," Parker said.

"Hold on a second. We just barely survived these guys and there's a whole bunch more of them at your LCC. Let's figure out what's going on first." Thorpe gently removed her hand. "You said that your partner was down in the LCC, right?"

Parker nodded. "Lewis. He must be with them. He pulled his gun on me and made me leave. I'm sure he's opened the vault door for them."

Thorpe had caught his breath. "There's nothing we can do about it right now," he said.

Parker stared at him. "Why didn't you want me to shoot at first?"

Thorpe checked the magazine in the weapon. "You might have hit me."

"I know how to shoot," Parker said.

Thorpe glanced at Bognar's body. "You hit him in the shoulder."

"That's where I was aiming," Parker said.

"Next time, shoot to kill," Thorpe said.

"I've never killed anyone," Parker said.

Thorpe spotted some grenades on the other man's vest and walked over and appropriated them. "Nine-millimeter ammo," he said, pulling some magazines out of pouches. He tossed a couple to Parker. "Reload." He also checked out that man's sub.

Parker took the offered submachine gun.

"Careful, there's a round in the chamber," Thorpe said. "Are you familiar with the H&K MP-5 submachine gun?"

"Yes."

Thorpe eyed her suspiciously. Parker took the weapon and spoke like she would to a recruit. "This is safe, this is semiautomatic, this is automatic. Keep it on safe and only fire on semi. Automatic is just a waste of bullets." Parker looped the sling over her neck, not giving Thorpe a chance to comment on her expertise. "Do you have any idea what's going on?"

"I was hoping you could tell me since it's your LCC they're after," Thorpe said. "I was just in the wrong place at the wrong time." He pointed at the corpses. "I do know these guys are ex-Canadian paratroopers."

"How do you know that?" Parker challenged him.

Thorpe showed her a tattoo on Bognar's forearm. A winged dagger with a barely legible inscription below it. "That's their airborne insignia. The other guy has the same tattoo."

"How do you know they're ex?" Parker asked.

"What, you think Canada's invading us?" Thorpe didn't wait for an answer. "Because their airborne regiment got stood down last year after getting accused of various war crimes. Torturing prisoners, that sort of thing."

Thorpe was thinking. "They're not the problem, though. The problem is the guy who had the big sniper rifle. He's American. An ex-Navy SEAL. He was medically retired this year. Name's McKenzie. He knows what he's doing and he's good."

"It's worse than that," Parker said. "The other man in the tree line with him, the older man, his name is Kilten. He's a civilian who works for the Pentagon, GS-God level. He designed the Omega Missile system and the LCC. He knows more about the setup than any man alive. Even more than my ex-partner down there."

"Great," Thorpe muttered. "Two fucking nutcases. You launched your missiles didn't you?"

"Only one," Parker said.

"Gee, only one nuclear missile?"

"The missile we launched didn't carry a nuclear warhead."

"Thank God for that," Thorpe said.

"It's worse than if we had launched a nuke carrier," she said, ending Thorpe's brief feeling of relief.

"Oh, great," Thorpe said. "How come nothing here is getting any better?"

Parker was almost talking to herself, replaying it in her mind. "We launched Omega Missile, but there was a nuclear strike on Barksdale! We saw it on video."

"I don't think that was a nuke strike," Thorpe said. "It was a big explosion and there was a mushroom cloud, but," he pointed at the two bodies, "they didn't seem very concerned about fallout and my bet is that they were the ones who made the big boom." He slapped himself on the side of the head. "The dump trucks!"

"What dump trucks?"

"There was a row of dump trucks parked on the outside of the post fence, near the flight line. I saw them as we flew out. They must have been loaded with explosives. Damn," Thorpe said, "the flight line has got to be a mess. I hope they got everyone under cover."

He thought of Lisa. She would have been frantic when she didn't find Tommy in the car. "We have to get back to my son," Thorpe said. "Then get in contact with the authorities."

"Your son?"

Thorpe quickly explained about Tommy stowing away and the helicopter crash.

"You left your son to head toward the sound of gunfire?" Parker asked.

Thorpe glared at her. "If I hadn't, you'd be dead." Thorpe was looking at the cuts she'd received from the concrete shards. "How do you know this Kilten guy?" Thorpe asked.

"I met him once."

"Well, he's on the wrong side now." Thorpe opened up a first-aid kit. "Any idea what they're up to exactly?"

Parker was lining up the pieces in her head. "He must be trying to get control of Omega Missile!"

"All right. Why don't you start at the beginning and get me up to speed. What's Omega Missile?"

LEWIS SAT at the REACT console, Kilten next to him. Cables from the back of Kilten's laptop were plugged into various jacks on the front of the console. McKenzie hovered behind both of them, watching Lewis work. Two ex-paratroopers were next to the elevator, standing guard. The doors slid open and Drake walked in.

"How's the satellite dish?" McKenzie asked.

"All set." Drake said. He walked over to a bank of radios next to the REACT consoles. "I've got it spliced into their stuff here. We can talk voice and transmit data through MILSTAR just like we're part of the system using the REACT here. We can talk to the Pentagon whenever you want."

Drake pointed at Lewis in his Air Force flight suit. "What's this?"

"Seems we had an ace in the hole that we didn't know about," McKenzie said. "Courtesy of the good professor."

Drake fingered his gun. "Can we trust him?"

"Yes," Kilten said. "He knows what we're doing and why we're doing it."

"Careful with that we," McKenzie said. He tapped Drake on the shoulder. "You keep an eye on him, make sure he does as he's told. What about Omega Missile?" he asked Kilten.

"We're in," Kilten said. "I have positive contact through MILSTAR."

McKenzie walked a couple of steps away. He punched in a number on his cellular phone.

THORPE HELD UP A HAND, interrupting Parker as the phone in his pocket buzzed. He flipped open the lid but didn't say anything. McKenzie's voice came out of the speaker. "Bognar? Reynolds? Are you there?"

"Hello, Chief McKenzie. This is Captain Thorpe. Nice of you to call. Your men are, shall we say, indisposed at the moment. Should I take a message?"

"Thorpe." There was a long moment of silence. "Well, isn't this a pleasant surprise?" McKenzie finally said.

"You fucked up," Thorpe said.

"I did?"

"Yeah," Thorpe said. "You didn't get into the LCC clean and you've got me here."

There was the sound of laughter. "You are so wrong," McKenzie said. "Right now, I'm standing directly behind the REACT computer and you are the one who can't get in, clean or otherwise."

"What are you trying to do?" Thorpe asked.

"By the time you figure that out, it will be long over," McKenzie replied.

The phone went dead.

McKENZIE SHUT THE PHONE.

Lewis looked up from the computer. "What's wrong?"

"Nothing for you to worry about," McKenzie snapped. How the hell did Thorpe end up here? McKenzie thought. He'd seen a man run out of the tree line and help the woman escape, but he hadn't bothered to try to identify him.

McKenzie knew the number one rule of any military operation was to expect the unexpected, contrary to Kilten's belief in planning. McKenzie absentmindedly rubbed his artificial arm, trying to scratch an itch that his nerve endings told him existed, but the metal arm reminded him didn't.

McKenzie reevaluated his plans, adding in the now known factor of Thorpe. After a few moments he felt better as he remembered the scuttlebutt he'd heard about the Special Forces officer. It didn't change much.

THORPE PUNCHED some numbers into the phone, but nothing happened. "Damn, he must have these on a frequency where they can only talk to each other. I can't get an outside line."

Thorpe flipped the phone shut and stuck it back in his pocket.

"Why didn't you try to find out what he was doing?" Parker asked.

"He wouldn't exactly tell me if I asked."

"What was the purpose of baiting him, then?"

"Now he has something else to worry about."

"What?"

"Me."

Parker shook her head. "Why don't you tell me how you know this McKenzie guy?"

Thorpe pointed. "We need to get back to the chopper and my son. I'll tell you about it on the way."

12

THREE HUNDRED AND fifty feet below the lowest level of the Pentagon proper was the Joint Chiefs of Staff's National Military Command Center, commonly called the War Room by those who worked there. It had been placed inside a large cavern carved out of solid bedrock. And while it was ten times larger and over three times deeper than the LCC Parker had been inside of in Louisiana, it was designed along the same principles. The complex could only be entered via one secure elevator and the entire thing was mounted on massive springs on the cavern floor. There was enough food and supplies in the War Room for the emergency crew to operate for a year. Besides the lines that went up through the Pentagon's own communications system, a narrow tunnel holding cables had been laboriously dug at the same depth to the alternate National Command Post at Blue Mountain in West Virginia.

When it had been built in the early sixties, the War Room had been designed to survive a nuclear first strike. The advances in both targeting and warhead technology over the past three decades had made that design obsolete. There was no doubt in the mind of anyone who worked in the War Room that the room was high on the list of Russian and Chinese nuclear targeting and would be gone very shortly after any nuclear exchange. Because of that, it had been turned into the operations center for the Pentagon.

The main room of the War Room was semicircular. On the front, flat wall, there was a large imagery display board, over thirty feet wide by twenty high. Any projection or scene that could be piped into the War Room could be displayed on this board, from a video of a new weapons system, to a map of the world showing the current status of U.S. forces, to a real-time downlink from an orbiting spy satellite.

The floor of the room sloped from the rear down to the front so that each row of computer and communication consoles could be overseen from the row behind. At the very back of the room, along the curved wall, a three-foot-high railing separated the command and control section where the Joint Chiefs and other high-ranking officers had their desks. Supply, kitchen, and sleeping areas were off the right rear of the room, in a separate cavern. The War Room had had its first taste of action during the Gulf War when it had operated full-time, coordinating the multinational forces in the Gulf.

Normally on a Sunday morning only a quarter of the desks in the War Room were filled by the duty staff, but over the last twenty minutes, new personnel flooded the room and the hubbub of activity indicated something more than a normal Sunday morning shift.

The elevator in the left rear opened and the president's national security adviser, Michael Hill, and General Lowcraft, the chairman of the Joint Chiefs of Staff strode into the room. Hill was still dressed for golf, but the general was in an immaculate set of green Class As, his rows of ribbons stacked on his left breast.

"What the hell is going on?" Hill demanded as they walked to the center desk and stood behind it. He had been informed on his cellular phone as he'd finished the eighteenth hole that there was a Class-1 Alert and he was required in the War Room as the senior representative of the administration present in Washington. A helicopter had swooped down into the parking lot of the golf course and carried Hill to the Pentagon landing pad. With Kilten's fax still in his pants pocket, Hill felt a new wave of anger toward the professor and Lugar surge through him.

"We'll find out shortly," Lowcraft said. They had met at the elevator doors upstairs and had not had a chance to talk.

Hill had other things on his mind. He grabbed the general by his elbow. "You told me there was no imagery from the Lebanon incident," he hissed.

Lowcraft stared at the civilian. "What are you talking about?"

"Don't jerk my chain," Hill threatened. "You'll find out who has the real power."

Lowcraft ignored Hill and turned to the War Room. "Give me a status report," he called out.

The senior duty officer, a full colonel named Hurst from the War Plans Division who had had the unfortunate luck of drawing duty this morning, had his position right below Lowcraft's desk. Hurst was air force and wore his blue uniform tightly on his slim body. He had white hair, combed straight back, and a thin, pinched face.

Hurst stood and turned. "We've got a red, level-four serious incident, sir. Omega Missile has been launched without authorization."

"Go through MILSTAR and get ahold of the Omega Missile LCC REACT to determine status and gain positive control," Lowcraft ordered.

"We've tried, sir. Someone's in the control facility, overriding. Omega Missile's MILSTAR link is locked into its LCC and we have no contact with the Omega Missile REACT. Barksdale Air Force Base received a nuclear strike alert that did not originate from any valid source and then was hit by a massive explosion. We believe the explosion was conventional."

"Who's in the Omega Missile LCC?" Lowcraft demanded. "The crew?"

"We don't know, sir."

Lowcraft stepped back as if hit in the chest. "Oh my God," he muttered, heard only by Hill.

"Will someone please tell me what the hell Omega Missile and REACT are?" Hill demanded.

Lowcraft turned to the civilian. "Omega Missile is a special Peace-keeper ICBM. It's the code name for the Emergency Rocket Communication System."

Hill held up his hands. "General, since I don't have a clue what you're talking about, why don't you just pretend I'm some guy in golf shoes and tell me what's happening?"

Lowcraft took a second to collect his thoughts, then spoke. "Omega Missile can communicate through MILSTAR with every nuclear launch platform this country has. Subs, missile launch facilities—it can even scramble strategic bombers and get them in the air.

"The emergency would be if every other normal mode of communication was knocked out. Omega Missile is the last-gasp means by which the National Command Authority can transmit launch codes and target matrices to America's nuclear forces if all other communication means are destroyed."

Hill nodded to indicate he had followed so far. "OK, so this thing has been launched and we don't know why. We can still communicate with all these same places, can't we?"

"Yes."

"Then get on the radio and tell them all to ignore any launch orders from Omega Missile."

Lowcraft ran a nervous hand across his chin as he thought. "It doesn't work that way. The point of all our training is for the crew never to ignore an EAM launch order from a valid source. Omega Missile is a valid source. In fact, it is the ultimate and final valid source. Did you ever read Fail-Safe?"

"Isn't that a movie? Henry Fonda plays the president?"

Lowcraft looked exasperated. "Yes. Just like in the movie, any launch officer will believe Omega Missile before they believe us. They would ignore even a direct order from their commander-in-chief."

"Bullshit," Hill snapped. "If we get the president on the horn, he'll stop this in its tracks."

Lowcraft raised his eyebrows slightly but didn't say anything. His entire demeanor indicated that he knew Hill still didn't understand what was going on, but there was nothing he could do about that now.

Hill leaned close. "Is this all a setup?"

"A setup?" Lowcraft stared at the other man. "I can assure you, Mr. Hill, we are facing a very grave situation right now."

"Don't fuck with me, General," Hill warned. "I don't know what you people are trying to pull, but I will come out on top, I can assure you."

"I don't have a clue what you're talking about," Lowcraft said.

"What about this explosion?" Hill asked, changing the subject. "How many people were killed?"

"So far there are no fatalities," the duty officer said. "The strike warning gave everyone a chance to take cover."

"We have to find out who is behind this," Lowcraft said to Hurst.

Hill wondered if that was one of the astute observations that had helped Lowcraft get appointed chairman. Hill already knew the answer to Lowcraft's question.

13

THORPE RUBBED HIS hands over his sharp, damp features and continued over his closely cropped skull. "Lady, how do you do your job?"

Parker, just finishing her Omega Missile briefing for Thorpe's benefit, reacted as if slapped. "That's a lousy thing to say, especially since you just shoved some guy's nose into his brain."

"He and I were both players and it was face-to-face. Him or me. This Omega Missile thing you're talking about is screwed up."

Parker had stopped. They were less than a quarter mile from the chopper crash site. Her eyes coldly fixed on Thorpe. "At least I can do my job sober."

Thorpe's reaction was swift. He reached over and grabbed the collar of her flight suit and pushed her up against a tree. He put his face into hers, his cold blue eyes fixed on her widening pupils. "I am not drunk. I do not drink on a mission. Never. Do you understand? Do you?"

Parker quickly nodded an agreement, ignoring the fact that the proximity of his breath belied his words.

As quickly as the anger erupted, it dissipated and Thorpe let go.

Parker edged away from him and her voice took on a cool, professional tone. "The system in the payload consists of two parts: a sophisticated computer and a powerful transmitter. The computer can hold all the launch codes, targeting matrices, and authorizations, while the transmitter accesses MILSTAR, a high-tech, frequency-jumping, secure global satellite network by which those codes and matrices are sent. It cannot be aborted by anyone else."

"REACT, the computer that runs everything, was developed to be totally self-sufficient for each nuclear weapon. Whoever has the proper code word has complete control and can't be superseded by anyone else, even if they have their own REACT computer. The real killer is that the Omega Missile REACT controls Omega Missile, which thus can control every other REACT computer in the arsenal."

"I have to assume that Kilten has control of REACT. Therefore, he has his finger on the button of this country's entire nuclear arsenal."

Thorpe was staring at her with a numbed, wounded expression, his mind still scurrying to catch up with all that had happened. "I'm sorry about grabbing you."

Parker shook her head. "Get your head out of your ass, soldier. Did you hear what I just said? This whole planet is on the verge of a meltdown and I really don't give a shit about you or your problems. I don't know how I'm going to stop Kilten, but I'm going to try. Just stay out of my way."

They both tensed as they heard the soft crackling of underbrush. Thorpe wheeled, the muzzle of his MP-5 leading the way. His finger tightened on the trigger.

Parker slapped the barrel of the weapon up. Thorpe cursed and was bringing it back down when he heard the low voice call out," Dad?" and then he saw Tommy stepping between two bushes.

"Oh, God. Oh, Jesus." Thorpe ran to the boy and scooped him into his arms. Burying Tommy's face in his neck, he returned to Parker, who waited silently. She watched the big man trying to control emotions that weren't meant to be controlled. His shoulders shook and his chest was heaving. If he cried, only the boy felt his tears. Parker knew it was her only chance.

"What's it going to be, Thorpe? Are you with me or are you going to give up like McKenzie? You think you lost the reason for what you do and who you are? Look at your son—doesn't he matter?"

Thorpe looked over Tommy's blond head and met Parker's softening gaze. "I'm sorry."

Parker sighed, scraping the toe of her boot in the dirt, anxious to keep moving. In her mind she could picture the Omega Missile system deployed in space. "I know."

Thorpe slowly put Tommy on the ground. He extended a hand to Parker. "Let's get him back to the chopper and figure out a way to get you into the LCC."

"I was just looking for you, Dad," Tommy said, regaining his composure. "The pilot passed out."

"It's OK, Tom."

They walked quietly, lost in their own thoughts while Thorpe held his son's hand tightly. When they arrived at the wreckage, Thorpe knelt down next to Maysun, who was unconscious.

"How is he?" Parker asked.

Thorpe pulled some smelling salts out of the first aid kit. "A slight case of shock," he answered. He wafted the salts under Maysun's nose. The pilot started awake.

"What? What's going on?"

Thorpe quickly brought him up to speed on what was happening. He didn't mention that Tommy had wandered away. When he finished, Thorpe turned back to Parker.

"Who would think up something like Omega Missile?" Thorpe asked.

"Kilten did. Or at least he did to the specifications given him by the Joint Chiefs."

"So they invented a way for us to finish off the whole world in case we get wiped out first? A machine to destroy the rest of the planet if we could no longer do it ourselves?"

"That about sums it up," Parker said.

Thorpe wondered aloud, "When did we get so sick?"

Parker remembered Sanchez's career-ending decision. She'd had her own epiphany in the past fifteen minutes and as much as she didn't like it, she accepted it. "When people like you and me become part of the machine. You can get pretty sick when you don't pay attention to your gut."

If Thorpe found her answer odd, he didn't show it. "So is there any way for you to just turn the machine off?"

"Only by getting back in the LCC and getting to REACT."

Thorpe gave her a determined, crooked smile. "Then that's what we'll do."

THE ATMOSPHERE in the War Room was not a pleasant one. "How come neither the president nor I know about Omega Missile? Or this REACT computer?" Hill demanded.

"It's in his strategic nuclear briefing packet that—" General Lowcraft began.

Hill snorted. "That damn packet is six hundred pages long. I sat in on the briefing you gave him before he took office and no one mentioned this thing!" Hill shook his head. "As I see it, you've taken the president out of the loop!"

Lowcraft clenched his teeth. "Omega Missile exists because of the very high possibility that the president and those immediately below him in the NCA chain will get knocked out of the loop in the first moments of any nuclear exchange. Omega Missile exists to keep our nuclear system from becoming immobilized if incapacitated by an enemy first strike."

"Oh, come on—" Hill began.

"You want to talk about the loop?" Lowcraft cut in angrily. "You know the red phone in the Oval Office?" The chairman of the Joint Chiefs of Staff didn't wait for an answer. "Well, after Kennedy had been in office a few months, he happened to look around and he couldn't find the infamous red phone. He was told that Eisenhower had kept the phone in his desk. They checked all the drawers and still couldn't find the damn thing. Turns out Jackie had switched desks and they'd simply unplugged the red phone and taken it out with the old desk. So maybe the guys who do the dying don't trust that you civilians necessarily have their best interests at heart."

Hill stared at Lowcraft. "That's over thirty years ago. Jesus, General, get—"

"You want to talk about the present administration?" Lowcraft poked a finger at Hill. "How many times have we tried to get the president to come down here to run a command post exercise? To at least let our people brief him on the SIOP in the football that follows him everywhere. Tell me that, Hill. Hell, do you even know what SIOP stands for?"

The officers nearby had all stopped working, and although military etiquette prevented them from staring at the two senior men, it was obvious that they were listening.

Hill simply stared at the fuming general for a little while, letting the other man calm down. From long experience he also knew that Lowcraft was right. The president, as had every recent president before him with the exception of Carter, who was an Annapolis grad, had had one briefing prior to taking office about the nuclear launch structure and the SIOP and that was the extent of their knowledge of the country's nuclear war plan and launch procedure.

Those in the administration defended that lack of interest by saying the president was a very busy man. It was hard to believe, however, that he could be too busy to study the plans that might end mankind. Hill knew that the main reason there was so little focus by politicians on nuclear war planning was fear. Even at the top levels of government, there was a distinct discomfort about focusing on the country's nuclear arsenal. If one stared too long at the product of over forty years of paranoia and fear, the underlying insanity became too obvious. So it was ignored like a crazy aunt kept in the attic. Ignored until times like this when the banging on the floorboards couldn't be ignored. Hill had only one priority right now: keep the banging from bringing down the whole house.

Contrary to Lowcraft's angry words, as national security adviser for this and two other previous administrations, Hill knew what SIOP stood for: Single Integrated Operation Plan, a misnomer if ever there was one. Hill had read the seventy-five laminated pages in the black football carried by a warrant officer that followed the president everywhere. The plan presented a multitude of retaliatory launch options for the president that Hill found stupefying. He was a ruthless man and the prospect daunted even him. He knew the president would be even more overwhelmed if the football ever had to be opened and used under the stress of incoming missiles with just minutes to make a decision.

On the other hand, though, the reluctance of those in the administration to look at the nuclear system allowed Hill the free hand to use the Red Flyer missions and events like Operation Delilah to further the U.S.'s interests in the political arena.

But Lowcraft wasn't done. "You asked me about the beach in Lebanon when you came in. We were left out of the loop on that one, weren't we?"

Hill stabbed a finger in the other man's chest. "You watch your mouth, General."

"What exactly was going on there?"

"None of your business."

Both men fell silent and glared at each other.

"All right," Hill finally said. "The only question is, General, can we control Omega Missile?"

Lowcraft's answer was carefully worded. "Right now it's not under our control."

"Then what's going on?"

"I don't know. I don't even know why it was launched. Barksdale Air Force Base reported a strike warning, but their headquarters in Cheyenne Mountain didn't send it. There was a large explosion next to the base that looked like a nuclear explosion, but there's no sign of radiation. Frankly, I don't know what's going on."

Hill ran out of patience. "Well, General, you'd goddamn well better find out what's going on before I have to talk to the president."

～

"Is our little demonstration ready?" McKenzie asked.

Kilten didn't say anything. He just sat in his seat, staring at McKenzie. The events of the day so far had sapped the sick man's strength.

McKenzie's mood abruptly changed as he slapped the desktop. "We're here now! We're committed. Do you understand?"

Still, Kilten didn't say anything.

"When you approached me with this, you said you were going to break the law for the greater good, do you remember?"

Kilten finally nodded.

"We've crossed the line," McKenzie continued. "We're criminals. That's not going to change. What can change is the results of our actions. If you stop now, the only result will be that those who died and will die, will have died in vain. There are many who died long before today because of this. And millions more will die if we don't follow through. That's what your own calculations say, correct?" He leaned forward until his face was only a few inches from Kilten's. "Hell, you're dying now. You have to follow through on your plan."

Kilten finally spoke, but it seemed as if he were talking to himself. "Yes. All right. Follow through on the plan. I can still do that."

Lowcraft was receiving reports from those in the front of the War Room every few seconds and interpreting the important ones for Hill. "We can't access the Omega Missile REACT through MILSTAR. Someone's in the launch facility and has locked out all outside transmissions, maintaining control through that REACT console which has override. The cable from Barksdale is down. Probably cut in the explosion."

"Can't you cut in? Or jam them?"

Lowcraft's fingers were pressing on the desktop. "You don't understand. We spent billions of dollars designing REACT, Omega Missile, and MILSTAR to prevent someone from doing exactly those things."

"Can you shoot the missile down?"

Lowcraft pointed to the front display. It currently showed the western hemisphere. A bright red dot was centered above Kansas. "That's Omega Missile. It's out of the atmosphere by now and in a geosynchronous orbit, always maintaining contact with a MILSTAR satellite so it can issue launch commands. We don't have anything that can hit it at that altitude."

"Does it stay up there forever?"

"No. It will reenter in a little under three hours and burn up on the way down. So unless something else goes wrong, we'll be all right in three hours. But we still don't know who set the blast off outside Barksdale and why ..." He paused as Colonel Hurst indicated he had something.

"Sir, we have an unauthorized transmission coming in on MILSTAR. It's from someone who says he has taken over the Omega Missile Launch Control Center."

Lowcraft briefly closed his eyes. "Put him on speaker."

The noise of activity in the War Room came to a halt as a voice boomed out of the speakers.

"This is Professor Kilten. With whom am I speaking?"

Lowcraft started as he recognized the name. "General Lowcraft. Professor Kilten, what the hell are you doing?"

Lowcraft didn't have time to say anything else as Kilten continued. "Good to talk to you again, General. Maybe you'll give me more time and attention now than at our last meeting. Who is there representing the National Command Authority?"

"This is Michael Hill. I'm the president's national security adviser."

"What a coincidence!" Kilten said. "Just the man I wanted."

Hill's voice was level, as if he were talking to an errant schoolboy. "What exactly are you doing, Professor Kilten?"

"I've taken over Omega Missile and its controlling computer, REACT."

"For what purpose?"

"So you'll listen to me: You're listening, aren't you?"

"Yes."

"See? It's working."

There was a long pause.

"All right, we're listening," General Lowcraft finally said. "What do you want?"

"First, for security reasons, if the radar in this facility picks up any aircraft within five miles of this location, I will have REACT order Omega Missile to fire a nuclear weapon from a submarine off the Atlantic coast at a target of my choice in the continental United States. The missile is already programmed with a target and the EAM is ready to be transmitted. Is that clear?"

Lowcraft signaled to Hurst to relay that command. "We'll keep the airspace free."

"Good. These are my demands.

"One. All U.S. nuclear systems except two nuclear submarines now on station, the Ohio and the Michigan, will be brought off-line at noon today."

"That will leave us defenseless!" Lowcraft sputtered.

"Let's be realistic, General, which is the whole point of this exercise. The Ohio and the Michigan, one in each ocean, have more than enough nuclear throw-weight between them to keep the Russians or anyone else from launching. Besides, the other nuclear powers have no reason to launch on us right now, do they? We are at peace, aren't we?"

Kilten didn't wait for an answer. "Actually, I'm making this easy on you. This first demand really isn't something you have to do anything about because I'm going to make it happen from here at noon. I'm just letting you know what's going to happen so there's no over-reaction."

"Second, I want all files on a mission code-named Delilah and an operation code-named Red Flyer to be declassified and released to the press."

Hill clenched his teeth as General Lowcraft turned a questioning gaze toward him. As Lowcraft opened his mouth to speak, Hill drew a finger across his throat and shook his head.

"Next, I want to speak to the president personally. I want him to read my memo, which Mr. Hill never forwarded, on both those items. I also want him to read the attached report on the lack of nuclear safeguards."

Lowcraft's face was red. "You son-of-a-bitch, you're making it all happen to—"

"General, there's something you should have read in my report. My basic hypothesis, which is universally supported in the scientific community, is that if something can happen it eventually will. Not just here with Omega Missile, but with every nuclear system and operation. Delilah is another wild card that will be played someday. And if it is played, then the Samson Option will be played also, won't it, Mr. Hill? The whole house of cards will come tumbling down."

"The Samson Option is fiction," Hill said.

"Oh, I don't think so, Mr. Hill," Kilten said. "You know what classified files I hacked into before you caught on and sent your little pet, Lugar, after me. Where do you think I've been the last several weeks? Holed up in a cave, saying my prayers and waiting to die?

"You need to listen to me very carefully. If a nuclear system exists, eventually it will be used, either by design or by accident. Either way, the result will be disaster. All I'm doing is making this one happen under my control. But I'm going to make a clean sweep of the board through this one incident. Omega Missile was the most vulnerable link for me to attack because I designed it, but it is a very powerful system as you are now discovering."

"The entire nuclear system was invented by man. I should know since I've been in charge of its design for the past ten years and worked on it for thirty-five years. And everything that man has invented, he has eventually used, whether deliberately or by accident."

"I am not alone in that thinking. Mathematical theorists have predicted that in the next five years there is a ninety-six percent chance that if nuclear weapons continue to exist, they will be used again."

"It is the same sort of scientific statistical projection that predicted the Challenger shuttle disaster. If something can go wrong, it eventually will. And of course, the world will continue to have nuclear weapons five years from now, won't it? Unless, of course, someone does something rather drastic to change that, which is the situation we're in right now."

"Trust me, in a week you, and the rest of the country, will be thanking me for doing this."

"I don't think so, you twisted—"

Lowcraft put his hand on Hill's shoulder. "Quiet. Let him speak."

"Good for you, General. You understand, even if Mr. Hill doesn't. Of course, he knows things you don't. Let me continue."

"I also want the president fully briefed on Omega Missile, Operation Delilah, Red Flyer, and the Samson Option. Our nuclear defense system cannot be used as a political tool. That introduces a variable that I never took into account forty years ago. I am forcing your hand to realize this very important truth."

"If you want an example, I give you the Red Flyer missions. Mr. Lugar told me they were tests, but imagine my surprise when I found out that their primary goal wasn't testing at all. Mr. Hill is using them as a way to threaten other governments with our capability to put an untraceable nuclear weapon inside their borders. You used it against Israel to counter the Samson Option."

The two men in the back of the War Room looked at each other in mutual suspicion as Kilten continued speaking.

"Omega Missile was designed to be used after Washington is nothing but a smoking hole in the ground and the civilian leadership of this country is wiped out. And Delilah was an operation conducted for political goals that ignore military and practical realities. I want a presidential inquiry. It's the same request I politely made in my report."

"I want my report to be published in the New York Times tomorrow along with the Red Flyer and Delilah papers. Not the entire thing, of course; that would be unreasonable. Just a synopsis of each. I want the American public to understand what sort of doomsday system the Pentagon has set up with their money. A system that will be used only after most of them are nothing but ash. I want the Samson Option outlined so the public will be aware of the threat. I want the people to know how their safety is compromised by people like Mr. Hill for political expediency. This is a democracy, gentlemen, and the people have a right to know."

Lowcraft and Hill just stared at the speaker. "I also want twenty-six-million dollars in used currency now being held pending destruction at the Federal Reserve Bank in Charleston to be packed into a Special Operations resupply pod. The pod—"

"You're just a lowlife thief, you—" Hill began, but again he was cut off.

"The money isn't for me, and, frankly, I wouldn't call anyone controlling this nation's nuclear arsenal a lowlife. It reflects badly on all of you in that War Room.""Mr. Hill, you are satisfied abusing your position for power; the men working for me are more interested in money."

"To continue. The pod is to be placed, as it is designed to be, into the warhead space of a Tomahawk cruise missile on board the USS Shiloh docked at Charleston Naval Base. A disk with flight path, radio frequency, and release code for the cruise missile is on my desk there in the Pentagon. The disk is to be used to program the cruise missile via modem. The missile is to be launched at exactly 1030 hours. I will have control of the pod ejection code. If these demands are not met by noon, east coast time, on the dot—"

Everyone in the War Room looked up at the red numerals on the digital clock above the main display, which read 0905.

"—I will launch nuclear weapons, unactivated, into the remote Pacific Ocean. One every minute. To prove to you that I am serious, please have the camera on board your KH-12 spy satellite presently over the mid-Pacific zero in on the USS Kentucky's location, currently heading toward Hawaii."

Lowcraft was rubbing his temples. "How do you know we have a KH-12 in orbit at that location? And where the Kentucky is?" he asked in a weary voice.

"General, please stop wasting time. There's not much of it left."

Lowcraft pointed and people got to work.

"It should take you no more than two minutes," Kilten said. "I will call back at that time."

The speaker went dead.

"What is he going to do?" Hill asked.

"He's going to launch." Lowcraft talked to a naval officer. "Get me the captain of the Kentucky on ELF radio immediately!"

"A nuclear missile?" Hill asked.

"Yes!" Lowcraft spat.

Hill picked up a red phone. "Patch me through to the president!"

"I have the Kentucky on ELF, sir," the naval officer called out.

"Who's the commanding officer?" Lowcraft asked.

The naval officer had a binder open in front of him. "Captain Rigby, sir."

"Put him on speaker," Lowcraft ordered.

There was a hiss of static. "Reception will be weak, sir," the naval officer said, "as the Kentucky is submerged."

"Captain Rigby, this is General Lowcraft."

The captain's voice was strained and rushed.

"General, we're in the middle of an EAM."

Lowcraft winced. "We have a problem, Captain, and not much time. Omega Missile has been taken over and launched by a terrorist force. I'm ordering you to stand down from your EAM and launch procedures."

There was a long silence, filled with the hiss from the radio, then finally Rigby's voice came back. "Sir, I have a confirmed Emergency Action Message."

Lowcraft spoke slowly and carefully. "I'm aware of that. But it has not been authorized."

Rigby's voice was implacable. "Sir, I have a confirmed EAM and launch order. I cannot confirm you are who you say you are."

Hill leaned forward toward the mike. "Captain Rigby, this is National Security Adviser Hill. I represent the president and I order you to stand down!"

There was another static-filled pause. Lowcraft could well

imagine the scene in the conning tower of the Kentucky. He felt for the bind Rigby was in.

Rigby's voice was firm. "Gentlemen, I have a confirmed EAM with launch in fifty seconds. My missiles have been programmed. I don't have a clue where they're going, but my orders are they go."

Hill's voice was threatening. "Captain, the president is ordering you to stop those missiles from launching."

"Sir, if you want to stop my missiles, you have to get the system to stop the EAM. Sir, my orders are to ignore any other message but an EAM once it comes through."

Lowcraft got very close to the mike and spoke in a calm, resigned voice. "Captain Rigby, terrorists have infiltrated the EAM system. You've got to stop the launch."

"And you could be the terrorist," Rigby replied. "I don't know what's going on, but I have authorized orders to launch. If this is some kind of test, you have twenty seconds to stop the launch! Regulations require I cease transmitting at this time." The hiss ended as Rigby cut the connection.

Hill slammed the mike into the desktop. "Damn it! It's like talking to a wall."

Lowcraft turned and gave him a disgusted look. "I told you these people are just following orders."

Hurst turned in his seat. "Sir, Kilten's back on the line. He says I should put him on now!" Lowcraft nodded.

"Gentlemen, are you ready?"

The screen in front of the War Room went blank, then a new image appeared: a blank expanse of ocean.

"Scale is power of ten," Hurst announced. "Directly over the Kentucky,"

"Kilten, don't do this!" Lowcraft pleaded.

"I think you are beginning to understand my point. Watch carefully."

The surface of the water broke and Trident missiles, one every three seconds, roared up into the sky until the entire ship's complement was away.

"You son-of-a-bitch!" Lowcraft exclaimed. "What's their target?"

"Don't have a coronary, General. I left them on their Broad Ocean Area," Kilten said. "Which for the Kentucky is empty ocean near Johnston Atoll. Relax, the warheads aren't armed. I just fired sixty-million-dollars worth of missile off with the push of a button from my seat here. Do you doubt my sincerity or my ability?"

"I'll give you a few minutes to reflect on it."

14

"WHAT CAN WE do?" Thorpe asked. They were lying underneath some bushes on the edge of the clearing around the Omega Missile LCC compound.

Thorpe had reluctantly left Tommy once again with Maysun. He had given his son strict instructions to remain hidden by the wreckage with the wounded aviator.

"There should be a reaction force from Barksdale heading to the LCC," Parker said.

"Kilten knows that, right?"

"Yes."

"You have to assume that everything Kilten knows, he and McKenzie have prepared for." Thorpe had been thinking about the situation. "So far, you and I are the only wild cards in this plan."

Thorpe could tell from the look she gave him that she would have preferred a different card than his and he was stung by the implied criticism. He tried to recall a time when someone had so doubted his abilities and could not. Then he remembered his wife. He pushed those thoughts away and, using years of practice, focused on the matter at hand.

Parker looked out at the Humvees with machine guns mounted

on top. "Even if we get past those guards, Kilten will have shut the vault door. We can't get in that way."

"How did you get in this morning?" Thorpe asked.

"I had a duty code. It can only be used once, then the code recycles."

"How would the security forces get in?" Thorpe asked.

"They'd have an override code."

"Can we get them on the radio or by phone and get the override code?" Thorpe wanted to know.

Parker shook her head. "Standard operating procedure for the override code is that it can not be transmitted by any electronic medium for fear of intercept."

"Even when the LCC is taken over by an enemy force and the good guys need to get in?" Thorpe was incredulous.

Parker shrugged. "There are no exceptions that I know of. The chance of the code getting intercepted or the duty officer being tricked into transmitting the code is too great. The other danger is that the same override code controls all of Barksdale's LCCs. You have to remember there are nine other LCCs that control their own missiles around here."

"Jesus!" Thorpe hissed. "The bad guys are already in the only one that counts."

"I didn't make the rules," Parker said.

"No, Kilten did." Thorpe thought for a few seconds. "What good is an override code then?"

"The security force will be given a hard copy of it by the EOC duty officer to take with them. They're the ones who are supposed to get into the LCC if bad guys take it over."

"Is there another way to get to the LCC?" Thorpe asked.

"No."

"There's always a way. You know this place. Think like a bad guy. Speaking of which." Thorpe pulled the cellular phone out. He flipped it open and looked at buttons. "I would be willing to bet that McKenzie's phone is number one in the memory. Want to bet?"

"My last bet was with my mom," she said. "That I couldn't get into the Air Force Academy. I'll pass, thanks."

Thorpe punched in memory one.

McKENZIE PULLED the phone out of his vest and flipped it open. "McKenzie," he growled.

"McKenzie, you little prick, how are you doing?"

McKenzie glanced around. Kilten was focused on Lewis who was banging away at the computer keys like he was writing Moby Dick. McKenzie walked away from the others and lowered his voice to a low, harsh whisper. "Thorpe, it's quite a surprise hearing from you."

"Wish it would have been enough of a surprise to give you a coronary," Thorpe said.

"I heard about you, Thorpe," McKenzie said. "Shouldn't you be drying out somewhere? Why don't you tell me where you are and I'll send some of my men to pick you up and take you to Betty Ford's."

THORPE PACED WITH ANGER. "Shut up, McKenzie. I've never been more sober in my life and right before I kill you, I'll prove it."

Parker was leaning close, listening to the conversation.

Thorpe got himself under control. "Hey, how's Kilten?" Thorpe asked. "You and him hanging together? Getting along OK?"

There was a long pause.

"Cut the shit, Thorpe."

Thorpe glanced at Parker. "All right, McKenzie. Just tell me what the hell you're doing." Parker reached out and tapped his arm, then signaled for him to calm down.

"You wouldn't understand," McKenzie said. "You've got your head so far up the government's ass you can't see reality. Even when it hits you in the face, like on that beach, you blind yourself to the truth.

Keep drinking, buddy. Maybe you'll get lucky and it will go away. But I don't think so."

"Why don't you help me see reality?" Thorpe asked.

"I don't need to help you understand, Thorpe. You're not important. You're not a decision maker. It's the people in Washington that have to understand. You wouldn't believe the shit they're into."

Thorpe tried another tack. "Why are you doing this?"

McKenzie's bark of laughter cut through the phone "Why? You should be the last person I have to tell why. They've fucked me over for twenty-two years. Well, now I'm on top. I paid for every dime they're going to give me with my flesh and blood."

"You're nuts," Thorpe said.

"And you're not?" McKenzie replied. "Didn't you see it, there on the beach? Didn't you realize that you would have been one of those guys unloading that hovercraft if you'd been ordered to? You have no personal ethics, no morals. You do what you're told to do. Well, not me."

"This isn't the way to do it. You don't kill people to help people."

"Tell that to Churchill and the people of Coventry. You saved my butt once, so I'll save yours," McKenzie said. "Stay away."

"You know I can't do that," Thorpe said.

"You can't? Why not? You know what was in that missile your little friend launched?"

"Yeah."

"You want to protect something like that?"

"A lot of innocent people could get hurt," Thorpe said.

"That's exactly why I'm doing this!" McKenzie's voice was louder. "Some are going to have to die so the rest of the world can live. There's no other way. You can't ask people to change, you have to make them. When enough have died, then the world will demand change."

"Come on—" Thorpe began, but he was cut off.

"You try to stop me and I'll kill you, Thorpe."

Thorpe tried putting a lighter tone into his voice and the conversation. "Yeah, yeah, yeah, I've heard it before. You've got to catch me first."

McKenzie didn't bite. "Nice try. But I'm exactly where I want to be, and you're not." "You have to come out sooner or later, and when you do, I'll be waiting."

"It'll be much too late by then."

"Say hi to Kilten for me. I'll be seeing him, too." Thorpe flipped the phone shut.

Parker was staring at him. "What now?"

"We see if McKenzie reacts. He's nuts enough, he just might. And if he does, we need to be ready."

McKENZIE SLOWLY PUT the phone back into his vest. He stared across the room at Kilten and Lewis for a few seconds, then walked over to them.

"That other officer. The woman who got away. Did you know her?"

Kilten nodded. "Major Parker. I brought her down here specifically to be on the crew. As I did with Lewis here, except he was on the inside. She was brought here because she would launch, given the right stimulus. It was all part of my plan," he added. He looked at the cellular phone in McKenzie's hand. "She's out there, isn't she? She's still alive?"

"Not for long."

Kilten absently nodded to himself. "She's smart. Very smart."

"Smart can't outrace a bullet." McKenzie said. He opened up his cellular phone and called his senior man on the surface. "Send a patrol out." McKenzie briefly described Thorpe and Parker. "They'll be close by. I'll try to bring them up on the cellular again and you get them on your tracker. Find them and finish 'em."

HILL LIT a cigarette and threw the match on the floor. "Can we stop Kilten?"

General Lowcraft figured this wasn't the time to tell the national security adviser that the War Room was a 'no smoking' area. Before speaking, Lowcraft glanced at the main display, which now showed a map of the Pacific. A series of very close, parallel red lines were heading toward empty ocean southwest of Hawaii: the Trident missiles the Kentucky had launched.

"The Omega Missile system, because it was designed as a weapon of last resort, will resist all our attempts to stop the launch codes and orders from being transmitted," Lowcraft said. "Kilten knows the system better than any of us and he knows we can't stop him unless we get to the REACT computer in the Omega Missile LCC and reprogram it."

Hill sighed. "Even I am beginning to see his reasoning. Why have this system if it controls everything and you can't take control back? It doesn't matter that he invented Omega Missile. It would be just as impossible if he were any flake off the street."

General Lowcraft hated hindsight. "It's a catch-22 that we do our best to insure doesn't happen. The launch control system—the REACT computer, the MILSTAR communications system, and the Omega Missile—has to be as secure as possible so that it will work under the most extreme of conditions, nuclear war, yet not so secure that we can't correct an internal mistake."

"Looks like you came out on the wrong side of the equation this time," Hill said. "And I think catch-22 is a very appropriate metaphor. This is insane."

Lowcraft's face was like a slab of chiseled granite. "I didn't invent the world situation. I just do my best to maintain the peace."

"Well, your best obviously wasn't good enough."

Heads in the War Room were beginning to turn again. "Please stop acting as if I designed and built these missiles by hand. Nuclear weapons are the spawn of civilian intelligence. We just keep them safe and in place. Military men have continued to die on conventional battlefields for forty years to keep them from being used." Lowcraft jabbed a finger at Hill. "What's this Operation Delilah that Kilten is talking about?"

"Nothing you need concern yourself with," Hill said.

"If it affects what's going on now," Lowcraft said, "then I ought to know about it. Does it have anything to do with what that SO/NEST team saw in Lebanon?"

"That team should never have made it back," Hill said.

"We don't abandon our own," Lowcraft hissed.

That brought an ironic grin to Hill's face. "You do when it's in the national interest. A couple of lives here and there against the needs of the nation?"

"Who determines those needs?" Lowcraft demanded.

"I do," Hill said. "I take responsibility, which is more than you can say for most people. I do what has to be done."

"Who elected you?" Lowcraft asked.

"General," Hill said, "you don't have a clue about the realities of the world political situation. It's a game of power and nuclear weapons are part of that. I play the game well and I do it with my own country's best interests at heart. Wasn't it a military man, Clausewitz, who said war was a continuation of politics by different means?"

"He said that almost two centuries ago," Lowcraft noted. "The face of war has changed rather drastically since then, particularly since total warfare and nuclear weapons have entered the picture. You can't play political games with nuclear bombs."

"What else are they there for?" Hill asked. "They exist, they are a reality and they exist for a purpose. I use that purpose. As a carrot when I have to and as a threatening stick when necessary."

"So the Lebanon delivery was a carrot for the Israelis?"

"Good guess," Hill said sarcastically, "but if it makes you feel any better, I've held the big stick over their heads, too."

"I ask you again," Lowcraft said. "Who elected you?"

Hill ignored the general and looked at the clock. "We have an hour and twenty minutes to get that cruise missile loaded with the money and flying. Let's at least get that prepared while I brief the president."

"You're not going to pay these terrorists, are you?" Lowcraft was shocked.

Hill pointed at the red lines on the display board. "Like he said, General, he just fired off sixty million dollars worth of missiles and warheads. God knows how much this is going to cost before it's over. Right now, twenty-six million seems cheap compared to what he's already cost us."

Hill picked up the red remote phone and walked into a small room off the main area. Lowcraft looked out at the assembled staff. "Do we have anyone near the Omega Missile control facility?"

Colonel Hurst fielded the question. "I'm in contact with the Barksdale EOC. The blast destroyed the aircraft to carry the reaction force at Barksdale. Even if it hadn't, we can't fly anybody in the five-mile zone covered by their radar."

"What about getting some people in on the ground from Barksdale?" Lowcraft asked. "How far is it to the Omega Missile LCC?"

"Eight miles, sir," Hurst said.

"Get them moving!"

"I'll get them on it, sir." Hurst hesitated. "The situation is pretty confused there. The base has been heavily damaged and apparently there is some panic among the local civilian population. Most people still believe the blast was nuclear."

"Tell Barksdale EOC their number one priority is to get into the Omega Missile LCC. Is that clear?"

"Yes, sir."

"What about other forces?" Lowcraft asked.

Hurst gave the report. "Delta Force is alerted, but flight time from Fort Bragg is too long. This will be over before they get there. The nearest army forces are at Fort Polk, about eighty miles away from Barksdale. We've got them getting some Cobra helicopters up in the air to cover the airspace and make sure there are no accidental intrusions. Also we've got all their Medevac choppers ready to help in case they're needed. Some mechanized and infantry forces are also being mobilized, but again, if you take out landing them by chopper, then they have to get in there by ground and it will take awhile."

Hurst was handed a piece of paper by an enlisted woman. He read it. "This is interesting, sir. It seems there's a Special Operations NEST team at Fort Polk. They were doing some security checks on storage sites in Louisiana."

That was the first piece of good news that Lowcraft had heard since coming to the War Room. "Are they ready to move?"

"Yes, sir. But we still have the problem with the radar."

"Get a C-130 on the airstrip at Polk," Lowcraft ordered. "We can at least get them closer by moving them to Barksdale."

Hurst paused. "Sir, I have a suggestion."

"Yes?"

"We can have our people start dismantling nuclear warheads manually."

Lowcraft stared at him. "Do you know how long that takes? In three hours you could dismantle, what, maybe two or three percent of the total arsenal?"

"About that, sir. But it's better than nothing."

Lowcraft thought about it. "All right. Get your people working on it at every nuke site."

BARKSDALE WAS INDEED the scene of massive confusion. Fire still burned in a fuel storage bunker and fire trucks were on the scene. Unfortunately, the fire chief didn't believe the senior duty officer that the blast they had experienced was not a nuclear explosion. He insisted on keeping his men in full protective gear which greatly hampered operations.

The Security Police detachment responsible for the 341st LCC and silos had gathered together as many men and women as could be found on a Sunday in addition to the platoon on duty.

The duty officer, Major Mark Ferrel, looked over the military policemen and women gathered in an empty hangar. "All right. Right now all we know is that someone has taken over the Omega Missile LCC. The missile has been launched. No nuclear armed missiles have been launched from our silos, but you and I know that if they control Omega Missile they control all the other missiles.""Therefore, while Alpha Platoon will have the Omega Missile LCC as its objective, the rest of you will be split up with missile maintenance personnel to go to our other missile sites and dismantle all nuclear warheads."

"Jesus, sir," a senior sergeant in coveralls called out. "It takes over an hour just to get the hatches off a missile to get to the warhead. Omega Missile's only got a three-hour flight time. I only have enough men to do two missiles at a time. We won't even get a tenth of our warheads disabled in that time."

"I know that, but it's better than sitting around with our heads up our asses," Major Ferrel replied. He looked at the platoon leader for Alpha Platoon. "Lieutenant Cruz, since all aircraft are down you have to go by road. Take the Peacekeepers."

Cruz was a twenty-four-year-old Hispanic woman, dressed in camouflage fatigues and sporting the blue beret of the Security Police with a single silver bar indicating her rank on the front of it. She was chewing a piece of gum and slid it to the side of her mouth. "Ah, sir, how am I supposed to get into the LCC? Have we heard anything from the crew?"

"We have no idea what the status of the crew is," Major Ferrel said. He handed her a piece of paper with a red TOP SECRET cover on it. "This is the override door code to get into the LCC."

"No idea about the threat, sir?" Cruz asked.

"We're getting some information forwarded from the Pentagon. We'll radio it to you, but right now you need to get moving."

"Yes, sir."

Cruz and the twelve men and women of her platoon ran out of the hangar. They broke into three groups of four and got into three lightly armored Humvees with M-60s mounted on top.

Cruz stood in the top hatch of the lead vehicle and waved her arm. The convoy rolled toward the airfield gates.

INSIDE THE SECURITY POLICE HEADQUARTERS, a distraught Lisa Thorpe had to be sedated after her second attempt at tearing off the straps binding her down so she could go look for her missing son. An alert was put out to all personnel to look for Tommy Thorpe.

15

"COMPANY," THORPE ANNOUNCED as three heavily armed men walked to the gate of the LCC surface compound and piled into a Humvee. "McKenzie swallowed our bait. Let's move," he said to Parker. They headed deeper into the woods at a trot.

The phone in Thorpe's vest buzzed. "He wants to track us by the cellular phone."

Parker shook her head. "Does he think we're so stupid that we'll answer?"

Thorpe took the phone out. "No, he knows we're that desperate. Let's bring the fly to the trap. Take your place," he ordered Parker.

They were next to a dirt road, about a quarter mile from the LCC. Trees hugged both sides of the road and the branches interlocked overhead, making the road a dark, green tunnel with limited visibility. Thorpe and Parker had already talked out what they were going to do. She moved down the road to her position while Thorpe settled into his.

"I knew you'd call back," Thorpe said upon opening the phone.

"How are you and the lady major getting along?"

McKenzie asked. "Parker is her name isn't it? How does she feel about being paired up with a has-been?"

"You're really pathetic, McKenzie. Good thing you have Kilten with you or you couldn't figure out how to take a leak. I know for sure that he's the brains behind this operation." Thorpe knew McKenzie wanted him to stay on the line while his men in the Humvee closed in on his transmission.

"You really don't understand, do you?" McKenzie said. "I'm doing a good thing."

"A good thing?"

"In three hours, the threat of annihilation by an accidental—or deliberate—launch of nuclear weapons will be gone. In fact, if things go the way I plan, the people of the world will demand that nuclear weapons be done away with altogether."

"Is that Kilten's plan?" Thorpe asked.

"We have the same general objectives."

"Uh-huh," Thorpe commented. "So you're single-handedly going to disarm the world? Listen, McKenzie, my wife and kid live on Barksdale."

"No one was hurt there," McKenzie said. "The good professor made sure of that. We sent a warning and they should have gotten everyone under cover. If they didn't, well, that's not my fault. What's a little personal sacrifice in the face of the greater good?"

"Not your fault?" Thorpe repeated. "You started this whole thing! You're responsible."

"No, I didn't start this," McKenzie said, "but I am going to finish it."

Thorpe pulled the phone away from his ear. He could hear the sound of a vehicle engine getting closer. "Sorry McKenzie, gotta go. Call you back in a bit."

He could hear McKenzie's voice even as he hung up. "I don't think so."

Thorpe was hidden behind a log angled off the side of the road. He settled the stock of the MP-5 into his shoulder. The engine was much closer now. The front end of the Humvee appeared around a bend in the road fifty meters away. Thorpe could see two men inside and a third standing in the turret, manning the M-60 machine gun.

Thorpe waited until it was within twenty meters then fired, stitching a pattern of hits into the windshield, shattering it. The M-60 gunner returned fire and Thorpe ducked as chunks of wood went flying from the log. He peered around the edge of the log. The Humvee had halted and the two men had gotten out, leaving the one in the turret to cover them.

In the branches above the Humvee, Parker used an underhand toss to throw a grenade right into the hatch past the gunner. She immediately pulled the pin on a second one and threw it behind the two men on the ground.

The M-60 gunner saw the first grenade tumble right in front of him. He immediately vacated the turret, throwing himself over the rim onto the ground.

The second grenade exploded, knocking the two gunmen to the ground. They were trying to get back up as Thorpe rose over the log and fired two quick bursts, killing both.

The machine gunner stayed prone and reached for his holster. His body was pounded into the ground by bullets from directly above as Parker fired her pistol six times.

Thorpe slowly walked forward as Parker climbed down. She stared at the bodies. "I've never killed anyone before," she said.

"You mentioned it." Thorpe looked tired and worn. "It gets easier, believe me."

She looked up from the bodies. "How can you say that? Look at you, you're an emotional wreck. Whatever's going on inside of you is going to win if you don't start feeling something."

"I feel it," Thorpe said.

"You don't act like it."

"Now's not the time," Thorpe said.

"If it isn't now, when is better?"

"How come the grenade in the Humvee didn't blow?" Thorpe asked, changing the subject.

"I didn't pull the pin," Parker said.

Thorpe stared at her. "You what?"

"I thought we might need the ride."

"And if the M-60 gunner hadn't jumped out?" Thorpe asked. "I was the one he was aiming at."

"But he did." Parker looked at him. "Now we're even. And admit it —I had a better idea."

Thorpe ignored her and pulled the phone out of his vest and punched in memory one. "Told you I'd be back," he said as the other end was answered. "Scratch three of your bad boys," he said, then he flipped the phone shut.

"Are you trying to piss him off?" Parker asked.

"Most definitely," Thorpe said. "Anger is a great equalizer. Besides, he could have killed my wife or Tommy at Barksdale."

"Your family lives at Barksdale?" Parker was surprised. "I—"

"We're separated," Thorpe explained.

"Your son is very sweet," Parker said.

"He's a good kid. He's having a hard time dealing with the separation. He just wants to go home. That's how come he stowed away on the chopper."

"I think he stowed away on the chopper to be with his dad," Parker said.

Thorpe didn't say anything.

"Which came first?" Parker asked. "The separation or the drinking?"

"Let's cut the personal stuff, OK?" Thorpe looked around. "We need to get into that place. We've got to stop this before it gets out of control."

"This nickel-and-dime stuff isn't getting us any closer to REACT," Parker pointed out.

Thorpe slammed a fresh magazine into the weapon. "But it's putting fewer obstacles in our way if you ever figure out a way to get in there. I'm doing my part, you do yours. Get us in there!" He pointed at her vest. "While you're figuring that out, let me borrow your radio."

Parker took her survival radio out of the vest. It was identical to the one Thorpe had left with Maysun at the chopper. He turned the frequency knob, then pressed send. "Maysun, you hear me?"

"This is Maysun. Loud and clear."

"How's Tommy?"

"Fine."

"Have you gotten ahold of anyone?"

"Not yet, but I'm at the aircraft and I just about have this radio working. It has better range than these little ones. What's happening? I've heard a lot of firing."

"You get that radio up, there's someone I want you to call. His name is Dublowski and he'll be listening on . .." Thorpe proceeded to relay to Maysun the necessary information. While he was doing so, Parker had been sitting on the hood of the Humvee, deep in thought.

"Come up with anything?" Thorpe asked as he turned off the radio.

"If, as you say, they took out the flight line, the security force for our missile wing will have to come here by vehicle," Parker said. "They'll have the vault door override code with them."

"You can be sure McKenzie's thought of that."

Parker nodded. "There's only one road they can take to get from Barksdale to the Omega Missile LCC."

"Ambush," Thorpe summarized.

"Right." Parker slapped her hand on the hood of the Humvee. "And that's why we need this."

"Let's roll," Thorpe said. "McKenzie might have set up an ambush, but I doubt he'll have it pointing both ways."

"Let it go, McKenzie," Kilten said. "We've got more important things to worry about. Thorpe and Parker are not going to be factors in this."

"Thorpe isn't going to just sit around," McKenzie argued.

Kilten waved a hand around the LCC. "Even if he can deal with the men up top, there's no way he can get in here. Believe me."

"You let me worry about security," McKenzie said. He pointed at the REACT computer. "Are we all set?"

It was Lewis who answered. "We have complete control of REACT and Omega Missile with the laptop."

"We've got their attention," Kilten added. "They'll give in. It's working just as I planned."

McKenzie nodded. "Good." He pointed to the other side of the room. "Could you show me how to operate the thermal surveillance cameras? Despite what you say, I'm concerned about Thorpe running around up there."

Kilten and Lewis got up and walked with McKenzie around the front of the consoles. Lewis began explaining the working of the surface security system.

As soon as they stood up, Drake slid over to the laptop and pulled a 3.5-inch disk out of his vest. He put the disk into the REACT laptop and began typing.

The screen cleared and then a prompt appeared:

To access target matrix from drive A hit enter

Drake hit the enter key. A listing appeared on the computer screen:

TARGET: GRID: WARHEAD
   Tel Aviv, Israel: FTR295867: 20 megaton
   Arlington, Virginia: PUY859345: 20 megaton

To confirm target matrix, press enter.

. . .

DRAKE HIT THE ENTER KEY.

TARGET MATRIX ACCEPTED AND PROGRAMMED.

DRAKE CLEARED the screen and ejected the disk. He slid it into his vest and moved his seat away from the laptop.

16

"SIR, WE HAVE inquiries coming in from the National Security Agency about the Kentucky launch," Colonel Hurst announced. "They say the Russians have picked it up and tracked the missiles. The Russians have moved up one level of strategic preparedness."

Lowcraft looked at Hill. "If Kilten keeps this up, we're going to have the Russians or the Chinese or both launching on us."

Hill pointed at the red phone. "I'll inform the president. He can contact the Soviet president and the Chinese premier." Hill paused. "Do you have any positive news I can give the president?"

"The EOC at Barksdale has sent out a contingent of Security Police to the Omega Missile LCC," Lowcraft said. "They're moving on ground so it's going to take a little while."

"When will they reach the LCC?" Hill asked.

Lowcraft turned to Hurst who answered, "Forty minutes, sir."

Hill kept his focus on Lowcraft. "And when they get there? Can they do anything?"

"They have an override code for the vault door,"

Lowcraft said. "If they get in, they can abort Omega Missile."

Hill nodded. "All right. I'll tell the president."

"ARE WE SET?" McKenzie asked Drake in a low voice.

"Matrix is in," Drake said.

McKenzie looked at Kilten, who was back at his place at the main console. "I think this will get the message across."

"And satisfy our clients," Drake added.

"Fuck them," McKenzie said. "I ain't doing this for them."

Drake raised an eyebrow. "They paid for all the gear and their money is the reason the Canadians signed up."

McKenzie ignored the issue. "What about the silo? You know what to do?"

"Yes. It won't take long."

McKenzie slapped him on the shoulder. "Get going. Time's-a-wasting."

Drake walked to the side of the LCC where several waist-high panels were bolted in the wall. He began unscrewing the bolts to one of the panels.

"What is he doing?" Lewis demanded.

"Mind your business," McKenzie snapped.

Kilten had been typing at the laptop when suddenly he looked up. "What is going on?"

McKenzie walked over and stood behind Kilten.

Kilten was reading the screen. "Someone's programmed a target matrix for two missiles!" He spun to Lewis. "Did you do this?"

"No!"

"Who did this?" Kilten demanded.

"My friend Mr. Drake did it," McKenzie smiled. "You had Captain Lewis as your wild card, I have my own. You didn't think I was going to rely completely on you, did you?"

Kilten pointed at the REACT computer. "This wasn't part of the plan!"

McKenzie shook his head. "Here we go again. No, this wasn't part of your plan. It's part of mine. How do you think I was able to get all these fellows here and purchase all this gear? On the promise of a payoff? Using my credit card?"

"I've got other clients who have paid very well, up front, and they want those two locations targeted and hit. If those assholes in the Pentagon weren't going to pay, and there's a good chance they won't, then I made sure the men and I would be taken care of regardless."

Kilten reached for the keyboard. "I won't allow it."

McKenzie grabbed him by the shoulder and spun the seat about. "You no longer have any say in things. You've served your purpose. You've accessed Omega Missile for me through REACT." He pointed at the laptop. "That's all you were necessary for."

Lewis pulled his pistol and pointed it at McKenzie. "Let him go!"

"Oh, the traitor speaks," McKenzie said. His own guards had their weapons pointed at Lewis. Drake paused in opening the maintenance hatch. "Did our good professor get to your sense of moral responsibility or your wallet?" McKenzie asked.

Beads of sweat stood out on Lewis's forehead. "Just back off. No one's supposed to get hurt."

"Too late for that," McKenzie said, "I'm afraid it must be you who backs off." McKenzie drew his silenced pistol. "You fail to realize that you weren't part of the original plan and you're not part of my plan. Therefore, as far as I am concerned, you are not what I would call essential personnel."

Lewis shifted his gaze to Kilten, then back at McKenzie. The muzzle of his gun wavered. "Hey, I just want my money. There's no need for us to be turning on each other."

McKenzie's weapon was centered on Lewis's forehead. "You've seen too many movies," he said. "Where both parties lower their guns, shake hands, swap a few brews, and live happily ever after. Do you know what they teach us to do in a situation like this in Special Operations training?"

Lewis held up his free hand. "Hey, I don't think—"

His words were cut off as McKenzie's gun spouted flame. A red dot appeared in the center of Lewis's forehead. The captain's body slumped down in its seat.

Kilten was surprisingly calm. "You're crazy."

"I imagine they're saying the same thing about you right now at the Pentagon. In fact, I think you're crazier than I am," McKenzie added. "You don't really care about the money or if you get away. In fact, you want to get caught. You think the president is going to sit and calmly listen as you explain all the flaws in the nuclear launch system? That they're going to publish your report and all that classified material in the New York Times? After all you've done?"

"They published the UNAbomber," Kilten said.

"And look where he ended up," McKenzie said. He jabbed a finger in his own chest. "I'm nuts, but at least I know I'm nuts. I accept it. I just want to be a rich nut. And make some of the people who screwed me over feel what it's like to hurt a little."

"Hell," McKenzie continued, "those two targets getting hit will make the whole world sit up and take notice. You'll get the results you want then. Real results. Not a bunch of people spouting bullshit and at the end we still have the status quo. You wanted real change, I'm giving it to you. All right." He pointed the pistol at Kilten. "Time to finish this."

"They're going to give you your money," Kilten said.

"True, and thanks to me you got the president's notice. So we both succeeded."

Kilten had a strange smile on his face. "Very true."

"Any last words?" McKenzie asked.

Kilten folded his hands on his lap. "You know, of course, that I can't let you explode those nuclear weapons."

McKenzie shrugged. "I don't see that you have much choice in the matter anymore. We have the computer and we have control. You and your dead friend got us in and Drake can take it from here."

"Do you know what a gambit is?" Kilten asked.

McKenzie frowned. "What?"

"At the direction of the Joint Chiefs I first designed Omega Missile five years ago. I initially called the system Final Gambit. More appropriate given its function and mission, but the Joint Chiefs didn't buy off on that. Too fatalistic they said."

McKenzie's gun hand was steady as he listened.

"A gambit is an opening move in chess where a pawn is sacrificed for strategic gain," Kilten said. "Putting the word final before gambit is an oxymoron, but no one noticed that. Do you play chess?"

"You done?" McKenzie asked impatiently.

"You should play chess," Kilten said. "The most intellectual game man has invented because of the requirement to plan and project both your own moves and the opponent's. That's how I got involved in strategic planning in the first place. The same rational requirements satisfy both endeavors." Kilten shook his head. "I don't think you're going to succeed. The odds are against you."

"I've already succeeded," McKenzie said.

"No, you haven't. Your gun doesn't bother me since I'm dying anyway. This was the most likely outcome for me personally so I accepted it when I committed to doing this. Your gun only shortens things by a week or so. And they would have been very painful days anyway."

Kilten's voice firmed up. "Go ahead and shoot. I'm ready. Of course my plan doesn't die with me. Any good chess master can play long after he's gone if he's prepared. There are only so many moves you can make and so many permutations of those moves that—"

McKenzie fired and the round hit Kilten in the heart. He slumped over, held in place by the shoulder straps in the control seat. There was a sad smile on his face.

Drake finally had the panel off. "What the hell was he talking about?"

"Get going," McKenzie growled as he unbuckled the body from the seat. "We don't have much time."

HILL TURNED TO LUGAR, who had just arrived in the War Room, a stack of file folders under his arm. He placed them on the desk at which Hill was seated. In the muted roar of the War Room they could speak in a low tone and not be heard by others.

"Tell me about Kilten," Hill ordered him.

Lugar pulled a file from the pile. "Kilten's classified file. His psych profiles."

"Tell me about the man. Is there anything we can use to negotiate with him?" Hill asked. "Or for damage control after this goes public?"

"Kilten's a genius. His IQ is in the top one percent of the top one percent. His first government job was—"

Hill held up a hand. "Give me something personal. Is he married?"

"No. No relationships." Lugar grimaced. "He's one of those guys who gets as excited over his job as most guys do over a beautiful woman."

"And he has nothing to lose thanks to you," Hill said. "Give me something we can use to discredit him. Any hobbies?"

Lugar flipped through the file. "He plays chess. This says he's a world-ranked amateur. He worked on something called Deep Blue." Lugar turned a page. "That's a computer program designed to play chess."

"If he's so focused on his job, why'd he take the time to do that?" Hill asked.

"I don't know," Lugar said.

Hill was about to say something more when a communications officer interrupted him.

"Sir, it's the president on your secure line."

Hill picked up the phone and listened for a few moments. He put his hand over the receiver and spoke louder to Lowcraft. "The president wants your professional opinion as to the possibility of success of the security force from Barksdale getting into the Launch Control Center and stopping this."

Lowcraft sighed. "Kilten and his people seem well-organized. They took out the aircraft, you can be sure they'll have something prepared for people coming on the ground. There are a lot of variables in an operation like—"

"A percentage rating of success," Hill demanded. "Now!"

"Less than twenty-five percent," Lowcraft said.

Hill relayed that, then listened. The only words he said were, "Yes, sir," Then he hung up.

He turned to Lowcraft. "The president has authorized getting the money in the air. As for the rest of it, well, he's not ready to negotiate. He wants other options beyond the security force."

Lowcraft gave a little laugh of disgust. "One thing's for sure, we can't nuke it. All control has been shifted over to Omega Missile. That's the way the system works."

Colonel Hurst had been listening in and cleared his throat. When Lowcraft looked at him, he spoke. "Sir, actually, I do believe we could hit the Omega Missile LCC with a tactical nuclear strike."

"How?" Lowcraft snapped. "Omega Missile has control of all our nuclear weapons. We're locked out."

"Well, sir, since we've got people manually disabling warheads, we could also manually arm a nuclear warhead that's in a stockpile at one of our bases waiting to be dismantled. Since it was already taken off-line it wouldn't be under REACT control."

"Omega Missile not only controls the nukes, it also controls their delivery platforms," Lowcraft said. "How do you propose delivering a nuclear warhead to the LCC?"

"B-2 bomber, sir," Hurst said succinctly. "It can come in fast and won't get picked up on radar."

"They'd have to manually drop the thing," an air force officer said. "That would be hard."

"Can it be done?" Hill demanded, stepping in.

"Yes, sir," the air force officer said, "but that facility is over a hundred feet underground with forty feet of reinforced concrete on top. The entire capsule is suspended on springs to sustain shock. It was designed to withstand an almost direct hit by a nuclear blast."

Hurst put his hands on the railing. "The key word, sir, is 'almost'. What if we hit right on top of the LCC with a conventional bunker-buster dropped by an F-l 17 Stealth fighter? That should dig down about twenty feet, then follow it right away with a twenty-megaton bomb from a B-2 right into that hole?"

Lowcraft looked at the other air force officer for an answer.

"That might do the job," the officer reluctantly admitted, "but it will also devastate the countryside for five miles all around and we have to take into account the fallout pattern."

"When you say 'do the job,' " General Lowcraft repeated, "what do you mean?"

"Take out the LCC completely," the air force officer said.

"That will stop them, won't it?" Hill asked.

"Unless they've already programmed Omega Missile to do something," the air force officer said.

"We're talking about dropping a nuclear weapon on American soil," Lowcraft said. "I don't—"

"We have to examine all possibilities," Hill cut in. "What effect will dropping such a bomb have?"

"Put a map of the Omega Missile LCC area on the screen," Lowcraft reluctantly ordered.

The map came up.

"If we put a twenty-megaton nuke center point on top of the LCC," Lowcraft said, "show me flash, blast, EMP, and fallout effects."

There was a pause, then several different colored circles appeared around the site. Hill looked at them, then slowly nodded. "It's worth at least preparing. Get the aircraft and bombs ready to target the Omega Missile launch facility. Have Barksdale begin evacuating the entire area. I want projections on delayed fallout, particularly with regards to New Orleans."

Lowcraft held up a hand. "I don't think you want to go to the president with a recommendation that we drop a nuclear weapon on the Louisiana countryside, Mr. Hill."

Hill glared at the general. "With all due respect, I don't want to drop a nuke on Louisiana either. But Kilten, and whoever's in there with him, can launch any of our nuclear weapons against any target in the world, whenever they feel like it! They've shown us that. The president understands the severity. He's discussing the severity of the Kentucky launching its missiles right now with the Russian president. I can assure you he understands this very well."

"I asked for options," Hill continued. "You've given me one. When this gets down to the wire, it might be the only one we have." Hill picked up the red phone.

17

RAISING HER LEFT fist, Lieutenant Cruz signaled for the convoy of three Humvees to halt. She was riding in the top hatch of the lead vehicle along with her platoon sergeant, Technical Sergeant Everson. It was tight, the two of them standing side by side, but it allowed them to work as an efficient team.

Everson was a man's man, over six feet tall and solid muscle. Although he was only twelve years older than Cruz, he treated her like a daughter. In the six months since she'd taken over Alpha Platoon he'd shepherded her through the trials and tribulations a new platoon leader had to face. His ebony face crinkled as he looked ahead at the dump truck parked in the middle of the bridge.

"I don't like it, L.T.," he said.

"We can go around it," Cruz said. "There's room."

"Yeah, but why's it there?" Everson asked. "I suggest we send one Humvee across to check the far side and keep the other two back to cover it."

"All right," Cruz agreed.

Everson turned in the hatch and pointed at the vehicle behind them. He put two fingers to his eyes and then pointed across. The squad leader nodded. The Humvee drove around their truck and toward the bridge. Everson pulled back the charging handle on the M-60 machine gun as the third Humvee pulled up to their right to give supporting fire.

The Humvee was moving slightly faster than a walking pace and passing the dump truck when the entire bridge disappeared in a flash of light. The shock wave hit Cruz and Everson a second later, knocking them back against the rear of the hatch. When the smoke cleared, the center span of the bridge and the Humvee were gone.

"Goddamn!" Everson wiped a hand over his face, getting the dust off. He shook his head trying to clear the ringing. Dimly he heard a chugging noise that he knew was familiar, but he just couldn't get a clear idea of what it was at the moment. He looked across the river and spotted a line of small, black objects in the air looping toward him.

"Grenades!" Everson screamed as he grabbed Cruz and pulled her down into the interior of the Humvee. At that moment, the first grenade exploded on the right flank of the vehicle and then all hell broke loose as 40-mm grenades landed every second on and around the Humvee, sprinkling it with shrapnel. The other Mark IX grenade launcher was doing the same thing to the other Humvee.

Everson heard Cruz cry out and he felt something warm and wet on his hands. He looked down. A jagged piece of metal was stuck in her throat and blood pulsed around it. "Ah shit, ma'am," Everson muttered as he tried to stop the bleeding.

THORPE HEARD the explosion and then the firing of the grenade launchers. "Faster!" he yelled at Parker.

She pressed down on the accelerator and they fishtailed around a turn and then the river was there, the bridge upstream a shattered ruin. He could see the two Humvees on the far side being peppered by 40-mm grenades from Mark IX launchers.

Thorpe swung the gun around, searching for the source of the firing on this side. He spotted a man to the left, an RPG on his shoulder. The man was standing on a small rise and aiming across the river at the two Humvees that the grenade launchers near him were suppressing from behind the cover of the rise.

Thorpe pulled the trigger and felt the familiar vibration of the M-60 in his hands. He walked rounds up and into the RPG man, blowing him down in a splatter of blood.

"Get out!" Thorpe yelled to Parker as one of the line of grenades turned toward them.

Instead, Parker gunned the engine and charged the ambush site. She was greeted by the streak of flame from another RPG that hit right in front of them. Thorpe felt the left tires lift and then the entire Humvee was up on its two right tires, balancing, then going over. Thorpe ducked down into the turret and barely escaped being cut in half as the Humvee came to rest upside down.

EVERSON COULDN'T STOP the bleeding. He heard an explosion across the river and more firing. He stuck his head through to the driver's seat and cursed. Their driver was dead, his head mangled by a grenade that had exploded right in front on the hood.

Looking across the river, Everson could see the upside-down Humvee. As he watched, a man in black fatigues stood with an RPG launcher and fired. Everson flinched, then realized the rocket was aimed at the other Humvee in his platoon. It hit and the other vehicle was gone in a fireball. Everson knew they were next.

"The code," Cruz whispered. Everson turned back to her. She had a blood-stained piece of paper in her hand. "Take the code for the vault door and get out of here," she said.

Everson ignored his platoon leader's words. "I can't leave you, ma'am."

"That's an order, sergeant," Cruz said.

"Sorry, I can't follow that order," he said. He picked her up and carried her out the rear door. They rolled onto the ground. The Humvee burst into flames as an RPG rocket hit the engine.

"WHEN I SAY GET OUT, I don't mean go forward," Thorpe hissed at Parker as he crawled in the wreckage and grabbed her shoulders, pulling her through the backseat and out the rear, putting the Humvee between them and the ambushers.

"Sorry," Parker said. "I thought—"

"We need to get out of here," Thorpe said. "Your Security Police got wasted and the bad guys will be here next to finish the job." He lay on his stomach and looked around the edge of the Humvee. He could see two men standing, one with an RPG launcher in his hands.

"Let's go!" Thorpe said. He stood and sprinted, Parker at his heels, heading for the safety of the trees on the right side of the road. They made it as someone belatedly fired a machine gun in their direction.

Thorpe led the way fifty feet into the woods along the river bank and halted. "Damn," he said. "Another thirty seconds and we'd have hit the sons-of-bitches from behind."

Parker tapped him on the shoulder and pointed. There was a large black man in Air Force camouflage fatigues on the far bank, twenty meters away, looking at them. He had a body in his arms.

"Major Parker," he called out.

"Sergeant Everson," Parker replied, recognizing him from the security briefing where launch officers met the security personnel.

"The lieutenant's got the override code," he yelled. With that, he ran into the river and began wading across.

Thorpe glanced upstream. The ambushers were probably coming. Thorpe made sure he had a round in the chamber of the MP-5. He fired a burst as a man in black fatigues and red beret appeared, moving cautiously down the bank.

Everson was crossing mid-channel, holding the lieutenant above the surface of the water.

Thorpe saw the splash of rounds as he heard the sound of the machine gun firing. "No!" Thorpe yelled, standing and firing upstream, trying to suppress the firing. The man with the red beret fired back at Thorpe while his partner continued to fire the M-60 at Everson.

Everson had crossed mid-channel as Thorpe hit the man with the red beret, killing him, but the man with the machine gun was protected from Thorpe's firing by a log. Water churned around Everson as he continued.

"Fuck!" Thorpe yelled and then he sprinted forward toward the log.

Thorpe vaulted the log with the trigger pulled back, killing the machine gunner even while the man was targeting Everson. Thorpe kept going, ignoring Parker's call for him to stop. He ran along the bank, slipping between trees. He dashed across the road leading to the bridge, not even aware of his breathing, his entire being focused on the weapon in his hands and the men ahead.

The three surviving ambushers were reloading their grenade launchers and RPGs when Thorpe came running up the small slope in front of their position. They were momentarily stunned by his sudden appearance. As they began to react, Thorpe fired, right to left. He killed the first and second, but the MP-5 ran out of ammunition before he reached the third one, Mitchell. Thorpe didn't stop, dropping the submachine gun, and drawing his knife.

Mitchell was fumbling, pulling his pistol out, then abandoning the effort as Thorpe closed the remaining ten feet. Mitchell went to a fighter's stance. The impetus of Thorpe's charge smashed through Mitchell's guard and Thorpe slammed his knife home to the hilt into Mitchell's chest. The ex-paratrooper died with a confused look on his face, not even knowing how he'd been bested.

Thorpe grabbed one of the M-60s from the ground and spun about, searching for more targets, his eyes wild. A figure moved along the bank downstream and Thorpe's finger tightened on the trigger.

"Thorpe!" Parker called out. "It's me! Parker!"

Thorpe's body shook as a shiver went through him and sanity returned to his eyes. He slowly lowered the muzzle of the M-60. Parker ran up to his position and stopped, staring at the carnage. "Jesus, Thorpe," was all she could muster.

Her black flight suit was soaking wet. She grabbed his shoulder. "Come on. Come back with me. The lieutenant's hurt."

Thorpe followed her along the bank. Everson was kneeling next to Lieutenant Cruz, bandaging her wounds. In her hand was a blood-soaked piece of paper. "The door code," Cruz whispered.

Parker took it out of her hand. At that moment, Cruz's eyes lost their focus and her hand slumped down on the grass. Everson slowly reached up and closed her eyes, tears flowing down his cheeks.

Thorpe looked across the body and met Parker's gaze.

FOUR MILES AWAY, Maysun had dragged himself over to the wreckage of the Blackhawk and had been working on the chopper's FM radio with Tommy's aid. He finished wrapping some severed wired together, then picked up the handset.

"Any station this net, any station this net, this is Army Helicopter Seven-Eight-Six. Over." He waited a few seconds then tried again. "Any station this net, this is Army Helicopter Seven-Eight-Six. Come in please. Over."

The radio crackled, then a voice came out of the speaker. "Army Helicopter Seven-Eight-Six, this is Cobra Twelve. What is your location? Over."

Tommy handed Maysun a map. "Cobra twelve, this is Seven-Eight-Six. I am located at grid square thirty-four eighty-six. I say again, grid square thirty- four eighty-six. Over."

"Seven-Eight-Six, this is Cobra Twelve. You are to immediately vacate that area on a vector of one eight zero degrees. If you do not comply, you will be shot down. Over."

Maysun rolled his eyes. "I'd like to comply guys, but I can't. Because I've crashed here. Over."

"You're on the ground at that location? Over."

"That's what crashed usually means. Over."

"Wait one while I contact higher. Out."

"Wait one," Maysun said to Tommy. He shook his head and spun the frequency dials. He keyed the mikes. "Sergeant Dublowski, are you monitoring?"

There were a short pause, then a strong voice came over the radio. "This is Master Sergeant Dublowski. Who are you and what are you doing on my net?"

THORPE SAT NEXT to Parker on the hood of one of the Humvees. They had left Cruz's body, covered by a poncho, where she had died. Everson was shaken, but ready for action. "Let's get to the LCC," Everson said.

"McKenzie's got a dozen men sitting guard at the door," Thorpe said. "Without the help of your platoon," Thorpe gestured at the burning Humvees on the other side of the river, "there's no way we can get in the vault door. We can't take them down with just the three of us."

"I say we try!" Everson said, his large hands were wrapped tightly around his M-16.

"There's got to be another way into that control center." Thorpe grabbed Parker's shoulders. "Think! Is there any other opening? An air shaft? Anything?"

Parker was shaking her head, when suddenly Everson held up a hand. "What about the maintenance tunnels?"

"You have to get into a silo or the LCC to get to the maintenance tunnels," Parker said. Then she sat bolt upright. Parker was thinking about Everson's suggestion as she slowly spoke. "The facility is designed to stop a terrorist from getting in and launching. But we've already launched Omega Missile."

"So?" Thorpe asked.

Parker was excited now. "The Omega Missile silo is empty. The silo doors are open. There's an underground inspection crawlway from every silo to the launch facility!"

"Where's the Omega Missile silo?"

Parker jumped into the driver's seat. "I'll get us there."

18

CHARLESTON NAVAL BASE is the Navy's third-largest homeport after Norfolk and San Diego. Over forty ships were currently anchored or docked on the Cooper River, just north of the city of Charleston. While the rest of the port was at its normal Sunday morning level, one ship was a beehive of activity.

The USS Shiloh was a Ticonderoga-class cruiser, more commonly referred to as an AEGIS guided-missile cruiser. It was a cousin of the infamous Vincennes which shot down an Iranian airliner in the Persian Gulf. The Shiloh was an even more advanced version than that older ship. The sophisticated ship was a far cry from the cruisers of an earlier age that had boasted eight-to ten-inch guns as their main weapons. The Shiloh only had two single-barrel five-inch guns, one on the forecastle and one on the quarterdeck at the rear. For armament, the ship relied on missiles and it carried quite a punch in that department. It boasted eight Tomahawk cruise missiles in each of its two VLS missile launchers along with numerous other surface-to-surface and surface-to-air missiles.

At the present moment, above the rear, deck of the USS Shiloh, a SH-60 specially modified Blackhawk helicopter was being guided down to a landing by a crewman in a bright orange jumpsuit. As soon as the helicopter's wheels touched down, the side doors were opened and several large bags were thrown out. Crewmen picked them up and carried them forward to the ship's captain, who was standing next to a special operations resupply pod. The pod was six feet long and two feet in diameter, painted dull black.

The pilot handed a computer disk out his door to the ship's weapon's officer before it took off.

"All right, pack them in," the captain ordered.

The crewmen had just begun doing so when one of the canvas bags broke open and stacks of worn hundred dollar bills fell onto the deck. All work paused as they stared at the money.

The captain's voice cut through the pause. "Pack the bags in the pod, gentlemen."

A petty officer looked up at the captain. "We're going to fire this off, sir?"

"If we get ordered to, we will."

The petty officer shook his head. "Someone on the Joint Chiefs retiring or what?"

"I don't know," said the captain honestly, "and I don't think I want to know." He turned to a petty officer. "Chief, is the Tomahawk ready to receive this pod?"

"Yes, sir."

The captain nodded. "All right. As soon as the money is in, load it."

The petty officer snapped to attention. "Aye-aye, sir."

Drake came back in the access panel, leaning it back in place behind him. McKenzie walked over and they talked quietly, so the other guards couldn't hear.

"Are we all set?" McKenzie asked.

Drake handed McKenzie a small device that looked like a TV remote with a cover. It had a thick, bright red nylon strap attached to one end, allowing it to be worn around the neck. Drake flipped open the cover and showed McKenzie a series of buttons. "I've programmed this manually so it's out of the Omega Missile loop." He lightly touched one button. "Green and the silo opens and the missile preps up. Blue and the missile takes off. Red and you arm the warhead and it goes off when the missile lands. Yellow is abort." He pointed to a last black button. "That's the bugaboo. Push black and that warhead goes off no matter where it is, whether it's flying or still sitting in the silo. As you can see, they're all labeled so we don't make a rather big mistake and push the wrong button."

McKenzie took the device and slipped it over his head, hiding it inside his shirt. "And the missile is targeted correctly?"

"Straight up and down isn't that hard to program."

"The flight time?"

"Thirty minutes give or take a few seconds."

McKenzie smiled. "Excellent."

NATIONAL SECURITY ADVISER HILL walked out of the small office to the rear of the War Room. He seemed to have aged years in the hour he'd been in the War Room. "If we cannot stop Kilten by any other means, the president has approved the nuclear strike at five minutes before the deadline is up. That's only if you can assure him the area has been evacuated and there will be no civilian casualties."

General Lowcraft had been looking through various printouts. "I've already given the orders to prepare the aircraft and to get the evacuation started. Our readout on wind and fallout indicate New Orleans won't be affected."

Colonel Hurst called out. "Sir, we've got radio communications with a helicopter that crashed inside the radar zone of the Omega Missile launch facility. They were knocked out of the sky by the explosion that took out Barksdale. The pilot says he had a Special Forces officer on board and the man is checking out some shots fired in the area. They've also made contact with one of the crew from the Omega Missile LCC."

"Can we talk to them?" Lowcraft asked.

"The pilot says the SF officer is supposed to radio him in a couple of minutes and he'll patch him through."

Hill looked at Lowcraft. "What can one man do?"

Lowcraft shrugged. "It's one more than we had."

"Still, what can one man do?"

"Ask Kilten."

PARKER PULLED to a stop in the tree line next to a fifty-square-meter clearing. The concrete cover for the Omega Missile silo was tilted back inside of a fence.

"How's it guarded?" Thorpe asked.

Parker pointed. "Two thermal cameras, there and there at opposing corners of the compound. Ground sensors along the fence projecting out twenty feet. Slave-driven chain gun, 7.62-mm, activated by the Omega Missile LCC is there. The one at the LCC tracks movement and fires at it. This one tracks movement of thermal signatures and fires at anything with a mass large enough to be a person inside the perimeter. It's the best-guarded silo in the inventory."

"Great," Thorpe muttered. Thorpe looked at the weapons mounted on a twenty-foot tower in the center of the compound. They had a clear field of fire over the fence at the entire clearing.

Thorpe checked his watch. "Hold on a second." He took out Parker's survival radio and pushed the transmit button. "Maysun, this is Thorpe."

"Thorpe, hold on a second. I got ahold of Dublowski and he's monitoring. There's someone else who wants to talk to you right away, though. Let me patch you through."

There was a short pause, then a new voice came over the air. "This is General Lowcraft. Who am I speaking to?"

Thorpe knew who General Lowcraft was. "Captain Thorpe, Fifth Special Forces Group on detached assignment to the Department of Energy Special Operations NEST team, sir. I also have Major Parker from the Air Force here. She's with the Three Hundred Forty-First Missile Wing."

"How the hell did you end up there, Captain?"

"Bad luck, sir," Thorpe replied. "My chopper was flying in to Barksdale for fuel and a spare part and we got caught."

Lowcraft was direct and to the point. "We have a problem."

"Yes, sir, we're aware of that. Major Parker is from the Omega Missile crew and we saw both Kilten and McKenzie go down into the launch facility."

"You certainly are up to speed on this problem. In fact, you seem to be ahead of us on some of it. Who's McKenzie?"

"Ex-Navy SEAL," Thorpe said. "He worked with me on the SO/NEST teams before he retired. They've also got a bunch of Canadian ex-paratroopers for their muscle."

"We have to stop them," Lowcraft said. "You're aware of what they control?"

"Yes, sir," Thorpe said. "We're working on it."

"Work harder, soldier."

Parker indicated she wanted the radio. "What are they asking for, sir?"

"Twenty-six-million dollars and for the president to review the country's nuclear weapons system safeguards and some classified files."

"Are you giving them the money?" Thorpe asked.

"We don't know yet. You do what you can. You've only got two hours."

"Then what, sir?" Thorpe asked.

"You let me worry about that, son."

Thorpe keyed the radio. "Sir, may I make a suggestion?"

"Fire away," Lowcraft said.

"We think we have a way of getting into the launch facility. We also have the override code for the vault door to the LCC. The air force security people got ambushed and wiped out."

"Goddamn!" Lowcraft exclaimed.

"But we're heavily outnumbered and outgunned," Thorpe continued. "We could use some help. If you could get the rest of my NEST team here, they could go for the LCC itself through the vault door.

There's a Master Sergeant Dublowski standing by at Fort Polk, ready to go."

"We've been in contact with your team and we have a C-130 arriving at Polk shortly to pick them up," Lowcraft said. "The problem is that Kilten has threatened to fire off a nuclear weapon if he spots an aircraft on the radar in the launch facility," Lowcraft said.

Thorpe turned to Parker. "What's the range on the radar in the launch facility?"

"Five miles," Parker said.

Thorpe spoke into the radio. "Sir, the team can jump in. They can go high, offset their release point five miles and HAHO in."

There was a brief pause, then Lowcraft's voice came back. "I'll get on it, Captain Thorpe. You monitor this frequency and do what you can to get into the launch facility."

"Roger that, sir." Thorpe waited a few seconds. "Maysun, you still there?"

"Where am I going to go with a broken leg?"

"How's Tommy?"

"Fine."

"Patch me through to Dublowski," Thorpe said.

"Wait one. OK, he's on."

"Dublowski, this is Thorpe."

"What's up, sir?"

"You guys ready?"

"Roger that. I've got the boys standing by. We've got a C-130 landing right now. Anything else?"

Thorpe snapped his fingers at Parker. "Give me the code."

"You can't send it over the radio!" Parker exclaimed.

"What, some terrorist is going to intercept it and break into the LCC?" Thorpe said. "We should be so lucky."

Parker shook her head. "That's the rule."

"Rules got us into this mess," Thorpe said. He looked at Everson. "Can you take the code and wait by the surface entrance, out of sight?"

"Yes, sir." Everson said.

Thorpe keyed the radio. "Ski, there will be a Sergeant Everson waiting for you on the ground with the override code."

"Roger."

"Do you have any demo just in case the code doesn't work?"

"We've got some charges," Dublowski said.

"Watch out for the machine guns on top of the LCC. They fire at movement when activated."

"Great," Dublowski said.

"I'm going underground in a few minutes to try to get in a different way and stop those guns from firing. Once I go down, I'll probably be out of touch. Good luck."

Parker was shaking her head as he hung up.

"What?" Thorpe asked.

"No way they're going to be able to blow that door," she said. "It's designed to take a nuke strike."

"They can try," Thorpe said.

"Even if they take down McKenzie's men," Parker said, "Kilten and McKenzie can stop them using the remote controlled chain guns on the top of the LCC surface entrance before they make it in the first door. They're just like the guns here."

"Is there any way we can short-circuit the guns?" Thorpe asked.

"From inside the LCC. There's a master control panel."

"Then I suppose we'd better make damn sure we get into the LCC, right?"

He turned to Everson. "Go put surveillance on the LCC and wait for my team. Use your survival radio to monitor."

Everson saluted and headed into the woods.

Parker pointed across the field. "After you."

Thorpe was looking in the back of the Humvee, taking out equipment the ambushers had in there. He appropriated a rope and sorpe grenades. "Any way you know of that we can beat the cameras and the sensors?" he asked.

"Not that I can think of," Parker said.

Thorpe looped the rope over his shoulder. He looked at the cameras. "Thermal right?"

Parker nodded. "That's so they can see at night without having to light the silos up and give away their location to overhead imagery."

Thorpe nodded. He reached into his vest and pulled out two small foil packets.

"What are those?" Parker asked.

"Survival blankets," Thorpe said as he ripped one of them open. "We put them over us and crawl to the silo. They reflect heat back so we shouldn't show up on the thermals."

Parker eyed the blankets dubiously. They looked like strips of aluminum foil. "What about the sensors?" she asked.

"They might think they've been tripped by an animal. Do you know what weight sets them off?"

"No," Parker said, "but we have had deer set them off."

"Well, they won't know what to make of us under the blankets, so let's go."

"Doesn't sound like much of a plan," Parker said, hesitating and looking across the way at the lurking menace of the machine guns.

Thorpe pulled the blanket over his shoulders, lowered himself to the ground, and began crawling away from the tree line toward the compound.

AFTER GENERAL LOWCRAFT finished giving a flurry of orders, he was finally able to answer the question Hill had asked after the conversation with Thorpe.

"HAHO stands for High Altitude, High Opening parachute drop. They jump at thirty thousand feet, open their parachutes immediately, and fly them to the drop zone. The parachutes won't get picked up on radar."

"Can the team get in there?" Hill asked.

"I don't know."

"But it's worth a try?"

"Yes, it's worth a try, but it puts us in a rather difficult position. If I HAHO an SF team on top of the launch facility and they don't make it in, then there's no way I can get them out before you hit that place with your nuclear strike. It's condemning those men to death."

"Send them anyway," Hill said.

Lowcraft gave Hill a look he might use for something that he accidentally smeared on the bottom of his shoe. He reached for the mike. "I'm going to tell them of the planned strike."

"I don't see how it would help them," Hill said.

"It would give them the option of getting out of there," Lowcraft said.

Hill shook his head. "Options are not things normally associated with military operations. Even though it's a slim chance, the NEST team and Thorpe and Parker are our best shot at getting into that LCC."

"I'm going to tell them anyway," Lowcraft turned to the communications officer. "Get me Thorpe on the radio."

THORPE AND PARKER were halfway across the field when Thorpe heard a low voice on the radio in his pocket. Irritated, he pulled it out. "Thorpe here," he answered as Parker edged next to him, her head near his.

"Captain Thorpe, this is General Lowcraft. I want you to know that if you don't get to the launch facility by noon, we're taking it out with a nuclear strike."

Thorpe rolled his eyes at Parker. "Just get Dublowski and his men moving." Thorpe paused. "Sir, have you evacuated Barksdale?"

"We're working on it. The nuclear bomb will be proceeded by a bunker-buster bomb so the nuclear bomb will go off twenty feet down, which will minimize the effects."

"There are family members at Barksdale," Thorpe said.

"We're aware of that," General Lowcraft said.

"Just do your job and we'll take care of our end of things."

"Sir, you need to get the people out from the chopper crash. My son is one of them."

"Your son?"

"It's a long story, sir, but can you get them out?"

"I'll get a medevac chopper as close to the radar limit as possible. We'll get them out of there. You focus on getting the LCC under your control."

"Yes, sir."

"Good luck."

Thorpe put the radio away. He met Parker's gaze without a word.

"Someone will get Tommy to safety," she said.

"The question is, will there be any safety?" Thorpe asked. "We've got to get into this place."

They began crawling.

INSIDE THE LCC, McKenzie punched memory five in his cellular phone for the tenth time. The phone rang and rang with no answer. "Shit!" McKenzie exclaimed.

He turned to Drake. "We've lost contact with Mitchell so we have to assume our perimeter has been breached at the bridge. We're wasting time. They're up to something."

McKenzie keyed the microphone for the satellite radio. "General Lowcraft. I and my associates are becoming short-tempered. Has the president been notified and is the money on its way?"

"Who am I talking to? Where's Professor Kilten?"

"Just answer my questions, General."

"The president has been notified," a new voice replied. "He has a copy of Kilten's report and I can assure you he is reading it. The money has been transported to Charleston and is being loaded as we speak."

"Is this Hill?" McKenzie asked.

"Yes."

"Is your shithead aide, Lugar, there? The one who uses Loki as his call sign?"

Hill remained silent.

"Listen, Hill, I know your people are trying to get in here. We spot anybody and you're going to have a hell of a lot more problems than us. You got that?"

"Is this McKenzie?" Lowcraft asked.

McKenzie smiled. "So you've been talking to my friend Captain Thorpe, have you?"

There was no answer.

"Not very bright, General, but not a great disclosure either. How's Thorpe doing? What's he up to?"

"He's back at Barksdale debriefing our people," Lowcraft said.

"Oh, I don't think so," McKenzie said. "That's not the way Thorpe works. He's around here somewhere. Of course, he's not the threat he once was."

"McKenzie, why are you doing this? I've got your service jacket here. You've served your country for twenty-two years. Why have you turned against it now?"

"I've turned against the Pentagon and assholes like your friend Hill, General, not my country. I'm doing my duty to my country here. Protecting them from people like Hill."

"Chief McKenzie, I—"

"You think what I'm doing is wrong?" McKenzie yelled into the radio. "I'll show you people doing wrong things." He reached into his pocket and pulled out a CD. He handed it to Drake. "Send that to the sons-of-bitches."

Drake took the CD and slid it into the communication computer. He transmitted the data on high-frequency burst to the War Room as McKenzie spoke. "You've got some digitized data coming in, General. I suggest you view it."

IN THE WAR ROOM, Lowcraft turned his chair to face the front of the room. The front display cleared and then an out-of-focus image appeared. It showed a beach with some trucks parked.

Just as Lowcraft was getting ready to ask his technician to clean the image up, it cleared and he could see four military-style trucks parked on the sand. The camera panned and a tank came into view. Lowcraft immediately recognized the make; there was only one country in the world that made that tank and it had never been exported.

"What is this?" Lowcraft asked.

"Don't act stupid," McKenzie hissed. "Those are Israeli-made Merkava tanks. Your friend Hill knows exactly what this is."

One of the tanks turned on its searchlight and a hovercraft appeared on the water, sliding up onto the beach. Men began taking barrels off the hovercraft and loading them onto trucks. The camera zoomed in on one of the barrels and Lowcraft could see the markings on the side.

"Oh, shit," he muttered to himself.

McKenzie's voice came over the speaker. "I shot this digitized video while working for our government, General. As you can tell from the scene, those are Israelis receiving a shipment of plutonium. What you can't tell is that the people doing the shipping are CIA."

Lowcraft turned to Hill. "Maybe you can shed some light on this. We aborted that Lebanon SO/NEST team but you didn't tell me any of this."

McKenzie's voice boomed out again. "This was my last mission for our government. We had received information that there was going to be a transfer of weapons-grade plutonium along the coast in southern Lebanon. This information was correct. Unfortunately this was a case of the left hand not knowing what the right was doing, no pun intended." McKenzie gave a strange laugh.

"When we called for an air and ground strike on the exchange to get the plutonium back under positive control, the strike was canceled by Mister Hill's aide and we were ordered to abort," McKenzie said. "Then we got attacked by the CIA guards and the Israelis. I didn't let the debriefers know I had the video when I got back because I knew it would disappear and I'd have Agency dinks knocking at my door. So don't give me any crap. You people are the criminals!"

"So enough bullshit!" McKenzie exploded. "You do what you were told to do. I want the money moving. Now!" He cut off the connection.

General Lowcraft was rubbing his forehead. "This thing keeps getting worse and worse."

Hill had been thinking about something McKenzie mentioned. "If Thorpe was with him on that mission into southern Lebanon, maybe Thorpe's not on our side."

"Sir," Colonel Hurst said. "I've got Thorpe's file and I've also contacted the NEST headquarters. Thorpe's team was directed to check out security at nuclear weapons storage sites this weekend by direct request from the Pentagon." Hurst looked up from the papers in his hand. "The request was initiated by Professor Thomas Kilten."

Lowcraft took the orders and looked at them, then he threw them down. "Kilten may have wanted this team in the area for some reason, but Thorpe's on our side."

"How do you know that?" Hill demanded.

"Because his son's there," Lowcraft snapped. He glared at Hill. "Of course, there are those of us who would sell out our own children if there was something to be gained." He poked a finger at Hill's chest. "How are you going to feel when it's you who is being sacrificed?"

"Sir, there's more," Hurst said. "I've run a check on the Omega Missile LCC crew. Major Parker just came back to the Air Force after being seconded to a CIA unit called Red Flyer."

Lowcraft turned to Hill with eyebrows raised. "What's Red Flyer? That was part of Kilten's request."

"You don't have a need to know," Hill replied. "Suffice it to say it's part of that hammer I hold over the heads of the Israelis and others who fuck with the United States."

"You're still playing 'I've-got-a-secret' and we're standing on the edge of nuclear Armageddon," General Lowcraft said wonderingly.

Hurst had another file in his hand. "In Kilten's file it says he also worked with Red Flyer. It's apparently something compartmentalized between the Air Force and the CIA."

"I'm only the chairman of the Joint Chiefs," Lowcraft shook his head. "No one tells me what the hell is going on with anything."

Hill took Lowcraft's arm and led him out of earshot of the others. "Red Flyer took over the SADM mission from the Special Forces six years ago."

Lowcraft knew that SADM stood for Strategic Atomic Demolition Munitions. A fancy term for backpack nukes. He'd known about the mission being removed from the Special Forces, but he thought that was because the mission had been phased out given the accuracy of cruise missiles with tactical nuclear weapons.

"Why?" Lowcraft asked.

"There are times when we have to use the threat of a deniable tac nuke strike for diplomatic pressure," Hill said. "There's so much shit floating around now that a bomb going off can be pinned on terrorists if there is no trace of a missile or aircraft launch that can be back-tracked."

"So we have Red Flyer teams stationed around the world with tactical nuclear weapons to use to threaten those who need threatening," Hill concluded.

"How was Parker involved?" Lowcraft asked.

"I don't know," Hill answered. "She must have done a tour of duty with Red Flyer. We take some personnel with the necessary nuclear weapons background from the military to work on the teams."

Lowcraft rubbed his eyes in weariness. "Jesus Christ, Kilten sure has uncovered a cesspool, hasn't he?"

19

FOUR SAILORS MANHANDLED the pod with the money into the nose cone of the Tomahawk cruise missile. As soon as it was in place, a weapons specialist rigged the explosive bolts that would separate the nose cone from the missile and then the pod from the nose cone. As soon as he was done, the missile slid back on its rail into the launcher on the forecastle of the USS Shiloh.

The captain was in the fire control center, supervising as his weapons officer went through pre-fire procedures. They'd programmed the Tomahawk's guidance system using the disk from Kilten's desk at the Pentagon, the information sent by modem. The weapons officer had also programmed the firing of the bolts using the same disk.

"Stand by," the weapons officer announced. "Clear the firing deck."

The report came back. "Firing deck clear."

The weapons officer turned to the captain. "All systems green. Ready to fire, sir."

"Fire," the captain ordered.

The weapons officer flipped up the cover on a switch and threw the lever underneath. On the forecastle, the cover blew open on the

Tomahawk's silo and it leapt out. The missile dropped slightly, then the rocket kicked in even stronger and the telephone-pole-sized missile roared away to the southwest.

AT WHITEMAN AIR FORCE Base in Missouri, a helicopter landed on the runway, two hundred feet from a waiting B-2 bomber. Armed guards jumped out of the chopper, weapons at the ready. Ordnance personnel from the airbase ran up and pulled a large plastic case out of the chopper.

One of the men helping carry the case to the bomber was new to both his job and the Air Force, having just graduated his basic training a few weeks previously. He glanced over the top of the metal casing at his partner. "Hey, what's the big deal with this? Why all the guards?"

The other airman nodded his head at the case. "See those symbols on the side?"

"Yeah."

"That means there's a 'special' in there."

"A special? What's that."

"A nuclear weapon, you dumb shit."

The navigator-bombardier from the B-2 was waiting underneath the plane. He supervised the uncrating of the bomb and the loading inside the bowels of the bomber. He then hooked up all the required attachments.

"What's the flight time from here to the target?" the pilot asked him.

"If we go straight shot, about twenty-five minutes," the nav-bomb said. "But we're to fly to a hold point and wait for further orders."

The pilot hit a switch that slowly closed the black doors. "Man, I hope this is an exercise."

Drake smiled at the computer screen. He tapped McKenzie and spoke quietly. "I have confirmation of the cruise missile firing."

"Do you have payload control?" McKenzie asked in the same low tone.

"It's on the frequency Kilten specified."

"Very good," McKenzie said. "Time to go pick up our package." He pointed at the laptop. "Let's unhook that, Mister Drake. I'll take care of the destruct hardware."

On the far right console a red light began blinking, unnoticed in the scurry of activity. On the screen that displayed the thermal imaging from the Omega Missile silo, two small, round warm dots were in the vicinity of the gate to the compound. These too went unnoticed.

Thorpe rolled on his back and aimed his pistol. He fired and the lock on the gate to the compound blew apart. Thorpe pushed the gates slightly apart and crawled in, Parker following.

Thorpe quickened his pace, expecting a Humvee to come tearing up at any moment. He reached the concrete lip of the silo. The massive concrete doors were open wide and scorched. Thorpe looked down. The silo was empty, the walls black and sooty.

Thorpe slid over the large concrete block that made up one half of the lid. There was a thin lip surrounding the circular opening, where the massive doors used to rest. Thorpe threw aside the thermal blanket and looked around. Both doors appeared threatening, balanced, as if they might fall and crush him any second.

Parker joined him. "We made it!"

Thorpe looked down at her. "And now?" The only way down was to jump from the concrete ledge, about twelve feet out and five feet down, to a metal ladder. If he missed, he'd fall eighty feet to the bottom of the silo.

"Where's the access panel to this crawlway?" Thorpe asked.

"At the bottom."

"Of course," Thorpe said drily. "You see any way down? Other than falling."

"The maintenance ladder?"

"That's what I was afraid of."

Thorpe let go of the edge and extended one hand. "Ladies first."

"Oh, thanks." Parker didn't say another word, but surprised Thorpe by suddenly jumping. Her hands slammed on the top rung, slipped past, caught the second rung, held for a second then slipped again. She desperately grabbed the third rung and held.

"I was just joking," Thorpe offered as Parker caught her breath, hooking her arms through the ladder.

"Ha, ha," Parker said. "Your turn." Parker climbed down a few more rungs.

Thorpe jumped and caught the top rung. Parker immediately began climbing down.

EIGHT MILES AWAY, six hundred feet in the air, a Cobra gunship banked hard. Below it, a civilian Bell Jet Ranger was flying toward Barksdale Air Force Base.

NEWSFOUR was written on the side in large letters.

The Cobra pilot keyed his radio as he pulled up next to the civilian chopper. "Bell Jet Ranger, this is Cobra One. You are entering restricted airspace. You are to turn back immediately."

"This isn't restricted on any flight chart I've got," the civilian pilot replied.

"You have ten seconds to turn or you will be fired on."

Inside the chopper, the reporter in the right side spoke on the radio through his headset. "We know you people are up to something. You're evacuating everyone from this area. People saw the explosion. Has there been an accident with one of the nuclear weapons stored out here? We have the right—"

A string of tracers came out of the 7.62-mm minigun on the nose of the Cobra and flew across the front of the Bell Jet Ranger.

The Cobra pilot wasn't elegant, but he got his point across. "The next burst will be up your ass." The Cobra turned and was flying sideways, minigun pointed right at the cockpit of the other aircraft.

"They're serious," the news chopper pilot said. "I'm getting the hell out of here!" The Bell Jet Ranger banked hard and headed back the way it had come.

"THORPE'S GOT to be in on it," Hill insisted. "Why else would Kilten have put him there? He's in the right place at the right time."

Lowcraft had spent the last several minutes looking at Kilten's classified file, ignoring the arguing going on around him. He also had a copy of Parker's file. Finally he looked up. "Thorpe's another piece on the board," he said. "As is Parker."

"What?" Hill was puzzled.

"It's beginning to make sense now. Kilten's a chess master. This is the greatest game of his life and he's arranged the board. Thorpe is a piece. So is Parker. Both were handpicked." Lowcraft was nodding. "And I don't think Thorpe or Parker even know they're pieces. I don't believe either one is in on it, as you put it, but they are a part of it."

"Bullshit," Hill sputtered. "Thorpe and McKenzie were on that mission together. It can't just be coincidence that they're in the same place in Louisiana."

"I just told you," Lowcraft said, "that it's not coincidence. Thorpe is there on purpose; the question is, what is that purpose?" Lowcraft tapped the report. "Kilten is doing this for what he views as a good reason. McKenzie might have different goals, but it is very clear what Kilten's are. Somehow Thorpe fits into this. Kilten wanted Thorpe and his team close by when this went down. Hell, maybe Kilten wants to fail. He gets just as much publicity either way. Parker has a role to play also, I just don't know what it is yet."

Hill didn't have time for psychological delving. "Well, it really doesn't matter much either way at this point. Launch the aircraft."

Lowcraft looked up from the folders to Hill. "If Kilten loaded the board, he also picked the timing of this for a purpose."

"So?" Hill tapped his fingers impatiently on the desktop.

"That means you and I are pieces also," General Lowcraft said. "Launch the aircraft, General."

AT WHITEMAN, the F-l 17A Stealth fighter led the way down the runway, accelerating rapidly and then darting up into the sky. The B-2 followed, its sleek form slowly separating from the ground. It linked up with the Stealth at five thousand feet and both aircraft then banked and headed south toward Louisiana.

PARKER AND THORPE were kneeling next to a panel. Thorpe was using a Leatherman multipurpose tool from his vest to unscrew it. Over half of the bolts were off, and the amount of sweat pouring down his back showed how hard it was to use the pliers on the nuts.

"Do you think Lowcraft will order your team in?" Parker asked.

"He'll send the team."

"Even knowing this place is targeted for a nuclear strike? That's pretty coldhearted."

Thorpe was working as he spoke. "That's his job. Yes, it's coldhearted, but so is your job and, as you pointed out, so is mine. If we don't like it, we shouldn't be wearing the uniforms we're wearing."

He got the last bolt off. The panel slid off and he looked in. A steel tube extended as far as he could see. It was three feet in diameter and dimly lit.

"Shall we?"

A C-130 with its engines running had its back ramp opening even as it turned around and faced back up the runway. Six men wearing free-fall parachutes with weapons and rucksacks strapped to their bodies waddled out toward the plane. In the lead was Master Sergeant Dublowski, a barrel-chested man in his mid-forties.

He hopped up on the ramp, the crew chief lending a hand. As soon as the last man was on, the ramp began closing and the plane began accelerating.

MIDWAY OVER GEORGIA, the Tomahawk cruise missile with the money on board was flying comfortably at an altitude of two hundred feet. Designed to be able to hug the ground at less than twenty feet, this flight was no challenge to the on-board computer. The route that had been programmed into it was a winding one that followed the front range of the Appalachian Mountains. The indirect route put it thirty-five minutes out from the vicinity of the Omega Missile LCC.

DRAKE HAD unhooked Kilten's laptop and connected one of the leads to a small satellite transmitter. It was a rough-looking setup, but it worked. Drake had a special backpack, which fit the pieces in securely. He walked over to McKenzie, who had just finished battering the Omega Missile emergency destruct mechanism into a nonfunctioning mass of metal with his artificial arm.

He turned to face the guards he had brought down. "We're going to do a security check on the surface. Let no one but me back in. Clear?"

"Clear, sir," the senior Canadian ex-paratrooper said.

McKenzie and Drake moved to the elevator. The door shut and they headed toward the surface.

"You're not going back for them, are you?" Drake said.

"If they can get out, then they get out," McKenzie said. "It's a question of how long it's going to take them to realize that I'm not coming back."

"They have the same planned escape route we do. If they don't make it, then there's a bigger cut for you and me. The bottom line is that right up to the last minute, we have to make the Pentagon believe we're inside the launch facility. Otherwise, we'll never get away."

"Why do the men believe you?" Drake asked.

The doors opened and the vault door slowly swung wide. McKenzie turned to Drake as they waited. "Why does anyone believe anything? Hell, they got paid fifty thousand apiece up front. They think that makes me trustworthy. And they want the five hundred thousand payoff we promised each one."

They stepped into the foyer. McKenzie called in several of the surface guards and ordered them to go down and augment the two men already down in the LCC. The vault door swung closed. There were three Humvees left parked there. Two were manned by two men each. The third was empty and McKenzie led Drake toward it.

"Let's roll."

20

THORPE WAS LEADING the way down the tunnel when Parker grabbed his leg. "Hold on a second."

She climbed by him, sliding her body over his in the tight confines of the crawlway. She paused on top of him and gave Thorpe a strange look. "Excuse me!"

Thorpe wriggled slightly and his hand came up holding the device he had used on the bolts. "It was the Leatherman."

"Oh." Parker moved ahead of him. "There's a motion sensor right up ahead."

"I thought you said we could get in this way."

"We can get in this way. I didn't say we could do it without getting spotted. The security people wouldn't leave this totally unguarded." She inched forward, then stopped. "It's right here. Give me that tool of yours. I think I can disable it."

ON THE SURFACE, McKenzie and Drake got in the Humvee and drove off to the southeast. They left behind the two Humvees with M-60s manned, standing guard on the surface. In the tree line, Everson watched the vehicle drive away. One less machine gun to deal with.

MOVING QUICKLY TOWARD THE SOUTHEAST, four turboprop engines straining to the max, the C-130 cargo plane was gaining altitude as fast as possible. Inside, the special forces team led by Dublowski sat around an oxygen console.

A crew chief walked up to Dublowski. "We're passing through thirty thousand feet. We're going to depressurize in one minute."

Dublowski turned to the team. "Hook in to the console."

The men connected the hoses from their high-altitude rigs into portals on the console.

The crew chief was hooked into the aircraft. "Depressurizing," he called out, then settled his mask on.

The back ramp slowly cracked open, the gap widening until there was a level platform at the rear, open to the sky.

The crew chief was now speaking to the team over their FM radios. They each had an earplug in and small boom mikes in front of their mouths. "Five minutes to drop!"

THE HUMVEE LEFT a plume of dirt behind as it sped down the road. McKenzie was looking around when he spotted the shattered tops of several trees in the woods to the left. He spun the wheel, catching Drake by surprise as they raced in that direction.

They bounced along the forest floor until they came upon the crashed Blackhawk. McKenzie bounded out of the Humvee, weapon at the ready.

He saw the wounded pilot, pistol in hand, and the boy behind him.

"We're the good guys," McKenzie called out, dropping the submachine gun to hang on its sling and holding up empty hands. "We're here to help."

"Thank God someone got here," Maysun said, lowering his pistol. "We need some help. There's—" the next word froze in his throat as McKenzie fired one of his nerve darts and it hit the pilot in the neck. Maysun slumped over, unconscious.

"And who might you be?" McKenzie asked as he walked up to the young boy who had his hands on Maysun's shoulders. Tommy shook the pilot, trying to wake him up.

Tommy's hands left Maysun's shoulders and grabbed the pistol. He swung it up and pulled the trigger, but nothing happened.

"Whoa!" McKenzie yelled, snatching it easily from the boy's hands. "You have to take the safety off first." McKenzie's face split into a wide smile as he read the name tag on the boy's shirt. "Tommy Thorpe. I know your daddy. I'll take you to him."

Tommy tried to pull free. "My dad said not to leave here for any reason."

McKenzie had neither the time nor the inclination to be persuasive. He reached down, grabbed Tommy's arm and hauled him back to the Humvee. He had Drake tie the struggling boy's hands together and put him in the backseat.

He continued south of the LCC, paralleling the Anaconda River. McKenzie slammed on the brakes as a guard suddenly came out of the trees, weapon at the ready. The guard waved them onto an overgrown trail that led to the riverbank.

"Everything secure, Johnson?" McKenzie asked.

"Yeah," the guard replied. "We're good to go." He looked around. "Where are the others?"

"They'll be along," McKenzie said.

"Who's the boy?" Johnson asked.

"A bonus," McKenzie said.

As McKenzie unloaded the Humvee, Johnson began dragging a camouflage net over the top of it. McKenzie led Drake down the bank and the two of them pulled a camouflage net off two Zodiac boats tied to a tree. There were half a dozen other boats secured there.

Once the two boats were clear, McKenzie gestured at Drake to open the laptop.

"Can you pick up the cruise missile with our money?"

Drake's fingers rattled over the keys. "Yes. It's about two hundred miles out and coming fast. ETA in sixteen minutes."

McKenzie pulled the remote from inside his shirt and flipped open the cover. "Now, to open the silo you said push black, right!"

Drake's face went white. "No! Green. Black sets off the nuke! It says it right there!"

McKenzie smiled. "Just joking. Everyone seems to have lost their sense of humor. We're rich. Enjoy it." He pushed the green button and flipped the cover shut. "Let's go sailing."

"THAT SHOULD DO IT," Parker handed the Leatherman back to Thorpe.

"Should?" Thorpe asked.

Parker didn't reply. She resumed crawling, leading the way. They reached an intersection. A tunnel came in from the right.

"Where's that go to?" Thorpe asked.

"One of the other silos," Parker replied.

Thorpe paused, sniffing the air. "You smell something?" He wet a finger and held it up in the intersection. "There's air moving down this way from that silo."

Parker paused. "That shouldn't be. That silo is sealed airtight until it opens—" She stopped speaking as they both had the same realization.

Thorpe looked down and noted that there were tracks in the dust going down that tunnel. "Someone's been to that silo recently!"

Parker put it all together. "The access panel is open and the silo doors just opened. That's why we feel air moving. It's going to launch! Move!"

Thorpe pushed her as they scurried straight ahead.

McKenzie was sitting in the back of the boat, next to the motor. He checked his watch, then opened up the remote again. He pressed the blue button.

A rushing noise was the first indication of the launch for Parker and Thorpe. A story crossed Thorpe's mind that he had heard while training in maritime operations about how when drowned bodies from sunken boats were recovered, it was often discovered that some of the corpses had boot marks on their shoulders from their crewmates trying to get up ladders faster than them.

Thorpe pushed Parker harder. "Move!" he yelled.

Inside the missile silo, flames were pouring out of the bottom of the ICBM. The flame filled the entire silo and part of it rushed through the access panel that Drake had left off in his rush to get back to the LCC.

Flames billowed down the tube. Thorpe and Parker could hear it coming, a crackling, thunderous noise.

"Move! Keep moving!" Thorpe yelled, looking past Parker's shoulders, seeing only a long stretch of pipe, his heart pounding, knowing there was no way they would make it to the end.

Parker reached a drain opening. Her fingernails ripped as she pulled up the grate. The opening was two feet by two. It went straight down into darkness. The sides were smooth metal and there were no handholds or ladder.

"Go! I've got you!" Thorpe pushed her in.

Behind them, the fireball hit an intersection and split, going both ways with equal ferocity. As Parker slid in headfirst, terrified, she felt Thorpe's hands on her ankles. She freefell for a second, then came to an abrupt halt as Thorpe's grip held.

Lying on his stomach in the tube, Thorpe looked over his shoulder and saw the flames coming. He pulled his toes up and allowed Parker's weight to pull him into the drainage tube. As he felt his shins painfully go over the edge, he spread his feet, boots slamming up against the sides of the opening, still in the crawlway, holding him in place. Parker screamed at this second drop, thinking Thorpe had lost her, but she came to another sudden halt as his feet held.

Flames roared above them, searing Thorpe's boots and his camouflage pants. Thorpe felt the pain, but didn't loosen his hold on either end. Then the flames were gone.

On the surface, the ICBM was out of the silo, accelerating, heading straight up.

Parker's voice was muffled. "Are you all right?"

Thorpe's voice was strained from pain and exertion. "Yeah. Listen, can you press up against the side of this thing and hold yourself from falling? Like a rock climber in a chimney?"

"Yeah, I think so."

Parker spread her arms against the sides of the drainage tunnel.

"I'm going to let go of your legs now," Thorpe said. "As soon as I do, push them against the wall."

Thorpe let go and Parker locked herself into place. Thorpe pressed his arms against the walls and painfully extricated himself from the drainage tunnel. He rolled onto his back and looked down his body. The green canvas of his jungle boots has been partially melted into his socks. Thorpe took a deep breath and flexed his toes and feet, feeling the agony. The metal in the bottom of the boots had helped keep some of the heat out. Painful, but walkable.

Thorpe reached down and helped Parker back out of the drainage tunnel. When she got into the main tunnel she sniffed the air.

"Whew, that sure burnt things up."

"That's my feet you're smelling," Thorpe said.

Parker looked down. "Oh my God."

Thorpe pointed down the tunnel toward the LCC. "As long as we don't have to tango, I'll be all right. Let's get moving."

21

"S IR, WE HAVE another launch. An ICBM with a nuclear warhead." Colonel Hurst delivered the news in a monotone. Coffee spilled over General Lowcraft's hand as he slammed the mug he'd been holding onto his desk. "Son-of-a-bitch! What's the trajectory?"

Hurst stared at his computer screen a few seconds too long.

"I asked what the goddamn trajectory is!"

"Uh, vertical, sir."

Lowcraft stared at him. "What the hell does that mean?"

Everyone in the War Room had been stressed for too long. "That means it goes straight up, then straight down, sir," Hurst said. "It's targeted for the Omega Missile Launch Control Center."

Hill had been following this. "What's happening?"

Lowcraft ignored the national security adviser. "Time to impact?"

"Thirty minutes."

Hill pressed his hands down on his own desktop.

"Please explain what is going on. Why would they fire a missile at themselves?"

General Lowcraft was staring at the front screen, thinking. "I take it to mean that Kilten and McKenzie are covering their tracks."

Hurst spoke up. "But that doesn't make sense, sir. They have to stay in the launch facility to control Omega Missile."

Lowcraft shook his head. "Kilten's been one step ahead of us the entire way so far. I have no doubt that he's overcome that little problem. What's the warhead in this missile?"

"Forty megaton." Hurst said.

"Jesus!" Lowcraft exclaimed. "We were only going to use a twenty to take out the LCC. Give me an updated readout on what a forty-megaton blast would do."

The screen in the front cleared, then new circles appeared. Hurst summarized it quickly. "Blast and thermal effects would reach those four towns around the epicenter with over fifty percent casualties. Fallout would reach New Orleans within six hours with lethal doses of radiation. Ten percent fatalities of those exposed."

Lowcraft turned to Hill, who promptly picked up the red phone to get ahold of the president. While the national security adviser was doing that, Lowcraft began issuing orders to evacuate those towns and to contact the mayor of New Orleans.

An army officer near the front of the room stood up. "Sir, what about the Special Forces team? They're ready to jump!"

"They already knew there would be a nuclear weapon inbound," Lowcraft said. "They have to try."

"Order in the Stealth and B-2," Hill suddenly said, hanging up the phone.

"What for?" Lowcraft demanded.

"Just in case," Hill said. "This launch could be an attempt by Kilten to stop us from attacking. We need to keep control."

"Control?" Lowcraft snorted.

"You said this ICBM would take thirty minutes to go up and then come down and impact?" Hill asked. When he received an affirmative nod, he continued. "And our aircraft can attack in twenty minutes from where they are now, correct? Then we gain ten minutes. In that ten minutes there is the possibility that Kilten might launch another missile. I would also think that Kilten and his people will be trying to escape the area in that ten minutes since the money pod will be in that area around that time. We can catch them with our nuke."

General Lowcraft wasn't pleased with that reasoning, but Hill spoke for the president. He gave the order for the Stealth fighter and the B-2 bomber to release from their holding position and head toward the Omega Missile LCC.

"THIS IS NUTS," the navigator-bombardier of the B-2 muttered as he received the order to assume a bombing path toward Louisiana. He glanced across at the pilot. "You have any clue what the hell is going on?"

"Same as you do," the pilot said as he turned the bomber out of the racetrack they had been in and followed the Stealth fighter to the south. "We're to take out a hardened position at our target coordinates."

"But what position? Who's there?"

"I don't have any idea," the pilot said.

"We're going to nuke Louisiana?" the nav-bomb still couldn't believe what was happening.

"It's a test. They'll stop us before we drop," the pilot said confidently.

"And if they don't?"

"Then we drop," the pilot said succinctly, "and God alone can help us then."

INSIDE THE CARGO bay of the C-130, the loud sound of the engines and the air swirling in the open ramp made normal speech impossible. The crew chief leaned close to Dublowski and pointed at the front of the plane, then at his headset. He took it off and handed it to the team sergeant. Dublowski put it on over his FM plug.

"What's up?" Dublowski said.

The pilot's voice sounded in his ears. "This is Colonel Harrows. We've received word that there's been an ICBM firing from one of the silos around our target. The missile is targeted for the LCC."

"How much time until detonation?"

"Twenty-eight minutes."

"Anything on the B-2 or the Stealth?"

"Negative."

"All right," Dublowski said.

He took off the headset and handed it back to the crew chief. He then spoke to his team on the internal FM net. "There's another nuke inbound at the target area, but if we take the LCC we ought to be able to stop that."

The crew chief held up one finger.

"One minute out," Dublowski said.

Every man got up and disconnected from the console, hooking into their personal oxygen. They all moved toward the ramp, following Dublowski. The light turned green. Dublowski threw himself out into the air, and the entire team followed.

Dublowski assumed the freefall position, back arched, limbs akimbo. He stabilized, then pulled his ripcord. The square chute deployed above him.

"Give me a count," Dublowski said into his mike.

All the men checked in. Dublowski looked at the navigation board strapped to the top of his reserve. "Follow me on a heading of one-four-zero degrees."

The team was staggered above Dublowski. As he turned, they followed in sequence until the team was heading for the Omega Missile LCC.

THE LEAD ZODIAC was planed out, cruising at forty knots down the Anaconda. The second, empty one bounced behind it, half the time airborne. McKenzie had Tommy tied to the rope that ran along the top of the pontoon.

"My dad will get you," Tommy said.

"I don't think so," McKenzie replied. He looked at the boy. "You should be thankful. I'm saving your life. This whole area is going to be destroyed by a nuclear bomb in a little while."

"My dad will stop it. That's his job and he's the best at his job."

McKenzie's eyes dropped momentarily from the young boy's, then he turned to the rear of the boat.

"Faster!" As he turned, his pistol caught on the tarp next to him, revealing a green cylinder with HELIUM stenciled on the side. Tommy noticed that and the thick coil of nylon rope that lay underneath the cylinder. McKenzie quickly pulled the tarp back in place, after making sure that neither Drake nor Johnson had noticed. He failed to detect that Tommy had seen what was hidden.

THORPE AND PARKER had finally reached the panel leading into the LCC. Thorpe carefully pushed on it and the metal plate moved.

"Where's the control for the guns on the surface?" he asked.

"It's a gray panel on the right-side wall as you go in," Parker said. "About fifteen feet in and four feet off the ground."

"Will we have a clear shot at it?"

"I'm not sure," Parker said. "I doubt it."

"Then we'll have to make one when we go in. You ready?" Thorpe asked.

"Ready," Parker replied, pistol in hand.

Thorpe kicked the panel out and rolled into the control center, firing. He put two rounds into the first man he saw, dropping him. The remaining Canadians reacted with a blast of automatic firepower that pinned Thorpe and Parker behind a metal cabinet. They didn't have a clear shot.

Dublowski could see the surface entrance to the Omega Missile LCC below him. He could also see the two Humvees parked with machine guns manned. He rapidly began giving orders and the staggered formation broke apart as parachutists headed for their targets.

Below them, the Canadian paratroopers scanned the surrounding woods, oblivious to the death winging down from above.

The Tomahawk cruise missile reached the east branch of the Anaconda River and turned left, heading downstream, less than twenty feet above the surface of the water.

Thorpe was returning fire by sticking the muzzle of his MP-5 over the top of the metal cabinet and blindly pulling the trigger. He had no idea where his bullets were going, but he wanted to keep the Canadians occupied.

"Where's the control?" he yelled.

Parker pointed with the muzzle of her gun. "Over there, behind that console. What's the plan now?" she asked.

"We keep them pinned down until my guys get down here."

"Keep them pinned down?" Parker repeated.

Thorpe fired an entire magazine on automatic, then quickly changed magazines. "Yeah, then we take out the panel."

Dublowski landed on the front hood of a Humvee, firing the last ten feet he descended, his rounds smashing into the machine gunner in the turret. He shifted aim and shot the man who was seated in the driver's seat right through the windshield as his feet touched the hood.

One of the other men on Dublowski's team did the same at the other Humvee. In the space of two seconds, the entire security force on the surface was dead. The rest of the SO/NEST team landed, their chutes cut loose and floating free in the wind as the men sprinted into the compound.

One of them spun, weapon at the ready as a man came out of the tree line. "Hold your fire!" Sergeant Everson yelled.

THORPE LOOKED up at the security monitors. He could see Dublowski and the rest of the team landing. So could the Canadians. One of them threw a switch and activated the automatic machine guns on the roof of the surface entrance.

DUBLOWSKI SHRUGGED off his parachute harness. "Let's go," he yelled. Then he just as quickly dove into the dirt as the ground ripped up around him and the roar of machine guns filled the air.

One of the team members was hit in the first burst and his body was tossed backward into the grass, blood pouring from half a dozen holes in his chest.

"Don't move!" Dublowski screamed.

THORPE FIRED A SHORT BURST, then glanced up at the video screens. He saw Dublowski and the other men lying in the grass, frozen.

"Fuck," Thorpe hissed. Thorpe handed her the MP-5. "When I count to three, just stick the muzzle over the edge and fire in that direction." He pulled two grenades off his vest.

"What are you going to do?" Parker asked in a worried voice.

Thorpe pulled the pins off both grenades. He dropped the pins on the floor and held the grenades, counting silently to himself.

"Thorpe!" Parker exclaimed.

"One. Two." Thorpe tossed both grenades into the room. "Three."

Parker stuck the muzzle over the edge and pulled the trigger. Thorpe rose and sprinted for the console hiding the panel as the grenades went off. He felt pieces of shrapnel hit his side but he dove for the ground and rolled. He fired with his pistol, emptying all fourteen rounds into the panel as quickly as he could pull the trigger.

DUBLOWSKI HAD BEEN COUNTING to himself. After thirty seconds of not moving, he took his backpack and tossed it several feet away from him. His body tensed, waiting for the expected bullets, but there was only silence.

"The guns are down! Let's go!" Dublowski shouted, scrambling to his feet. He led the men into the surface entrance, through the door McKenzie had destroyed. They ran up to the vault door and came to an abrupt halt. Dublowski stared down at the keypad and ordered his men to prepare their charges. He turned to Everson. "You have the code?"

Everson took the bloodstained piece of paper and punched in the code.

The vault door slowly swung open. Dublowski signaled and two men ran into the elevator.

THE CANADIANS POPPED up from their covered positions and fired, spraying the room. Thorpe had scurried into the well of a desk and reloaded his pistol.

He blindly fired, trying to keep them from rushing his tenuous location.

Half of the Canadians turned at the sound of the elevator coming down, covering the doors with their weapons. As the doors slid open they fired in, tearing up the interior. They slowly stopped firing when they realized no one was inside, just a small green object on the floor.

Just as they recognized the device, the Claymore mine exploded, sending thousands of ball bearings throughout the room like a large shotgun. The Canadians were blown down, their bodies shredded by the mine. Thorpe heard the balls ping into the metal of the desk and whistle by.

"You OK, Parker?" he yelled.

"Yeah."

In the foyer above, Dublowski tied a rope off to a bolt in the top of the elevator shaft. He hooked it into a snap link in the front of his harness and rappelled into the shaft. Thirty feet above the shattered elevator, he dropped a satchel charge. It exploded, tearing a hole in the roof of the elevator. Dublowski finished the rappel through the hole, followed by the rest of the team.

"Whoa! Good guy here!" Thorpe yelled out, slowly unfolding himself from his hiding place and revealing himself.

Dublowski smiled upon seeing his team leader.

Thorpe pointed. "And there's a good guy over there." Parker gingerly edged herself around the corner of the cabinet. She stared in shock at the torn up bodies of the Canadians.

"What the fuck is going on, sir?" Dublowski demanded.

"I don't exactly know, but I'm sure we'll find out soon," Thorpe said.

Thorpe and Parker quickly searched among the bodies.

"I don't see McKenzie," Thorpe finally said.

"That's Kilten," Parker said, pointing at a body lying near the console. She looked at Lewis's body.

Thorpe checked both corpses. "McKenzie is running things now. I knew he'd have something up his sleeve." He turned to the console. "Can you abort Omega Missile?"

Parker walked over and looked at the battered machinery. "This was the abort controls here," she said. "Looks like they thought of that and made sure we couldn't."

"What about through the computer?" Thorpe asked.

Parker sat down and quickly worked on the computer. "I'm

blocked out of REACT. Without the destruct or access to REACT, I can't do anything."

"What about the missile that was launched?" Thorpe asked. "Can you find out what its target is?"

"Yeah, I should be able to. Wait a second. Let's see it's—oh shit! It's targeted for here!"

"Can you stop it?"

"I can't do a damn thing without control of REACT."

"How long do we have?"

Parker pointed up at a large digital clock with red numerals that were winding down. "That's it there. Twenty-two minutes."

"Is there anything we can do?" Thorpe asked.

"Find McKenzie. He has control of this through the satellites, through Kilten's computer. He also has to have some way to control the missile that is inbound here since he launched it remotely."

Thorpe turned to Dublowski. "You guys get out of here."

The team turned and ran for the elevator shaft. They began climbing their way out.

Thorpe sat down next to Parker and swung the mike for the radio close to his lips.

"This is Captain Thorpe calling the War Room. Do you read me?"

Lowcraft's voice rumbled over the speaker. "Thorpe, what the hell are you doing?"

"Sir, we've got control of the control center but Parker tells me we can't abort Omega Missile."

"There's a bomb headed right for you!" Lowcraft exclaimed. "Get out of there."

"We're working on that, sir. We also can't abort that missile from this location." He paused in thought. "Sir, can you get us a chopper? Right away? I don't think we have to worry about it getting picked up on radar anymore."

"I'll get you out of there, Captain." There was a moment of silence, then Lowcraft came back. "There's a medevac chopper nearby, picking up Captain Maysun and your son. We sent it in once we realized the missile was coming down there. I'll send it to your location as soon as it makes the pickup."

"Sir, you said that Kilten asked for money?" Thorpe inquired.

"Right."

"How was he to get that money?"

"There's a cruise missile with the money in a resupply pod flying right now. McKenzie has control of when the pod is released."

"How close to this location does that missile come?"

"Hell, it's flying straight down the Anaconda River right now." There was a pause, then Lowcraft's voice came back. "The chopper's landed at the crash site, but all they've found is Chief Maysun. He was knocked out with some sort of nerve agent. Your son isn't there."

Thorpe stood. "McKenzie!" he screamed in anguish.

22

D RAKE HAD THE laptop resting on the rubber pontoon that made up the side of the Zodiac. His fingers were poised over the keyboard. All three men were watching down-river. They heard the Tomahawk a few seconds before they saw it.

It roared in low and fast, catching them by surprise even though they were expecting it. Drake hit a key. The nose cone of the missile exploded and the pod popped out. A parachute deployed out the end of the pod and then it was down in the river, a quarter mile from their location.

"Let's go!" McKenzie yelled.

MOST OF THE team was up the ropes. Parker had been working the computer while Thorpe talked to General Lowcraft. Thorpe took a deep breath. "McKenzie's got Tommy."

"You have to get him back."

"What about—" Thorpe pointed at the console.

Parker nodded. "We've got a big problem in here, too. McKenzie's used REACT to program Omega Missile with a target matrix. With live warheads."

"How many?"

"Two. The Pentagon's one of the targets. Tel Aviv's the other."

Thorpe was torn between running for the surface and going after Tommy and finding out what was going on. "Oh, Christ. Have they been launched?"

"Not yet, but all McKenzie has to do is hit a button and they launch."

"Is there anything we can do?"

"You've got to go after McKenzie and keep him from launching," Parker said. "You don't need me for that." Parker turned in her seat to face Thorpe. "Kilten recruited me to be here when he pulled this off. He wanted people in here who would launch when he gave them the right stimuli, but I don't think he meant things to turn out like this. And since he's planned this for a long time I think I was put here for another reason. I see that now."

"But—"

"I might be able to do something. Maybe I can override his programming. Regain control of REACT."

"You told me Kilten designed and programmed the thing. How can you—"

Parker stopped him with a look. "I have to try. Just as you have to get Tommy away from McKenzie and abort this missile. Maybe I can beat his program. Kilten had to override this REACT computer to transfer control to his computer. Maybe I can do the reverse. McKenzie's the one running things on the outside. He's your problem." She turned back to the computer. "Kilten—his legacy— is in here. And this is where I have to beat him."

"All right," Thorpe said. "You know the Pentagon's got some heavy firepower coming this way."

"I'll radio them and see if I can get them to call it off," Parker said.

Thorpe turned and ran for the shattered elevator. He looked over his shoulder once as he grabbed the rope. Parker's head was down and her fingers were flying over the keyboard. She glanced over at him. Thorpe snapped her a salute, then began climbing.

McKenzie, Johnson, and Drake pulled the pod out of the water into the second Zodiac. They tied it off to the lead Zodiac with a length of nylon rope, then lashed it down inside the second with more cord. They resumed their way downriver.

Amid the dead in the Launch Control Center, Parker worked feverishly. She looked over at Kilten's body and swore as she reached another electronic dead end.

"Come on, come on, Kilten. You put an override into this. An override and a hidden program so you could take the other computer out. So what's the password?"

She pursed her lips in thought, then typed:

Omega Missile

The computer immediately replied in the negative: improper password She typed in:

Omega
   improper password

Parker looked up at the clock. Time was flashing by as the digits dropped second by second. She knew that McKenzie would launch the matrix soon and there was no way of knowing where the missiles would come from or what their flight time would be—Omega Missile would decide that.

She typed in:

KILTEN

COMPUTER SCREEN:
   Computer screen:
   Computer screen:

"DAMN!" Parker exclaimed.

DUBLOWSKI AND HIS team were deployed outside the LCC fence when Thorpe reached the surface. He ran out and joined them. They could hear a helicopter inbound.

"Where's the major?" Dublowski asked.

"She's staying. She thinks she can get the computer working."

Dublowski looked at the building, then back at Thorpe. "That takes guts."

Thorpe simply nodded. "McKenzie has Tommy."

"Fuck," was Dublowski's commentary on that. "Do you know where he is?"

"I have an idea."

"We're with you," Dublowski said.

"There's a warhead—" Thorpe began.

"We're with you." Dublowski's tone indicated no further discussion would be tolerated.

"McKenzie's programmed the computer to launch two warheads," Thorpe added. "One at Tel Aviv and one at Washington."

"Great," Dublowski muttered, watching the horizon for the helicopter they could now hear.

The helicopter came in low over the treetops. It was a Blackhawk with red crosses painted on the side. It swooped in to a fast landing. Thorpe and the team ran forward and jumped into the cargo bay. Thorpe noticed CWO Maysun lying inside on a stretcher along with a body wrapped in a poncho next to him.

"I'm sorry about your son, Captain," Maysun said. He was barely conscious.

"You did your best," Thorpe replied. He leaned between the pilots' seats and grabbed their flight map. He scanned, running his finger along the river, then he tapped the pilot on his shoulder, pointing at a spot on the map. "Get us to the river here, then fly downstream.

"I'm supposed to—" the pilot began, but stopped when Thorpe drew his pistol.

"Take us to the river."

∾

THE TWO ZODIACS were moving slower now with the weight of the pod in the second one. McKenzie turned to Drake. "Fire the target matrix."

Drake's fingers went to work on the keyboard and then he transmitted the message to Omega Missile.

"They're fired," he announced.

∾

INSIDE THE LCC PARKER watched red warning lights come to life on one of the panels indicating that the matrix had been initiated. She worked harder, typing in every code word she could think of.

While she was doing that, she pulled the mike for the radio close to her lips.

"General Lowcraft, this is Major Parker in the LCC. I know you probably have an attack coming on to this location. Please abort it. It would serve no purpose. The missiles aren't being launched or controlled from here."

Lowcraft's voice came back. "Major, you were supposed to get on that chopper and get the hell out of there."

"I can do more good in here," Parker replied. "If I can get control of REACT back, then I can stop all of this. I need time."

IN THE WAR ROOM, Lowcraft turned to Colonel Hurst. "Order the attack off."

As Hurst reached for the radio, Hill's voice cut through the room. "Hold on there! We continue as planned. Those are the orders of the President of the United States!"

THE USS NEBRASKA was the closest nuclear-missile carrying submarine to Israel when Omega Missile received the target matrix. The sub received the EAM to launch one missile and the crew ran through the proper procedures for launch.

When the final go came, a D-5 Trident II submarine-launched ballistic missile roared out of its launch tube to the rear of the conning tower, burst through the surface of the water, and angled up into the sky.

Israel was just over the horizon.

IN THE ATLANTIC OCEAN, the USS Wyoming had been chosen by Omega Missile for the Washington launch as it was returning from a tour of duty in the Atlantic and was only four hours steaming out from Norfolk Naval Base. It launched a single Trident II toward the nation's capital, the crew not even aware of the missile's target. They simply did what the electronic codes they received ordered them to do, the target programming done by Omega Missile.

23

"How long until the first one touches down?" McKenzie asked.

"The Israeli one is from a sub in the Med. Tel Aviv will be a parking lot in twenty minutes."

"Good," McKenzie growled. He'd been paid a lot of money by several Arab leaders to launch that missile, money that had funded this entire operation and paid for the Canadians up front, but McKenzie would have launched that missile at the Israeli capital for free.

"When do our friends in the Pentagon get fried?" he asked.

"Twenty-four minutes."

BEDLAM BROKE out in the War Room as the launches were noted.

"Sir, we've got two launches. Two missiles up!"

"Put it on the screen," General Lowcraft ordered.

In the front of the War Room, two red lines in addition to the red dot showing the missile headed for the Omega Missile LCC appeared. The lines began moving toward their targets.

"Give me the targets," Lowcraft demanded, although it was apparent where they were headed.

"Tel Aviv." The officer paused, as if that wasn't bad enough.

"And?"

"And right here. First missile will touch down on Tel Aviv in nineteen minutes! We get hit in twenty- three!"

"Goddamnit!" Hill exclaimed. "I thought our people were in the LCC!"

"Major Parker and Captain Thorpe said—" Lowcraft began, but Hill silenced him.

"They're in on it," Hill exclaimed. "They're all in on it. You get that strike down on their heads right away. We are going to end this!"

THE NEBRASKA LAUNCH was picked up by a U.S. Air Force J-STARR surveillance aircraft flying routine patrol over the Red Sea. The J-STARR was hooked in to the multinational peacekeeping force in the Sinai. As part of that agreement it was also linked to the Israeli Self-Defense Force headquarters.

Thus the first alert that the Israelis received that there was a U.S. nuclear missile inbound came from a U.S. plane.

THORPE WAS LEANING out the side of the Blackhawk, watching the river surface flashing by less than fifteen feet below. The pilots flew under a set of high-tension wires, narrowly missing them. He figured that McKenzie had a large lead on them, but the chopper was faster than any boat he might have.

THE CLOCK in the front of the room was down to sixteen minutes, but the missile heading her way wasn't the highest priority in Parker's mind. She rapidly typed a question for the computer:

How long until first missile strike?

Computer:

EIGHTEEN MINUTES; Target Tel Aviv

PARKER RAN her fingers through her hair and then pounded her fists on the console.

"Damn you, Kilten! You didn't want it to turn out like this. You must have had a way into the computer."

Her mind went back to the conference room in Cheyenne Mountain and the mission into Israel that had preceded it.

Parker typed into the computer:

SANCHEZ

THE COMPUTER SCREEN DISSOLVED, then two new words appeared:

PASSWORD ACCEPTED

INSIDE THE WAR Room the countdown was being called out as all eyes followed the red lines on the screen. "Sixteen minutes to touchdown Tel Aviv!"

One red line was over the eastern Mediterranean, approaching the shore of Israel. The other was in the Atlantic, heading toward Washington.

"How long do we have here?" Hill asked.

"Twenty minutes."

"And the LCC?"

"Four minutes until the B-2 strike."

THE ISRAELIS REACTED PROMPTLY. The president happened to be in a meeting with his Self-Defense Force commander when an aide came sprinting in with the word of the inbound Trident missile.

The president sat stunned for a second, then turned to the SDF commander, General Ariel. "Implement the Samson option."

"Why would the Americans—" General Ariel began, but the president waved a hand to silence him.

"It does not matter why. Do as I order. We do not have time to discuss this. We must act."

Ariel pulled his secure cellular phone out.

PARKER WAS READING the computer language, trying to sort through the hidden program. "OK, OK. I see what you did."

She began typing rapidly, trying to wrest control back from Kilten's laptop.

HILL WAS RECOVERING from the shock of the missile launches. He stared at the screen and then it really came home to him. Tel Aviv.

"Oh my God," he exclaimed as he desperately dialed numbers into the red phone.

"What's wrong?" Lowcraft asked. "The Samson Option," Hill muttered as he pressed the phone to his ear. "The what?" Lowcraft asked.

24

IN WASHINGTON, THE man who waited heard the tone screech and a red light flashed in the basement. He blinked, not believing after almost two years that the unthinkable had happened. He jumped off his cot and ran to the computer that was hooked to the satellite radio.

The decryption coding inside the computer was working on the incoming message. It didn't take long. The message was only two words:

ACTIVATE IMMEDIATELY

THE MAN, whose name was Isaac, turned to the metal casket that rested in the center of the floor. His fingers were shaking as he flipped up the lid, but his hands settled down as he ran through the routine he had memorized and practiced every day. His mind was detached. Two years of waiting and contemplating the possibility of doing exactly what he was doing now had formed a schism in Isaac's consciousness.

TWO BLOCKS AWAY, in the abandoned firehouse, one of the men picked up a cellular phone. He listened to Hill's voice on the other end.

"Prairie Fire alert and execution!" he yelled and the men were grabbing weapons and running for the back ramp of the Abrams Fighting Vehicle.

ISAAC KNEW about the men in the firehouse just as they knew about him. It was all a question of timing.

THE ABRAMS SMASHED into the old wooden doors and splintered them apart. It roared down the street, shocking the few drivers passing by. A cabbie made the mistake of screeching to a halt in front of the Abrams. The treads rolled up on the taxi and crushed it as the driver desperately rolled out his door and away from the treads. The Abrams continued on its way.

ISAAC HAD a row of green lights glowing on the control panel. He turned back to the computer screen. One by one numbers appeared.

THE ABRAMS ROARED up to the front of the red house. Forty-mm rounds spewed out of the turret, blowing the front of the house to pieces. The drug dealers next door, thinking they were under attack by the police, opened fire with automatic weapons, the bullets bouncing off the armor harmlessly. The Abrams crunched up through the front of the house.

ISAAC COULD HEAR the tank above his head. Six numbers glowed on the screen. He began entering them into the numeric keyboard in front of him.

The back ramp of the Abrams dropped and two men carrying a specially designed charge ran off. They slapped it onto the metal plate covering the stairs, then ducked for cover.

The charge blew a four-foot-wide hole in the metal.

THE BLAST KNOCKED ISAAC DOWN, but he quickly regained his place. He had one more number to enter. His finger poised above the final key, Isaac paused.

BLACK-SUITED FIGURES DROPPED through the hole, firing, spraying the room with bullets. Isaac's body was slammed up against the bomb casing, then slid down to the floor.

25

I N THE WAR Room, Hill was on the phone with the president, telling him not only of the two missiles, but also telling him that it was very likely that the Israelis had exercised the Samson Option.

Lowcraft was listening to him in disbelief. He was stunned that the Israelis had a nuclear weapon secreted in a house in Washington that the U.S. knew about and yet had done nothing.

"It's politics," Hill said in a dull monotone, putting the phone down. "The president will call the Israeli president and square it all away."

"Politics?" Lowcraft was stunned.

"You don't think they stayed out of the Gulf War just because we asked them?" Hill asked. "They snuck that bomb in years ago. We found out about it and realized we could use it for leverage against them by keeping it there. After all, the one you know about is better than the one you don't."

"We also had our Red Flyer teams to keep them on their toes. We sent a Red Flyer mission into Israel every six months or so just to show them we could penetrate their airspace with our Combat Talons any time we wanted to and put a tac nuke on the ground. For the exercises we'd leave a conventional bomb configured as a tac nuke in place as our calling card."

Lowcraft had a dumbfounded look on his face. "The Israelis having a nuclear weapon in Washington was leverage for us! And we've been running training missions into Israel simulating putting an SADM in? That's goddamn illegal!"

Hill wasn't concerned about Lowcraft. Now that the president was truly clued in, Hill knew his political life was over. There probably would be criminal charges, the lawyer part of his brain told him. To have it all end because one old man asked a question.

There was a buzz and Hill flipped open his cellular phone. Hill slumped back in the chair after hearing the report from the other end. "You don't have to worry about it anyway. A CIA strike team has taken out the Samson Option." He looked up. "How long until our airplanes take out the LCC?"

"Two minutes, thirty seconds," Colonel Hurst replied. "Sir, our planes will strike the LCC twelve minutes before Tel Aviv is hit," Hurst said.

"Will that stop the two ICBMs?" Hill asked.

"I doubt it," Lowcraft said.

"But it might?" Hill pressed.

"Anything's possible."

"Give the final go to the B-2," Hill ordered.

INSIDE THE B-2 the pilot and navigator-bombardier listened in disbelief as they received their final authorization to drop their weapon. The Stealth fighter was several miles ahead and already going into its final approach with the bunker-buster bomb in its payload.

"We're going to nuke Louisiana," the nav-bomb muttered.

The pilot said nothing. His concentration was on flying the aircraft. He didn't want to think about what they were about to do. "Arm the weapon," he ordered.

With a shaking hand, the nav-bomb flipped a red switch.

As Kilten's program scrolled up the screen, Parker desperately searched for a way she could wrest control back from the other computer. The clock in the front of the room was down to twelve minutes, but the missile heading her way wasn't the highest priority in Parker's mind. She rapidly typed a question for the computer:

How long until *first missile strike?*

Computer:

Fourteen minutes. *Target Tel Aviv*

Inside the War Room the countdown was being called out as all eyes followed the red lines on the screen. "Thirteen minutes to touch-down Tel Aviv! One minute LCC!"

The red line was nearing the shore, closing on the Israeli capital. "How long do we have here?" Hill asked.

"Seventeen minutes."

Parker's fingers were working furiously, her head beginning to nod as she found the program she needed.

She grabbed the phone. "General Lowcraft, this is Major Parker. I can stop them! I can stop the two missiles. Just give me some more time."

OVERHEAD, in the clear blue sky, the pilot of the Stealth fighter pressed a button on the side of his yoke, then pulled back hard on the stick as he kicked in his afterburners. He wasn't worried about getting away from the large black bomb that fell out of the bottom of the plane and was arcing its way toward the small building on the surface. He was worried about the inferno the B-2 thirty seconds behind him was getting ready to let loose.

The bunker-buster landed square on the LCC surface building. The delayed detonation fuse allowed the heavy bomb to crash through the roof and five feet into the floor before it ignited the specially designed charge inside.

A forty-foot-deep crater was ripped into the concrete protecting the LCC.

PARKER WAS THROWN against her shoulder straps as the sound of the explosion reverberated through the LCC. A large plume of dust came in the already buckled elevator doors and she could hear rock and earth crashing down in the shaft. She knew she was now buried in the LCC.

Parker prayed that she could still transmit. "General, stop the attack! You've got to trust me!" The message went into a cable then up to the alternate satellite dish that Drake had rigged.

"TWENTY SECONDS UNTIL LCC NUCLEAR IMPACT!" Colonel Hurst yelled as Parker's voice faded off the speaker.

In the War Room, Hill slapped his palm on the desk. "She's trying to save her ass. Fry the LCC before that missile hits here!"

"Abort the B-2," Lowcraft ordered.

"Ignore that order!" Hill yelled.

"I'm in command here," Lowcraft yelled back. "You're a damn criminal and I'm not going to listen to you spout orders one second longer."

"I'm in charge!" Hill yelled as he gestured at Lugar. The aide's hand snaked inside his jacket and came out holding a large caliber revolver.

In response, several officers at desks wheeled about, their own pistols in their hands.

Colonel Hurst met General Lowcraft's gaze, then spoke into his headset. "Abort!"

"Jesus!" the pilot yelled as he heard Colonel Hurst's voice.

The navigator-bombardier's thumb was less than an inch from the release button and heading down when the word came.

He jerked his thumb away. "Oh my God, oh my God," the nav-bomb muttered as he very carefully began the process of putting the nuclear weapon in their bomb bay back into an inert status.

"I'm going to have someone's ass for this," the pilot swore as he pulled back and banked away from the wreckage of the LCC.

Parker was looking up, waiting for the end. The clock kept ticking, the red numbers winding down. She grabbed the mike.

"War Room, this is Major Parker. Over."

"This is the War Room," General Lowcraft replied. He was watching military police handcuffing Hill and Lugar. "You've got your time, Major. Make it count. You're the only thing that stands between those nukes and Washington and Tel Aviv."

THE PILOT of the Blackhawk was pushing his skills to the utmost following the river, leaving behind a trail of spray from the rotors' downwash.

Thorpe was looking directly ahead. Less than two miles away he could see that there was a spread of open water. He looked at the map. It was a large reservoir formed by the main channel being dammed. Beyond and around it lay the swamp that stretched to the Intercoastal Waterway. There were several minor routes around the dike into the swamp. If McKenzie made it into the swamp with Tommy— Thorpe didn't want to think about that.

"There's something in the water," the pilot said over the intercom. "Dead ahead."

Thorpe looked closer and saw the two Zodiacs. "Let's get them!"

MCKENZIE HEARD THE CHOPPER. He turned and looked back the way they had come, then spun about and looked downstream. Within sight, the river opened into the lake. Two miles across the smooth surface of the lake he could see the dike blocking the main channel.

"Faster!" McKenzie yelled.

Drake had abandoned the computer and had his hand on the outboard engine throttle. He opened up the throttle all the way. The lead Zodiac was now half flying across the water but the pod was slowing them too much. Johnson held his submachine gun at the ready to fire if the chopper got closer.

McKenzie took the rope that was tied to the pod inside the second Zodiac and pulled on it, slowly bringing the second Zodiac closer until its prow was just behind the engine of his boat.

"Stop!" McKenzie yelled.

Drake cut the throttle and the two boats coasted to a stop. "Give me a hand," McKenzie ordered, stepping over the gunwale and into the second Zodiac.

"What are you doing?" Drake asked in alarm as McKenzie cut the ropes holding it in place and put his shoulder to the pod.

"Do as I tell you!" McKenzie shoved, and with Drake's assistance, the pod rolled over into the water where it bobbed on the end of its line. McKenzie reached back into the first boat and grabbed Tommy with his artificial arm and lifted him over into the second boat as he yelled and pounded futilely on McKenzie's arm.

"Shut up," McKenzie yelled at the boy as he quickly looped the rope binding Tommy's hands through the safety rope that ran along the top of the front pontoon. McKenzie quickly tied off several square knots.

THE BLACKHAWK WAS NOW LESS than twenty feet above the water. Inside, Thorpe manned the left M-60 while Dublowski manned the right one. They were less than a mile away from the two stopped Zodiacs and the lake.

"What are they doing?" Dublowski asked.

"I don't know," Thorpe's finger was itching on the trigger of the machine gun as he saw movement in the boats. He would have started firing already if Tommy wasn't out there.

MCKENZIE PUSHED down the outboard motor that had been canted up in the second Zodiac. He pulled the starter cord and it roared into life.

"Say hi to your dad for me," he said to Tommy as he twisted the throttle and locked it full open. His mechanical hand squeezed down on the metal, crushing it in place. As the Zodiac accelerated, McKenzie jumped into the boat with Drake in it. Tommy's Zodiac built up speed, rushing straight across the lake toward the dike two miles away.

"Let's go!" McKenzie yelled at Drake.

"WHAT THE FUCK!" Dublowski exclaimed as they watched the two Zodiacs part, one heading across the lake, the other turning to the right and driving toward the swamp on that side. They could see Tommy tied off in the first one and the men in the second.

"Which one do we go after?" the pilot asked in Thorpe's headset.

Thorpe looked from one to the other, then looked back in at Dublowski across the cargo bay. The older NCO said nothing and Thorpe knew he would back whatever decision he made one hundred percent.

"The one with my son," Thorpe ordered.

The Blackhawk swooped down to less than ten feet above the surface of the lake in pursuit.

MCKENZIE SMILED as he watched the Blackhawk go after the other boat. The beginning of the swamp and concealment beckoned less than a quarter mile ahead.

INSIDE HIS BOAT, Tommy was ripping at the ropes with his fingers, slowly undoing the knots that McKenzie had tied. He could feel the rush of wind across his face. Water spray from the Zodiac bouncing across the surface of the lake splashed up, blinding him when he tried to look forward.

Tommy looked over his shoulder as he heard the sound of a helicopter. His heart rose as he saw his dad leaning out the side, held in by a harness. He was waving at him, less than two hundred feet away.

"LOWER," Thorpe ordered.

The pilot had them down to less than ten feet above the surface of the water and he edged down a couple more feet. Thorpe looked past the boat they were rapidly gaining on and saw the dirt wall of the dike four hundred yards in front of Tommy.

"Put me right over the boat!"

The pilot did as he was told but another hundred yards went by before Thorpe could look down on Tommy, hair blown about by the rotor downwash. Thorpe met his son's eyes and could see the fear in them. Thorpe gave a thumbs-up, then unsnapped the strap across his chest.

He fell the ten feet, the forward speed of the chopper giving him enough velocity to match the boat. Still, he hit the left rear pontoon and had to desperately grab at the safety line to keep from sliding off.

"Dad!"

"I'll be there, Tommy," Thorpe said as he scrambled into the boat. He looked past his son at the rapidly approaching dike, now less than two hundred yards away. The chopper was following them, less than forty feet behind. Turning to the motor, Thorpe twisted on the throttle but it didn't move.

"Damn," Thorpe cursed as he saw that the metal had been crushed in place at full open. He drew his knife and moved up next to Tommy, wrapping one arm around his shoulders. "I've got you."

"Stop the boat, Dad," Tommy said.

"I can't," Thorpe replied as he sliced through the rope holding his son. The dike was now a hundred yards away. Thorpe knew he had less than ten seconds.

"We're going to have to jump overboard," Thorpe said.

"I can't, Dad. We're going too fast."

"Trust me, Tommy " Thorpe held him, poised on the edge of the pontoon. "We'll be all right. I'll make sure you don't get hurt."

Tommy looked at him and nodded, his chin trembling. "All right, Dad."

"Let's go," Thorpe said. He rolled over the side with Tommy in his arms. His back hit the water and the position cushioned his son from the impact. They went under and Thorpe kicked, pushing them to the surface. He cradled Tommy as he coughed and spit out water.

"We made it!" Tommy cried out, gripping him tight around the shoulders.

"Yeah, son, we made it," Thorpe said as he watched the zodiac smash into the dike and crumple, the weight of the engine flipping the boat end over end, smashing it into the earth.

The Blackhawk came to a hover over their heads and Dublowski lowered a line off a winch.

COLONEL HURST WAS READING a computer screen. "Our Patriot missile batteries near Tel Aviv are responding. Defensive launches are going up now."

Lowcraft was shaking his head. "Just great. Our own missiles are defending against a Trident launched from one of our own subs. And we don't even have any Patriots here to protect Washington."

"What are the chances the Patriots will take out the Trident?" Hill asked. He was under guard by the MPs, but still a spectator to the two red lines on the screen.

"Zero to none," Lowcraft said, "but the Patriot battery was a great political placebo you gave the Israelis." He pointed at Hurst. "Get me the commander of that Patriot unit," General Lowcraft ordered.

PARKER WAS WONDERING if what was left of the forty feet of reinforced concrete and large spring suspenders would work as they were advertised. The clock turned to 9:45, then 9:44. She knew that Tel Aviv would last only two minutes longer than her location, with Washington following four minutes after that.

The program was complicated. She'd known Kilten was a genius but this was almost beyond her. The key word was almost. She had the added spur of her—and millions of others'—very survival. Her fingers flew over the keyboard, her mind working furiously to unravel Kilten's puzzle.

DRAKE WAS DRIVING MORE SLOWLY NOW, NEGOTIATING the treacherous shallow water. McKenzie was carefully watching their route on the map, telling Drake which way to go. "Another two miles and we'll be at the floatplane. Then we'll be out of here," McKenzie said.

The lake was gone, hidden behind a wall of trees and the sky overhead was crisscrossed with branches. McKenzie knew they were safe.

"What about the others?" Johnson asked. "The guys at the LCC?"

"We'll give them thirty minutes," McKenzie said. "If they aren't there by then, we take off and they have to use the alternate plan."

A MILE away on the lake, Thorpe and Tommy were pulled into the cargo bay of the chopper.

THE CLOCK WENT DOWN to 8:00. Turned over to 7:59. Parker sat back in the chair and closed her eyes for a second as she furiously searched her mind for an answer to her predicament.

"Yes!" she yelled. "I see it." She leaned forward over the keyboard.

McKENZIE DID ANOTHER MAP CHECK, then picked up the bulky sniper rifle from the floorboards and put it across his lap. He slowly maneuvered the muzzle so that it pointed at Johnson, the third man in the boat. McKenzie pulled the trigger. The round blasted Johnson out of the boat and sent the body flying twenty feet, splashing down in a bloody mess in the swamp. Alligators immediately started sliding into the water for the meat.

Drake eyed McKenzie with a worried look.

"More money for each of us," McKenzie said. "Oh, don't look so concerned, Drake. I won't shoot you. You're my buddy. It's me and you the rest of the way. And remember, I need you to fly the plane."

THORPE WRAPPED a poncho liner Dublowski had handed him around Tommy. The Blackhawk had gained altitude and was hovering over the lake at five hundred feet. Thorpe looked to the southwest where McKenzie and the Zodiac had disappeared.

"We'll never find him under all that foliage," Dublowski was at his side, looking in the same direction.

"He's got to have a way out," Thorpe said. "A plan to get away."

"He has a balloon, Dad," Tommy said from deep inside the poncho.

"What?" Thorpe asked.

"He has a balloon. I saw the helium and some rope under a blanket in the boat."

Thorpe looked across Tommy at Dublowski and their eyes locked. "Helium and rope?"

They both said it at the same time: "Fulton rig."

Thorpe keyed the radio. "Head southwest," he ordered the pilot.

"HOW FAR TO THE FLOATPLANE?" Drake asked as he turned a bend in the small creek he was navigating and entered a small pond. The money pod dragged behind them, half submerged, the contents dry.

McKenzie had the map on his knees, covering the barrel of the large sniper rifle. "This is far enough," he said. "How are our missiles doing?"

Drake stared at the computer screen. "Seven minutes until the LCC gets hit. Nine minutes for Tel Aviv. Thirteen for Washington."

"Excellent." McKenzie smiled. "Then it's time to say good-bye."

"What?" Drake's face was a mixture of confusion and growing awareness. The look was wiped off by the half-inch-diameter bullet hitting him in the jaw and taking most of his head off as it continued its trajectory. The body flipped overboard, the laptop computer going with it.

THE CLOCK in the LCC was now down to 6:00. It changed to 5:59.

"Goddamn!" Parker screamed as her computer screen went blank before she could finish reprogamming and regaining control. McKenzie must have done something to the system. She knew she would have to reboot the mainframe in the LCC and that would take about six minutes. "Oh, God," she muttered as she hit the reboot button.

McKENZIE RIPPED OPEN the tarp in the back of the Zodiac. He checked his watch and speeded up the pace of his action. First he threw a small anchor overboard, locking the Zodiac in place in the center of the pond. Then he popped open the top on a long tube as he turned the valve on the helium canister. A blimp-shaped balloon slowly slithered out of the tube. The blimp was eight feet long and four feet in diameter, connected at the bottom to the climbers' 12-mm rope in the bottom of the boat.

McKenzie didn't bother to watch as the blimp rose, reaching up above the height of the weathered trees surrounding the pond. He was buckling on a monkey harness, cinching down all the connections. He grabbed the free end of the 12-mm rope and connected the sewn-in loop to the front center of the harness with a locking snap link.

Then he turned and untied the money pod from the back of the boat. He tied that rope off to another snap link on the waistband of his harness. He reached into his vest and pulled out an FM radio headset, settling it on his head. It was already set to the right frequency.

Finally he looked up. The blimp was still rising, another fifty feet of slack in the boat before it would come to a halt. Still it was already over three hundred feet up.

McKenzie spoke into the voice-activated mouthpiece. "Alpha Two, this is Alpha Six. Over."

FORTY MILES ABOVE THE SURFACE, the ICBM was coming straight down. The nose cone was just beginning to glow red from contact with the atmosphere. Through a haze of clouds, the Gulf of Mexico lay in an arc far below.

"SIX, this is Two, we are on course and one minute out. We have you in sight."

The C-130 was over twenty-five years old and had been bought fourth-hand from the Cambodian government. It had actually cost McKenzie more money than the plane's original price to add the special equipment that the plane now had. There was a specialized steel yoke that had been welded to the front of the plane like a pair of whiskers, along with a powerful winch and crane in the cargo bay that faced the rear ramp. There were also rubber fuel bladders in the front half of the cargo bay, bulging with enough JP-4 to take the C-130 to a country that didn't have an extradition law with the United States.

The pilot saw the orange blimp floating in the clear blue Louisiana sky and lined up the nose of his aircraft for the rope which he knew hung below the blimp.

THORPE and the pilots of the Blackhawk also saw the blimp.

"What do you want to do?" the pilot asked.

The copilot was looking out the left window. "We've got a One-Thirty inbound!"

Thorpe saw both the C-130 and the blimp. "Put us at the bottom end of that rope below the blimp." He knew exactly what McKenzie was doing and he knew that unless they acted quickly, McKenzie would succeed.

Thorpe grabbed the only thing handy, a parachute harness from the firewall of the cargo bay, and strapped it on as the Blackhawk swooped down toward the pond. He looped a snap link through the chest strap, securing it in place. The pilots slowed as they approached the rope, afraid of fouling the blades. Thorpe tapped Dublowski on the shoulder and pointed at his ruck, yelling in his ear what he wanted. Dublowski pulled out a small green bag and looped it over Thorpe's head.

Thorpe could see McKenzie seated in the boat, the rope coming down to him. "Lower," Thorpe said. He turned to Tommy. "Stay with Sergeant Dublowski . I have something I have to do."

Tommy had seen the Zodiac also. "He's a bad man, Dad."

"I know." When the chopper was less than twenty feet from the pond surface, Thorpe jumped.

INSIDE THE LCC the clock now read 3:20. Parker's hands were gripping the arms of her chair as the computer screen ran through its self-diagnostics as it powered back up. 3:19...3:18...

Like a mantra she repeated to herself exactly what commands she would have to type to abort the two missiles once she could access the computer again. The clock told her she wouldn't have that time.

"Sɪʀ," Colonel Hurst called out, "I have the Patriot battery commander on the line. He's reporting negative strikes on the inbound. They've shot their wad. It's going in. Four minutes, fifty-five seconds until Tel Aviv hit. Eight minutes, fifty-five until we get it."

Many in the War Room were watching the two red lines creep closer to their targets. Others, like those in a sinking ship, were writing notes to loved ones, despite the knowledge that such notes would most likely never be recovered. Some were desperately trying to get an outside line, trying to call their families.

General Lowcraft knew that discipline had broken down, but he understood that there was nothing they could do and that was precisely the reason people were reacting the way they were. He keyed the microphone.

"Major Parker, I don't want to disturb you, but it would be most helpful if you did whatever it is you said you could do to abort these missiles."

"You fucked up trusting her," Hill said, twisting uncomfortably in his seat, trying to adjust his cuffed hands.

Lowcraft turned to the former national security adviser. "As you said earlier, the most important thing is that I take responsibility. And I do."

MᴄKᴇɴᴢɪᴇ ʜᴀᴅ ʜᴇᴀʀᴅ the Blackhawk long before he saw it. He watched Thorpe jump into the water, even as the voice in his ear reported ten seconds out. McKenzie looked up and saw the C-130 roar by overhead.

Tʜᴇ ʀᴏᴘᴇ ᴡᴀs ᴄᴀᴜɢʜᴛ by the whiskers and dragged into the exact center. A sky anchor clamped down on the rope and held it in place, while just above the anchor a blade cut the blimp free.

THORPE WAS SWIMMING HARD toward the Zodiac. He was five feet away from McKenzie when the rope suddenly went taut and McKenzie's grinning face was yanked up out of the boat into the air.

Thorpe twisted and reached out, grabbing the rope leading to the money pod. He pulled in a bit of slack and pressed it through the snap link on the chest of his parachute harness. He was just in time, as the slack in that rope was ripped out of his hands and the rope, pod, and Thorpe were lifted into the air, the latter sliding down the rope until he slammed into the top of the pod.

Tied together, the two men and the money cleared the trees at the end of the pond and flew off to the south, dangling at the end of the rope tether leading to the C-130.

THE PILOT of the C-130 went into a steep climb, the rope caught in the sky anchor, now pulling back along the belly of the plane by both the plane's speed and attitude. In the rear of the C-130, the Colombian mercenary who McKenzie had hired for this job was watching the procedures from the back ramp. "Shit, man, we've got two people and the money! I thought there was only supposed to be one. We also got a helicopter trailing us!"

"Just grab the rope!" the pilot yelled.

The mercenary extended the arm of the crane and lowered a hook on a steel cable toward the rope.

"FUCK!" McKenzie yelled, seeing Thorpe ten feet below him. Wind whistled by at a hundred and thirty knots, twisting and turning the rope.

Thorpe reached into the green pouch and pulled out the small black box inside, slapping the metallic rear against the money pod and pushing a button. Then he wrapped both hands around the rope, getting both feet fixed on the top of the money pod. He began climbing.

PARKER LOOKED UP. The clock turned to two minutes and then below. The radio crackled to life again.

"Anytime now, Major, would be most helpful," General Lowcraft's voice was quite calm.

Parker watched the screen. She knew it was almost there, but not close enough. "I'll get it, General," she replied, her fingers poised above the keyboard for lack of anything else to do.

MCKENZIE LOOKED DOWN at the snap link on the waistband of his harness. His hand wavered over it. He knew if he released it, the pod and Thorpe would drop away and he would be free. Thorpe climbed closer, over halfway up the rope.

McKenzie kicked at Thorpe's face, narrowly missing. Thorpe grabbed hold of the foot and used it to get even closer, wrapping his arms around McKenzie's legs.

INSIDE THE C-130, the mercenary had hooked the rope. He threw a lever and the steel cable pulled up the rope until it locked in place in the crane itself. Then he threw another lever and the winch slowly began to wind the rope in.

DUBLOWSKI HAD both arms around Tommy and was watching from the Blackhawk, mesmerized as the two men dangled at the end of the rope. The helicopter was following the C-130, a half mile back. The brown line of beach and the sparkling blue waters of the Gulf of Mexico and international water beckoned just ahead.

"Fuck you!" McKenzie screamed, removing his hand from the snap link and reaching down with his artificial arm and striking at Thorpe.

"Give me the control for the nuke," Thorpe yelled back. "You're finished."

"Bullshit!" McKenzie replied. "You're finished."

They were less than fifty feet from the back ramp of the C-130 now and both could see a man standing there with a submachine gun in his hands.

"You don't have to blow the nuke," Thorpe pleaded.

McKenzie grinned and reached around his neck with his good hand and held up the remote on its red strap. "You're so fucking naive. You lose!" He pulled it off and tossed the remote away into the air.

Thorpe didn't hesitate, swiftly pulling the release on his chest strap and falling away from the rope.

In the Blackhawk, everyone gasped as the figure fell away from the line. The other figure and the pod moved more quickly now, gaining on the ramp.

Thorpe could see the red strap streaming behind the remote as it plummeted to earth. He arched his back and freefell headfirst in that direction. Below lay beach and surf. Thorpe prayed that the remote would hit the beach and not the water.

The wind whistled in his ears but he knew that he was falling as quickly as the remote and that their trajectory would be basically the same. He kept his eyes on the red streamer, less than four hundred feet above the ground. He held on until the last possible second, then pulled the ripcord, the chute billowing out, two hundred feet above ground all the while watching the red streamer go down and land on the sand.

Thorpe grabbed the risers, dumping air, going down faster than safety dictated toward the landing spot. He landed, feeling something in his lower left leg crack as he hit the ground too hard.

Thorpe cut loose the chute and pulled himself through the sand toward the remote.

THE CLOCK in the LCC was now down to 1:00. It changed to :59.

Parker had watched the computer boot up every day for the past couple of weeks during their daily checks. She knew the computer still had more than a minute before it was booted. Her hands were still poised, but her lips had stopped mumbling the programming and were now praying.

SIX MILES ABOVE THE SURFACE, the ICBM was coming straight down. The nose cone was glowing bright red from the speed. Directly below was the tiny square of the LCC compound with smoke drifting out of the shattered concrete.

MCKENZIE WAS NOW level with the back ramp, the rope pulling him in. His feet touched metal and he stood up inside the plane, unhooking himself from the rope. He joined the mercenary as the money pod bumped against the back ramp, then slid over and into the cargo bay.

"I did it!" McKenzie exulted. Then he saw the black box attached to the money pod. He knelt down and looked at it, then his eyes shifted out the ramp to the Blackhawk helicopter following a half mile back.

INSIDE THE BLACKHAWK, Master Sergeant Dublowski could almost see McKenzie's eyes looking back at them as he pressed the firing handle on the radio transmitter.

McKenzie had his hands around the box, trying to rip it off, when it exploded, blowing him to shreds. The explosion roared up the cargo bay and reached the fuel bladders.

The C-130 became one huge fireball, pieces of wreckage littering the clear sky.

INSIDE THE LCC the clock now read :20 above Parker's bowed head ... : 19 ... : 18 ...

THORPE'S FINGERS closed on the remote. He flipped the lid open. There were five different colored buttons, but their functions were neatly spelled out below each one.

PARKER LOOKED UP. The clock turned to :05 ... : 04 ...

THORPE MOVED his finger to the yellow button and pressed down.

THE MISSILE EXPLODED IN MIDAIR, barely a hundred feet above the LCC compound, scattering pieces of itself everywhere. The nuclear warhead slammed into the ground without detonating.

PARKER WATCHED the number turn to :oo. Nothing happened.

She looked back down at the computer screen as it ran through its final checks.

"NEGATIVE NUKE STRIKE, LOUISIANA!" Colonel Hurst called out.

General Lowcraft stood up from his seat and stared at the master board and the two red lights. "Come on, Major Parker, come on," he whispered.

"One minute, thirty seconds until impact Tel Aviv," Hurst announced. "Five minutes, thirty seconds, impact Washington."

THE SCREEN CLEARED and a prompt appeared in the upper left-hand corner. Parker's fingers flew as she reprogrammed.

THORPE FELT the warm sand against his back. He could hear the sound of a helicopter coming closer. He looked at his watch.

TEN SECONDS TO *touch down Tel Aviv.*

The computer announced.

.   .   .

PARKER STOPPED TYPING. "That's it. I think." She bit her lip, then struck the enter key with a long forefinger.

THE TRIDENT WAS over the suburbs of Tel Aviv when side thrusters kicked in, leveling the missile out, at three thousand feet of altitude. Afterburners kicked in and the missile headed back out toward the Mediterranean.

"IT'S AN ABORT! IT'S AN ABORT!" The duty officer was jumping up and down.

There was pandemonium in the War Room, people slapping each other on the back.

"What's happening?" Hill was standing also now.

General Lowcraft pointed at the board. "Parker's aborted the missiles."

Hill was still dazed. "Where do the missiles go? Do they just crash down?"

"No. The abort on a missile in flight has its afterburners kick in and the missile turns and heads straight toward open water. That way we can recover it."

"You mean we're safe?" Hill asked. General Lowcraft's jaw was tight. "For now." He turned to the MP. "Get him out of here."

PARKER PUSHED her chair back from the console. Lifting her head she scanned the room, taking in the bodies, bullet holes, and wrecked equipment. She looked up at the gray-painted ceiling, imagining the tons of smashed concrete and earth.

Slowly she began twisting the big ring on her finger back and forth.

THORPE FELT the pain from his broken leg throbbing. He could see the smoke from the explosion in the sky and the Blackhawk heli-copter heading his way.

The Blackhawk settled down in the sand nearby and the first person off was Tommy, running toward his dad with open arms.

EPILOGUE

THORPE WAS LYING in bed, his feet swathed in bandages, his leg in a cast. Chief Warrant Officer Maysun was next to the bed in his wheelchair, his own broken leg extended straight forward.

"Unbelievable," Maysun was saying. "They must have been packing a lot of JP-4 in that C-130. The largest piece the Coast Guard has picked up from the ocean floor so far was only about five feet long." Maysun shook his head. "All that money, too. Just gone. Poof. They've found some bills but most of it must have been shredded by the bomb."

"McKenzie could have cut the pod loose and saved himself," Thorpe said. "He was too greedy."

Maysun changed the subject. "Hey, you think we'll get Purple Hearts? I mean, we were—" He paused as Major Parker walked in, wearing her blue uniform.

Maysun turned for the door. "I think it's time for—" He scratched his head. "Well, something."

Thorpe held up a hand. "Hey, Maysun. I am sorry about Kelly."

Maysun's playful look disappeared. "Yeah. I talked to General

Lowcraft. He says no matter what, she gets the Purple Heart. Guess they'll pin it on her casket."

"She saved our lives, and by doing that she saved a lot of lives," Thorpe said.

"Yeah, I know that. Too bad she never got to know it. Later." He rolled out the door, nodding at Parker as he went.

Parker walked to the edge of the bed and looked down at Thorpe. He raised his arm and she took his hand and shook it.

"You look better."

"I feel better," Thorpe said.

"How long did it take for them to dig you out?" Thorpe asked.

"A day and a half," Parker said. "I'd have been here sooner but they kept me in Washington, testifying."

Thorpe nodded. "The shit's hit the fan."

"That's understating it." She sat down on a hard, wooden chair. "Kilten was right. If it hadn't been for McKenzie, maybe he could have made his point without anyone getting hurt. At the very least Kilten nailed Hill and his aide. They're going to jail for a very long time."

"I don't suppose anyone will ever know all that Kilten had planned now that he's dead," Thorpe said.

Parker nodded her head in agreement.

"What happened wasn't all bad," Thorpe said.

"No, it wasn't. It's changed a lot of things for me. The point is, from the way people are talking in Washington, it sounds like we're going to put the people back into the system. Thinking people. Feeling people. People who will be willing to take apart what Kilten spent decades putting together."

"People like you?" Thorpe asked.

"Like I am now," Parker corrected. "I'm staying. I can do more good from the inside."

But Thorpe was looking past her at the woman in the wheelchair and the child standing in his doorway.

"Dad!"

"Hey, Tommy!"

The young boy ran over and jumped up on the other side of the bed. Thorpe looked from the boy to the woman. "Hey, Lisa."

Major Parker looked from Thorpe to his wife and back. "I think you can do good somewhere else."

Thorpe nodded, his arm around Tommy and his focus still on his wife. "I think so, too.

THE END

AN EXCERPT FROM THE LINE, another Shadow Warriors book is after the bio and book info.

ABOUT THE AUTHOR

Thanks for the read!

If you enjoyed the book, please leave a review as they are very important.And recommend it to a friend!
The Shadow Warriors are five books, but each stands alone and they don't have to be read in any order.
The Line; The Gate; Omega Missile; Omega Sanction; The Gate
If you enjoyed this, you'll also enjoy The Green Beret Series. The latest in that are the books featuring Will Kane that start with **New York Minute** and are set in New York City in the late 1970s.
An excerpt from **THE LINE** follows author information.

Bob is a NY Times Bestselling author, graduate of West Point and former Green Beret. He's had over 90 books published including the #1 series The Green Berets, The Cellar, Area 51, Shadow Warriors, Atlantis, and the Time Patrol. Born in the Bronx, having traveled the world (usually not tourist spots), he now lives peacefully with his wife and dogs.

My free and discounted books, updated daily, are here: https://www.bobmayer.com/free-books-updated-daily/
My books, fiction and nonfiction, are here: https://www.bobmayer.com/books-by-bob-mayer/
My lists of suggested preparation and survival gear are here: https://www.bobmayer.com/survival-and-preparation-gear/

Questions, comments, suggestions: Bob@BobMayer.com
Blog: http://bobmayer.com/blog/

Subscribe to his newsletter for the latest news, free eBooks, audio, etc.

Thank you!

EXCERPT FROM THE LINE

ALEXANDRIA, VIRGINIA

25 NOVEMBER
1:00 P.M. LOCAL/1800 ZULU

The man in the high-backed chair was hidden in the shadows cast by the halogen desk lamp. A thin sheaf of laser-printed pages was the only object on the desk in front of him. A hand, the skin withered with age, slowly reached out and angled the first page so it could be read.

11 June 1930: U.S. Military Academy,

WEST POINT. NEW YORK

The smooth marble felt cool to Cadet Benjamin Hooker's hand. He gazed up the shaft of Battle Monument to the stars overhead, then up the Hudson

River where the hulking presence of Storm King Mountain loomed to the left, a darker presence against the night sky. It was a view that never failed to raise a strong feeling of attachment and sentiment in Hooker's heart.

That feeling was immediately followed with an uncertainty that had two causes. The first was that tomorrow he would graduate and be leaving his home for the last four years. The second was the written message he'd been given by a plebe earlier in the day. The words had been simple and direct: "TROPHY POINT. 2130 HOURS." There had been no signature, but the paper was written on stationery from the office of the Commandant of Cadets.

Hooker momentarily played with the notion that the note was an elaborate prank set up by his classmates; but he knew he dared not be here, on the chance that the message was legitimate. Although why the commandant would want to see him at such a strange place and time left him at a loss.

Hooker knew he held a special place in his class of 241 cadets. He was ranked second in academic standing and was the fifth recipient of a Rhodes Scholarship in the history of the Academy. Tall and thin, with an angular face that most of the women coming to the Academy for hops found appealing, there was about him a sense of intellectual reserve and emotional distance from others that counteracted his physical attraction. He had straight brown hair that was at the very limit the regulations would allow —unusual for a man who otherwise followed every rule and regulation to the letter. His eyes were black, and when they focused on an individual they had the ability to make that person feel that they had 100 percent of Hooker's attention. Many a long-suffering plebe had felt the power of that gaze during a hazing session in Hooker's room.

Those same eyes flickered across the Plain to the barracks where his classmates were spending their last night as cadets. There was a distinct feeling of excitement and anticipation in the air. Although Hooker shared in it, he had different expectations for the immediate future. While his classmates would go to various officer courses and then report to regular Army units scattered all over the world, Hooker was heading to England for two years of study at Oxford before becoming part of the "real" Army. Although the prestige of the scholarship was great, he was concerned about the possible negative effect those two years out of the active Army loop might have on his career.

"Good evening, Mr. Hooker."

The voice caught Hooker off-guard, his thoughts already halfway across the ocean. He stiffened as he recognized the figure silhouetted in the glow of lights around the Plain. "Good evening, sir," he automatically responded

Colonel William B. Kimbell's physical appearance was in accordance with his martial reputation. West Point, class of '14, Kimbell had been blooded on the fields of Europe in the Great War, earning a Silver Star for gallantry. The colonel had been wounded three times, but each time had returned to the fight until peace had arrived before a fatal wound. As commandant, Kimbell was in charge of the welfare of the Corps of Cadets, and because of that, ran every aspect of their lives outside the classroom.

"Beautiful, isn't it?" Kimbell said.

Hooker automatically knew that Kimbell was referring to the overall view—regardless of direction. To the north, the Hudson and Storm King framed a scene many artists had captured on canvas. To the east, across the river, lay Constitution Island, the far anchor point for the Great Chain that had been stretched across the river during the Revolution to stop the British from moving on it. To the west, at Plain-level, stood the cadet gym and above it and to the left, loomed the impressive edifice of the cadet chapel, overlooking the main Academy grounds, a slight concession by the planners that there might possibly be an institution more powerful than the Academy. To the immediate south was the billiards-table green surface of the Plain where Hooker had sweated through four years of innumerable parades. Beyond the grass were the barracks where the comraderie of four years of suffering had forged unbreakable bonds among the members of the class of '30.

"Yes, sir, it is."

The commandant turned and started walking, Hooker immediately fell in step, half a pace to the rear as required by etiquette. They passed the links of the Great Chain that were displayed and halted behind a collection of old cannon barrels. "Looking forward to Oxford, Mr. Hooker?"

"Yes, sir."

Kimbell glanced at him in the darkness. "It is an honor for the Academy to have had you selected for the scholarship."

Hooker let that pass without comment. He reined in his emotions and focused on the present. There was a sense of something important about to happen—something beyond graduation and the beginning of a new life.

"Are you worried about missing two years of time in the field?" Kimbell asked.

Hooker wasn't surprised that the commandant could guess his worry. Any officer would feel the same. "Somewhat, sir."

"Somewhat?" Kimbell snapped. "What does that mean?"

Equivocal answers were not acceptable at West Point. Hooker had had that lesson beat into him from the first moment he'd disembarked the train four years ago. There he had been given the four answers a new cadet was allowed: "Yes, sir; no, sir; no excuse, sir; sir, I do not understand! "

Hooker hastened to amend his mistake. "Yes, sir, I am concerned. While Oxford is certainly an excellent opportunity, nothing can replace spending two years with troops."

"Hmmph," Kimbell snorted. He reached into his dress uniform coat and pulled out a pipe and started filling it. "I've watched you, Hooker. I've looked through your records and talked to your instructors and tactical officer. They say you like working alone. That you possess a mind of the highest caliber, but that your leadership ability might leave something to be desired."

Hooker stiffened at the implied rebuke, because he knew it was true. He had a hard time dealing with subordinates who couldn't keep up with his thinking. He had little patience for those who could not meet his high standards.

"Major Whittaker in Engineering says that you are the type of person who would rather deal with conceptual problems than with people," Kimbell continued. "Is that true?"

Hooker had already been chastised once for a vague answer. "Yes, sir, it's true."

"Then two years away from troops won't make much difference, will it?"

Hooker felt himself being controlled into a position, although he didn't know what it was. "No, sir."

Kimbell's voice softened. "You know, Mr. Hooker, we all can't be at the head of regiments and divisions. The Army has other needs."

"Yes, sir."

"Especially in these hard times with all the cutbacks. There are dark clouds on the horizon. Not many see them, but I think you do, don't you?"

"Yes, sir." Hooker was surprised. Kimbell must have read his paper on German rearmament, otherwise why would he have made that comment? But why would the commandant be interested in a senior cadet's history theme paper?

"When do you leave for England?"

Hooker wondered about the change in direction of the questioning but promptly answered. "The tenth of July, sir."

"Where are you sailing out of?"

"New York, sir."

"Change it. Sail out of Savannah. I want you to go to Fort Benning before you leave."

Hooker remained silent, waiting for the commandant to clarify his command.

"Do you know Colonel Marshall, the deputy commander of the Infantry School at Benning?" Kimbell asked.

"I heard him speak in March when he came up here, sir. The topic was—"

"Yes, yes," Kimbell interrupted. "I was at the lecture too. Marshall is a most fascinating man. He has some interesting ideas," he added cryptically. "And he's not even a graduate, did you know that?"

"I understand he graduated from the Virginia Military Institute, sir."

"That's correct. Not quite the same thing as the Academy but they do an adequate job with what they have," Kimbell conceded. "Indeed, it's to our advantage that Marshall's not a Graduate."

Our advantage? Hooker thought. He felt a slight trickle of sweat run down the back of his stiff dress gray uniform coat.

Kimbell was looking up the river. "Marshall's got vision, Hooker. He's no fool. He was in the war with me and he saw what happened afterwards.

Even with two years to prepare, we weren't ready for France. We lacked the proper training, and we most certainly did not have the proper equipment. Many good men died because of that. And then we came back, and the first thing they did was gut the Army. And we're back where we were before the war, even worse in many ways.

"This Briand-Kellogg Act," Kimbell shook his head. "As if by signing a piece of paper they can outlaw war. Hell, Hooker, I don't like war but my job is to be prepared to fight and to win. Now the President signs this treaty and seems to think everyone else in the world is going to abide by it. Well, you and I know they will not. So it is our job to be prepared, no matter what those damn civilians in Washington think.

"They use the state of the economy as an excuse to justify what cannot be justified. The national defense must always be the number one priority. It cannot be tied to the vagaries of those fools on Wall Street. We must be beyond that."

Colonel Kimbell let loose a few puffs from his pipe. "What do you think, Hooker?"

Hooker didn't have to think about his answer. "I agree, sir. It's our duty to defend our country and that means being as well prepared as possible in peacetime, as well as being ready to give our lives in war if that is required."

Kimbell nodded. "Yes, but that first task is difficult, given the short memories of most of our politicians." He reached out and tapped Hooker on the shoulder. "Colonel Marshall and I talked for a long time in March. He's in a very good position at Benning. He's in charge of all tactics instruction and not only does he see the students who go through the Infantry School, he also gets to know all the instructors."

Kimbell turned back and faced Hooker. "Every few years we are going to select someone—someone special—among the Corps. Someone to do a different sort of job that will be very important." Kimbell paused and Hooker felt his heartbeat slow down and time seem to stand still. He felt on the verge of a great destiny. One that had been written just for him.

"I told you that not all of us can be at the front of the troops. That's why I want you to see Colonel Marshall. Why I've chosen you to be the first one. Colonel Marshall will tell you what is expected of you. What your country expects of you. Do you understand?"

"*Yes, sir.*"

Kimbell slapped Hooker on the shoulder. "Good. Good. Well, you need to go back to the barracks and get some sleep. You've got a big day tomorrow. The biggest day of your life so far, if I remember my graduation correctly."

"Yes, sir." Hooker watched as the commandant walked off toward the officer quarters on the northwest side of the Plain. Alone again with his thoughts, he realized that the past four years had prepared him for this moment. The rigorous academics, the physical conditioning, the hazing, the forge of high demands that had made him what he was. And now the future beckoned for him to serve his country—his army—in the way his abilities were best suited.

He didn't know what Colonel Marshall would ask of him, but Hooker knew he was prepared to give all just as the 2,230 names inscribed on Battle Monument—the name of every officer and enlisted man of the Regular Army killed in the Civil War—had given all. He also understood from the recent conversation that the statue at the top of the monument, representing Fame, was not to be his lot. He was going to be asked to serve in another capacity and, while it brought a momentary rush of regret, he also accepted it with the same fortitude that had served four hard years on the Plain.

Hooker used his right hand to remove his class ring from his left ring finger. West Point was the first school in the country to adopt the use of class rings, beginning with the class of 1835. The Academy tradition was that while still a cadet, the ring was worn with the class crest turned toward the heart. After graduation, the ring is turned and the Academy crest is closest to the heart. Hooker turned the ring in the moonlight, watching the stars reflect off the black onyx stone, then he slipped it back on, the Academy crest turned in toward his heart.

"FANCIFUL BUT DANGEROUS," the old man muttered, removing his reading glasses. "We have all copies?" he asked in a louder voice from the shadows, holding the pages up.

The aide had stood silently on the other side of the large wooden desk, unmoving while the pages had been read. "We have all that were sent out, sir. The author still has the original."

"Is this all of it?"

"That's all that was sent, sir."

"And this is being submitted as fiction?"

"Yes, sir. It's just a book proposal right now. We believe that's all that is written."

The gnarled fingers crumpled the pages. "You were right. This must be stopped." As the old man threw the wad of paper toward the trash can, the light glinted off the black onyx set in the large ring on his left hand. "We need to know where she got this information. Then take care of it and the author."

"Yes, sir."

Airspace. The Ukraine: 28 November

2:32 A.M. LOCAL/ 0432 ZULU

"One minute! Lock and load!"

In the glow of his night vision goggles, Major "Boomer" Watson could see the hand gestures reinforcing the words of his executive officer, Captain Martin—one finger up, then palm slapping the magazine well of the AK-74.

The Soviet-made Mi-24 Hind-D shuddered as the pilots reduced airspeed and crept even lower to the heavily wooded Ukrainian countryside, until they were flying less than twenty feet above the highest treetops. Boomer reached up and slightly adjusted the focus on his AN-PVS-7 night vision goggles, using the forward bulkhead separating the eight Delta Force troopers from the pilots up front as his reference point. In the green glow of the inner eyepieces, the other occupants of the blacked-out cabin showed up clearly, the men similarly outfitted in long Soviet-style overcoats, night vision goggles, AK-74s, and combat vests bristling with the tools of death.

Boomer knew the pilots were wearing their own goggles up front in order to fly the Russian aircraft well below minimum safety zones. He wasn't overly worried. The pilots were from the top-secret 4th Battalion of Task Force 160—the Nightstalkers—and were more than proficient in their job of flying captured and "appropriated" foreign aircraft.

Instinctively, Boomer slid a thirty-round plastic magazine out of a side pocket of his load bearing vest, slipped the back lip into the magazine well, then levered it forward, locking it in place. He smoothly slid back the charging handle on the right side, chambering a 5.45mm round. His thumb flicked over the safety, ensuring the weapon was still on safe.

"Ten seconds!" Martin yelled from the right door.

Boomer stood, letting the folding-stock AK dangle on its sling and grabbed both sides of the open left door. He peered out, ignoring the chill night air blown down by the rotor wash. Getting oriented, he recognized the landing zone from the satellite imagery they'd hurriedly been fed minutes before loading at their base in northern Turkey. On time and on target.

The LZ was on a mountainside and the only way the pilots could get in close without having the tips of their blades hit dirt, was to put the nose in, touching the front wheels, while keeping the tail up in the air. As soon as the wheels touched, Boomer jumped out, landing in waist-high grass. He ran to the side ten paces and hit the ground, weapon pointing into the darkness. As soon as the last man was out, the sound of the turbines increased and the helicopter lifted and was gone, leaving a deep silence.

Boomer got to his knees and pulled a global positioning receiver (GPR) out of the top flap of his backpack. He popped up the small integrated antenna and twisted the activating key on the side. No larger than a portable phone, the GPR fit in the palm of his hand. The small screen quickly glowed with data received from the network of satellites the Department of Defense had blanketing the planet. By finding the best four satellites in the night sky, the GPR could pinpoint their location to within ten meters. Boomer punched the POS key and was rewarded with grid coordinates confirming that they were exactly where they were supposed to be.

Despite the visual confirmation prior to landing—and trust in the pilot's navigating skill along with the chopper's own GPR—Boomer had long ago learned the importance of double-checking. "Assume means make an ass of you and me!" Boomer had heard more than once in his twelve years in the Special Forces and Delta Force, and he'd had those words confirmed on several missions. He punched the NAV button and the route information he had memorized was displayed:

235 D MAG. 2.3 KM
2.1 HOURS TOT
EL + 256M
STEER RIGHT

BOOMER STOOD and turned clockwise until the bottom line changed to read ON COURSE. He glanced over his shoulder to make sure the other members of his team were all accounted for, and then he moved off in the indicated direction. They had slightly over two hours to get to their target, and it was downhill most of the way.

The team had been dropped off along a mountainous ridge line in the southern Ukraine that ran parallel to a two-lane asphalt road between the town of Senzhary and the province capital at Barvenkovo. The road was their goal. Their target would be traveling this road between 0430 and 0530. Or at least that's what the Intelligence thinks doing the mission briefing had assured Boomer. He himself had little trust in the wisdom of those who kept their rear end comfortably ensconced in chairs and didn't have to live—or die —based on the accuracy of their information.

That was left to Boomer and his team. He grimaced slightly as he remembered the colonel from the Joint Chiefs of Staff office, his nametag identifying him as Decker, who'd given them the mission briefing. Decker assured them that their target would be traveling along this road. In Boomer's opinion, the man would have been more comfortable in a three-piece suit on Wall Street than wearing camouflage fatigues at a secret forward staging area in the mountains of northern Turkey.

Boomer especially remembered the flash of the large diamond set against black hematite in Decker's West Point ring as he slapped the pointer on the satellite photo of the ambush area. Boomer couldn't remember the last time he'd worn his own West Point ring. As a matter of fact, he couldn't quite remember where the ring was. Hopefully it was somewhere in the one-room apartment he kept back at Fayetteville, North Carolina, for the few weeks in the year he was actually back at his home base.

The terrain steepened. Boomer could see the dark snake of the road ahead and below. He halted briefly, the team mimicking his actions, and did another GPR check. Checkpoint One. On course and ahead of schedule. Less than a thousand meters from the road.

"Let's split," Boomer whispered, the acoustic mike built into the transceiver clamped on his head transmitting the message on low power FM to the other seven men. The whisper did little justice to his normally deep voice. It was a voice that instilled confidence in listeners. An advantage for a man who led others into death and destruction.

Boomer and his commo and security men—Headquarters Element—moved to the left, the two men falling in place and covering his flanks. Captain Martin, the team executive officer, went off to the right with the remaining four team members to set up the kill zone.

The Headquarters Element scrambled down the hillside, staying hidden under the pines that covered the rock-strewn ground, until they reached a small knoll overlooking the road. Boomer crouched behind the trunk of a tree, one of his men going off to the left to provide far left flank security, the other settling next to the team leader. Boomer scanned the deserted stretch of road fifty meters away and ten meters below.

"Bronco, are you in position? Over." He asked over the FM radio.

"Roger, Mustang," Martin replied. "In position. At my mark, I'll turn IR on for your identification."

Boomer peered off to his right.

"Mark. Over."

Boomer spotted the brief glow as Captain Martin illuminated an infrared flashlight—invisible to anyone not wearing goggles—then just as quickly turned it off. "Roger, Bronco. I've got you. How's it look? Over."

"Good field of fire. Good cover. Palamino Element is at the road installing their toys. Over."

"Roger. We'll keep an eye open for the target. Mustang out."

Boomer lay down on his stomach in the pine needles at the base of the tree, pulling the Russian overcoat in tight around his neck. It was cold, somewhere in the low thirties. He looked to his lower right along the road and spotted the silhouettes of the demolitions men, Palamino Element, at work. He checked the time on the GPR: 0413. Seventeen minutes before the estimated target window. Boomer tapped the shoulder of the man lying next to him. "Are we up on Satcom, Pete?"

Staff Sergeant Peter Lanscom nodded. "Five by." He handed over the small handset for the satellite communications radio.

Boomer pressed the send button on the handset. "Thunder Point, this is Mustang. Over."

The reply from Turkey was immediate. "Mustang, this is Thunder Point. Go ahead. Over." Boomer recognized Colonel Decker's voice.

"We're in position. What's the latest from the eye in the sky? Over."

"We're getting live downlink from an Intelsat on your target, Mustang. You've got two vehicles en route your location. A car in the lead and a bus following. Just as briefed," Colonel Decker couldn't help adding. "They're approximately twenty-two klicks from your position, moving at about sixty kilometers per hour. Over."

"Roger. Out." Boomer replied. He returned the handset to Lanscom. The math was easy: twenty-two minutes, give or take a couple. Nothing to do but wait. He glanced down the road. The demo men were done.

Boomer hissed in a lungful of cold air, trying to still the churning in his stomach. The flash of white teeth was framed in the moonlight by his naturally dark skin, an inheritance from a grandmother on his father's side who had been a full-blooded Cherokee. His black hair, a few inches longer than allowed by regulations, had just the slightest tinge of grey at the temples. His eyes were so dark as to appear black, but more unusual was the warmth they emanated regardless of Boomer's mood. While Boomer's overall reputation as a calm, likable individual was valued by friends and acquaintances, it mattered little to the organization that received the bulk of his time and attention.

Boomer was a long way from home. He'd grown up on the Upper West Side of Manhattan, where the George Washington Bridge touched New York City. Boomer's earliest memories were of his mother taking him on walks in Fort Washington Park along the banks of the Hudson beneath the high arch of the bridge. She'd taken him there when he was ten years old after receiving the telegram that his father had been killed in action in Vietnam. That was in 1969, prior to the Army instituting the policy of having notification officers deliver the grim news. At that time, the Army had simply sent telegrams and had them delivered by cab drivers.

Virginia Watson had had the driver take them down to the park and drop them off, the piece of yellow paper gripped tightly between her clenched fingers. The news of Michael Watson's Medal of Honor for actions on the last day of his life would come many months later, but on that bright fall day nothing had mattered other than the intense grief Boomer could feel and see in his mother. Boomer's emotions were more complex. His father had been gone for eight of the first ten years of his life and Boomer's memories of him were blurry images of a large man dressed in a uniform with a strange green beret that he wore cocked at an angle.

Just as Boomer had sensed the grief that day, seven years later, he had sensed his mother's disapproval of his decision to accept the automatic offer of an appointment to West Point that every child of a Medal of Honor winner was given. Boomer's attitude had been that at least something good had come from his father's death. Besides, he had rationalized, she couldn't really afford to send him to college anywhere else. The idea of a free education *and* pay more than satisfied his seventeen-year-old mind.

His mother had already gone into debt to send him to Cardinal Spellman Catholic High School in the Bronx. And though she would have preferred more bills rather than give another man to the Army, Boomer was not to be swayed. His easygoing attitude was blunted in this regard, and she accepted his decision.

She'd seen this tenacity on the basketball court at Spellman. Despite his—by basketball standards—relatively short height of six feet, he'd earned a starting slot on the Spellman varsity team by outworking all the other players on the team and impressing the coach with his hustle.

What had really caught the coach's eye though, was Boomer's actions as a sophomore in a game against perennial New York basketball mecca Power High School, alma mater of Kareem Abdul-Jabbar. Boomer had been sent in after the starting backcourt had fouled out trying to guard Power's all-city forward, later an NBA player. The coach had told Boomer to let the Power forward have no free shots. Boomer had promptly stuck to the more talented player like glue, hacking him severely every time he handled the ball, to the point where the Power player had lost his temper and took a swing at Boomer. The fight that erupted had cleared both benches and half the stands and resulted in Boomer and the Power player being ejected, but not before Boomer had returned the swing and decked the other player. The action had surprised the coach, but not Boomer's mother in the stands. She knew that, like his father, her son had a hard streak in him.

The years had passed and now Boomer was lying in wait, a familiar but always nerve-wracking position as far as he was concerned. As the countdown to action continued, Boomer was shifting to his action mode, his nerves freezing over and a wary calmness settling in. He grabbed the handset for the Satcom radio again. "Angel, this is Mustang. Over."

The reply from the pilot of the MI-25 was instantaneous. "This is Angel. Over."

"Status? Over."

The pilot's laconic southern drawl was reassuring. "At hold position. All clear. We can be there in a jiffy to pick ya'll up. Over."

"Roger." Boomer checked the time display on the GPR. "We're probably going hot here in five miles. We're going to need you real quick then. Over."

The Russian-made aircraft, appropriated from Saddam Hussein's air force during the Gulf War years previously, and the Soviet made weapons and uniforms, were a subterfuge to influence any possible survivors of the ambush—or anyone who might be in the area—that the events that were about to occur were the work of a renegade Ukrainian militia group of which there certainly were many. The only pieces of equipment that were not endemic to the area were the GPR, night vision goggles, and satellite radios, but if any of them were captured, there would most certainly be a body captured also, at which time the foreign origin of the equipment would no longer matter and diplomatic denial would take over.

The muted roar of the helicopter blades sounded behind the pilot's voice. "No sweat. Over."

"Mustang, out." Boomer glanced down the road, trying to catch the glow of the oncoming vehicles headlights in his goggles, where they would show up like brilliant spotlights. Nothing yet.

Boomer spoke into his FM radio. "Bronco, this is Mustang. Status? Over."

Martin's reply was swift. "All set. Over."

That meant Martin's team had the Soviet made PK machine gun set up and their RPG rocket launchers ready. Contrary to the movies,

Boomer knew a good ambush consisted of setting up the kill zone, then backing off so that the weapons can effectively cover the killing ground which must be too far from the ambushers for the victims to overrun. In this case, Boomer was satisfied his men had all the little checkmarks in the manual of efficient killing ticked off.

A faint glow appeared in the hills to the south: the reflection of the headlights. Boomer picked up the handset for the Satcom. "Thunder Point, this is Mustang. Over."

"This is Thunder Point. Over."

"Request final mission authorization. Over."

"Your mission is a go, Mustang," Decker said. "Authorization code Victor Romeo Two Four. I say again, your mission is a go. Code Victor Romeo Two Four. Out." The radio went dead.

"There's gonna be some hurting puppies in a few minutes," Lanscom whispered, the snout of his NVG pointed down the road, picking up the glow, as he fingered his AK-74. This was Lanscom's first live mission, and Boomer could understand the younger man's nervousness. He himself had been on several, but that didn't necessarily make it any easier. In fact, having witnessed the effects of modern weapons on the human body did little to relieve the anxiety of being on the receiving end.

Boomer didn't bother trying to allay Lanscom's fears. Now that he had the final go, his job was to concentrate on the mission at hand. The bus was carrying members of one of the factions of the newly formed Ukrainian parliament. A faction that was vehemently opposed to following the guidelines of the standing agreements on nuclear arms reduction between the United States and the Ukraine.

NATO inspection teams in the Ukraine to ensure treaty compliance had recently been forced to curtail their activities. The political situation was growing unstable. A NATO team had been attacked two days earlier by a mob, and the U.S. Congress was getting very vocal about sending 200 million dollars a year to the Ukraine to dismantle nuclear weapons when the job wasn't being done. The Ukrainian parliament, defying the Ukrainian president's signing of the START II Treaty, was making vague threats of nuclear blackmail as the country's economy slid into a morass. It was the politics of the late 1990's, and since military force was an extension of politics, Boomer was here to extend the wishes of the United States government.

Thirty-six hours ago, the issue reached crisis level. A Ukrainian Backfire bomber flying low toward Iraq had been intercepted over Turkish airspace by two American F-16s assigned to NATO. The Backfire had refused to land, and the F-16s had attempted to force it down. The result had stunned the world as the Backfire disintegrated in a nuclear fireball, taking with it the two American jets.

According to the intelligence analysts, the Backfire had been caught while trying to smuggle a nuclear weapon to Saddam Hussein's regime in exchange for desperately needed cash. When confronted with the possibility of capture, the crew of the Backfire had chosen suicide. The Ukrainians claimed the aircraft had wandered off course during a routine training mission and an on-board accident caused the explosion. It was a feeble excuse at best. No one seriously believed that the plane could be that far off course and the experts pointed out that nuclear weapons did not explode by accident.

The incident infuriated Congress. Claiming treachery and deceit, it demanded that the START II Treaty be scrapped. Boomer knew that in the biblical tradition of an eye for an eye, he was here to inflict hurt on those that had harmed the United States. In this case the radical politicians who had sent the Backfire on its fateful mission. Intelligence had placed them in a bus on this road. Boomer and his team were here to kill them.

Boomer wasn't exactly sure how his team's mission was going to affect things, but in a few minutes there would be fewer people opposed to NATO gaining positive control over the nuclear stockpile. Boomer, like most of his comrades in arms, drew no ethical lines when it came to nuclear weapons in the hands of extremists. Using the cold calculations of the professional military man, the potential body count of a rogue nuclear bomb weighed against the lives of the men approaching his kill zone left him with no qualms.

The lead car came around the bend and into sight, closely

followed by a bus. Boomer twisted the focus knob on his goggles. The Ukrainian flag flapped from the radio antenna on the right rear of the car. It roared by, rapidly approaching the ambush area. Boomer looked at the bus and blinked. There was some sort of emblem pasted to the right side of the bus, next to the door. As the bus rumbled by below him, he tried to make it out; he could almost swear it was the globe/compass marking of NATO.

The car had entered the kill zone, and the bus was less than thirty meters away from the point of no return. Boomer knew he had less than two seconds to make a decision.

"Abort!" he hissed into his radio. There was no immediate reply. "Martin, abort! Answer me, goddamnit!"

A bright flash split the night sky, followed immediately by the roar of an explosion as a remotely detonated mine went off under the front tire of the lead car. The blast lifted the car twenty feet into the air and tossed the crumpled machine off the road. A line of fire seared from the area of Martin's team and slammed into the bus—the warhead of the RPG rocket detonating on impact. Designed to stop tanks and armored personnel carriers, the warhead tore through the thin metal skin and exploded inside, blasting apart flesh and machine with equal ruthlessness.

"Abort!" Boomer yelled helplessly.

Green tracers licked out from the hillside disappearing into the ravaged body of the bus, the crack of the PK machine gun filling the silence left by the explosions. Boomer could see men crawling out the windows of the bus, trying to claw their way to safety.

"Get the chopper here!" Boomer ordered Lanscom. He got to his feet and ran along the hillside toward Martin's position. He slipped and fell, grabbing onto a sapling to keep from rolling down the hill. As he got to his feet, he could hear the snap of AK-74s adding to the din of the PK machine gun.

Just as Boomer arrived at the kill team's position, the firing suddenly stopped. In the sudden absence of the sound of killing, the screams of the wounded echoed up the hillside.

The members of Martin's team were standing, peering down,

weapons at the ready, the barrel of the machine gun glowing bright red. Boomer grabbed Martin on the shoulder, and the captain turned, startled, a glazed look in his eye.

"Why didn't you obey me?"

Martin blinked. "What?"

"I ordered you to abort, goddammit!"

Martin shrugged and pointed downhill. "They were in the zone. There was nothing else we could do. It was too late."

"You didn't have to fire up the bus," Boomer retorted.

"What's the big deal?" Martin asked. "This was what—"

They both froze as an eerie voice floated up the hill, crying out in English: "*Oh God, help me!*"

"That's why!" Boomer yelled. "That was a *NATO* bus."

The members of the kill team stared at him. Boomer was looking down the hill, thinking furiously. Flames were flickering out of the engine of the bus. He could make out some movement among the bodies lying around the shattered vehicle. There appeared to be one or two unwounded men down there, dragging the hurt to the shelter of the drainage ditch on the far side. Lanscom and the other man from his headquarters element came running up.

"Chopper's inbound, sir," Lanscom informed him. "Two minutes out."

Boomer reached out and grabbed the handset for the Satcom radio. "Thunder Point, this is Mustang. Over."

"This is Thunder Point. Over."

Boomer's voice was harsh as he reported. "We've got a fuck-up here. We hit the target, but it was a friendly. Looks like a bus full of NATO inspectors. Over."

Colonel Decker didn't hesitate. "Get out of there ASAP. Over."

"There's wounded down there. We need to help them. Over."

"Negative, Mustang. Over."

"Let me talk to my six. Over," Boomer said, trying to get a hold of his commanding officer.

"Your six is not available. Exfil immediately. You are not to render any assistance. You are not to compromise your presence. That's an order. Over."

Boomer held the handset, unable to reply. He felt the gaze of the other members of his team upon him.

Colonel Decker's voice took on an edge of anxiety at the lack of reply. "Mustang, do you hear me? Mustang? Confirm that you will comply with your orders. Over."

"Let's get down there," Boomer ordered his men, dropping the handset.

"Thunder Point says to exfiltrate," Martin objected, pointing at the radio.

"And I say let's get down there and help who we can. We'll put the wounded on board the chopper and take them back to Turkey."

Martin shook his head. "I'm sorry, sir, but we have to obey orders."

Boomer stared at his executive officer. The sound of helicopter blades started to override the cries of the wounded.

Martin half lifted his AK-74, in a vaguely threatening gesture in Boomer's direction.

"You're going to have to shoot me in the back if that's what you're thinking," Boomer snapped. He turned and started downslope. Behind him, Martin lowered the weapon and grabbed the handset for the Satcom radio, rapidly speaking into it.

Boomer was less than twenty feet from the road, when the Hind-D changed its landing pattern, roared up the road, and the 12.7mm Gatling gun in the nose opened fire. Boomer threw himself to the ground as bullets tore through the carnage his team had wrought, effectively finishing the job. The survivors were caught in the open and thrown about like rag dolls as the heavy metal-jacketed bullets tore into them. The helicopter banked and flew back, doing another gun run, taking care of those who had hidden in the drainage ditch. The aircraft flared just beyond the wreckage of the bus and slowly settled down to land.

Boomer stood and stepped out into the road. He bent over the closest body. There was no doubt the man was dead, his chest was torn open and half his head gone. Boomer checked the pockets, then quickly ran to the other bodies. All dead and most unidentifiable. The rest of his team came running down the hill toward the beckoning doors of the helicopter. Reluctantly, Boomer turned and followed them, stepping up and through the door into the waiting womb of the cargo bay. The helicopter immediately lifted and headed south to safety.

Boomer had something in his hands, a small piece of plastic. Turning it toward the red glow of the cargo bay, he read the lettering. He briefly froze and a look of anguish coursed across his face. He stuffed it back into the pocket over his heart.

Boomer spent the rest of the return trip in silence, ignoring the other members of his team. The one time Lanscom nudged him, holding out the handset of the Satcom to answer an incoming message from Thunder Point, Boomer simply pointed at Captain Martin. Lanscom took the radio over to the executive officer, who spent a good portion of the trip speaking into the handset. Boomer unhooked his FM radio and stuffed the earpiece into his vest pocket.

The noise inside the helicopter, loud enough to drown out any attempt at normal conversation, made the ride a curiously silent one. Each man was coming off the adrenaline rush of the action, and each was weighing the potential consequences.

At the airfield in northern Turkey, the helicopter landed and was immediately directed into a secure hangar where the doors swung shut as protection from prying eyes. The helicopter came to a halt. The sound of the engines decreased as the pilots began shutting the bird down. The side door opened and a soldier stuck his head in. "The Colonel's waiting for you."

As the other members of the team stood up to exit the bird, Boomer grabbed Captain Martin's arm and pulled him down into the seat next to him. "What the fuck happened back there, Pete?" he asked, finally able to be heard.

"What do you mean?" Martin asked, jerking his arm out of Boomer's grip.

"You told the pilots to strafe, didn't you?"

Martin couldn't meet his commanding officer's eyes. "Those were our orders."

"We killed our own," Boomer said. "You damn near killed me."

"You shouldn't have gone down there, Boomer," Martin said. The younger man shook his head. "It was messed up, but once the shit starts hitting the fan you got to play it out as it lays."

"That's what you call it?" Boomer asked incredulously. "Strafing wounded friendlies? Playing it out?"

Martin nervously shrugged.

Boomer poked him hard on the shoulder. "You ever pull a weapon on me again, I'll kill you."

Martin exited the aircraft without another word. Boomer angrily got to his feet and followed. In the hangar he walked to the brightly lit corner where the communications console was set up and the maps were tacked to plywood walls. Colonel Decker was there along with Colonel Forster, Boomer's immediate superior in Delta Force. Boomer's hand slid into the pocket of the greatcoat he was wearing and reappeared with two pieces of cloth. He threw them down onto the folding table in front of the two senior officers without a word. A small, blood-stained American flag with a Velcro backing along with a NATO blue beret lay there, frozen in the bright glow of the overhead lights.

Forster glanced at the patches, then at Boomer. "I heard. I'm sorry."

Boomer's eyes were locked on Colonel Decker's. He ignored the other members of the team as they gathered around, Captain Martin keeping a safe distance away.

"Do you have a problem, major?" Decker asked, breaking the uncomfortable silence.

Boomer stiffened. "No, sir, *you* have a problem. The target that you identified and confirmed for destruction was a busload of NATO officers from one of the inspection teams in-country. I took that shoulder patch and beret from one of the bodies. An American body."

"It was a mistake," Decker said. "We received some bad intelligence."

"Bad intelligence?" Boomer was stunned. "I counted at least six bodies outside that bus, and God knows how many were inside."

"It's done," Forster quietly said. "It was a mistake and it's done. Let it go, Boomer. There's nothing we can do right now."

Boomer twisted his head. "Let it go? Sir, my men just killed some of our own." His finger pointed at the patch, shaking with emotion. "How the fuck could Intelligence get that screwed up? You were tracking that damn bus since it left—."

"But we couldn't tell who was in it," Decker quickly interjected. "That was your job on the ground."

Boomer stepped back in surprise at the last comment. "My job? It was oh-dark-thirty in the morning there. Those vehicles were moving about forty miles an hour into my kill zone. You gave me final authorization for a go on the mission. I tried to abort," he said, throwing a hard look at Captain Martin, "but it was too late by the time I recognized the markings on the bus."

"Sounds like *you* made the mistake, major," Decker said.

Boomer took a step toward Decker, his eyes blazing.

"Listen," Forster said, holding both hands up and moving between the two men. "Let's not be getting into a pissing contest about whose fault things are. It's done. We've run seven different ops here into the Ukraine and this is the first one that went wrong. I don't like it. Nobody likes it, but our luck was bound to run out sooner or later. Let's be glad you all made it back all right, and we'll make damn sure something like this never happens again."

Decker picked up the flag and beret and stuffed them into his fatigue pants pocket, then turned an emotionless gaze on Boomer. "Your boss is right. We don't like it, but that's the way it goes sometimes. There are things going on that you aren't cleared to know. We were obviously fed false intelligence on this mission. It might even have been a deliberate setup. A lot of strange things have been going on since the interception of that Backfire. But it's done, and we need to make the best of it."

"The best of it?" Boomer asked. "How can you make the best of it?"

"That's not your concern, major."

"It damn well is my concern," Boomer replied angrily.

"Major!" Decker snapped. "That's enough." He turned to Forster. "I want this man relieved of duties immediately."

Forster bristled. "This is *my* command."

"It won't be much longer if you don't do what I say," Decker warned.

Forster glared at the other officer for several seconds before replying. "I'll take care of it. *You*," he added, still looking at Decker, "watch what you say to my people. This was *your* mission and you take responsibility for what happened."

Decker pointed at Boomer. "I want him out of this area of operations before close of business today." With that he turned and strode out of the hanger.

Forster waited until he was gone, then faced his subordinate. "I'm sorry, Boomer."

From the tone of his commander's voice, Boomer knew what the words meant. He was stunned. "You're going to let that asshole dictate what you do?"

"He works directly for the Joint Chiefs, Boomer," Forster explained. "I think the best thing to do is to get you out of here before someone goes headhunting to lay blame for this mission. It's for your own good. I'll cover your ass and take care of things here."

EXCERPTED FROM THE LINE, another Shadow Warriors book.

Cool Gus Publishing
www.bobmayer.com

ISBN: 9781621253075

❀ Formatted with Vellum

www.ingramcontent.com/pod-product-compliance
Lightning Source LLC
Chambersburg PA
CBHW052044240626

47153CB00006B/2204